BEATING WINGS

Novels by ROBERT W. CHAMBERS

WAR PAINT AND ROUGE
GITANA
THE RAKE AND THE HUSSY
THE PAINTED MINX
THE SUN HAWK
THE DRUMS OF
  AULONE
THE MAN THEY
  HANGED
THE MYSTERY LADY
THE GIRL IN GOLDEN
  RAGS
AMERICA
THE HI-JACKERS
ERIS
THE TALKERS
THE FLAMING JEWEL
THE SLAYER OF SOULS
IN SECRET
THE LITTLE RED
  FOOT
THE CRIMSON TIDE
THE LAUGHING GIRL
THE RESTLESS SEX
BARBARIANS
THE DARK STAR
THE GIRL PHILIPPA
WHO GOES THERE!
ATHALIE
THE BUSINESS OF
  LIFE
THE GAY REBELLION
THE STREETS OF
  ASCALON
THE COMMON LAW
THE FIGHTING
  CHANCE
THE YOUNGER SET
THE DANGER MARK
THE FIRING LINE
JAPONETTE
QUICK ACTION
THE ADVENTURES
  OF A MODEST MAN
ANNE'S BRIDGE
WHATEVER LOVE IS
THE YOUNG MAN'S GIRL

WHISTLING CAT
THE HAPPY PARROT
THE ROGUE'S MOON
BETWEEN FRIENDS
THE BETTER MAN
POLICE!!!
SOME LADIES IN
  HASTE
THE TREE OF
  HEAVEN
THE TRACER OF
  LOST PERSONS
THE HIDDEN
  CHILDREN
THE MOONLIT WAY
CARDIGAN
THE RECKONING
THE MAID-AT-ARMS
AILSA PAIGE
SPECIAL MESSENGER
THE HAUNTS OF
  MEN
LORRAINE
MAIDS OF PARADISE
ASHES OF EMPIRE
THE RED REPUBLIC
BLUE-BIRD WEATHER
A YOUNG MAN IN A
  HURRY
THE GREEN MOUSE
IOLE
THE MYSTERY OF
  CHOICE
THE CAMBRIC MASK
THE MAKER OF
  MOONS
THE KING IN
  YELLOW
IN SEARCH OF THE
  UNKNOWN
THE CONSPIRATORS
A KING AND A FEW
  DUKES
IN THE QUARTER
OUTSIDERS
SECRET SERVICE
  OPERATOR 13

THE GOLD CHASE
LOVE AND THE LIEUTENANT
THE GIRL IN GOLDEN RAGS
BEATING WINGS

BEATING WINGS

BY

ROBERT W. CHAMBERS

To

FLORENCE MORRIS

A SYMPATHETIC MIND
A LOYAL FRIEND

CHAPTER I

FOR a century the submerged sex had been getting ready. The first shot in the World War cleared the track.

As at a concerted signal they threw away their corsets. Long skirts and long tresses fell to earth. Millions of shorn heads lifted brightly; millions of freed bodies straightened. Millions of flying feet cleared the first ditch. Suddenly the whole world swarmed with clear-eyed, supple multitudes, gaily, carelessly overrunning the heritage to which all children are born—the world we live in.

Ancient prejudices vanished. Limbs became legs, and legs of no more significance than arms. In the saddle, on the beaches, across country, blew the ever freshening winds of freedom stirring the curls on millions of bobbed heads.

The reactionary sex roared disapproval; but the immemorial cult of the seraglio was already crumbling into dust, blown across space by a world-wide gale of girlish laughter.

Woman, unfettered, unencumbered, unafraid, stood as she was made, unashamed of her anatomy.

On the contrary, enjoying it and the disconcerted world that was discovering she had any. Woman admired herself, and was naïvely willing that men should share her admiration.

No more leers. There was nothing to leer at, now. The

cannon of the Marne blew the bluff out of "civilization."
The cannon of the Argonne blew sex nonsense to pieces.
Pigs long had been pigs. Legs at last were legs.

For the first time in the history of the world the submerged sex found itself free to make good or go under.
For the first time woman's opportunities equalled man's.

They now had just as much chance to make of life a
success or a failure.

For youth there were no restrictions except limited
parental control, self-control, and the laws of the land.
The liberated were to govern themselves and make their
own codes. No more man-made laws; no inhibitions. They
were to vote as they chose, dress, behave, think, live—and
love as they liked.

Compared to men, probably a higher percentage would
make good. The minority, like men, would make a mess of
it. What of it?

However, the elder generation lifted a mighty bellow
and proclaimed modernism anathema.

But all over the world millions of bobbed heads and
supple bodies were already flying across the world on
winged feet, eager, intoxicated with freedom, on fire to
learn what is the real goal, the real prize and its value; and
to reach and grasp it unaided and alone.

There is no goal. The prize is Death. The sporting effort,
only, is worth the race to the stars.

CHAPTER II

WHEN Harry Lessing, as usual, went South to follow the races, his wife, Helen, and her little daughter, Eleanor, remained at home in the Bronx flat.

Harry Lessing's business was to follow the races. His wife's business was to take care of the apartment on the Grand Concourse and look after Ellie. God only was qualified to do that.

For the family history was not one to inspire confidence in the future of Ellie Lessing.

The child inherited good blood and mongrel. A host of conflicting inclinations lay latent within her. Suggestion and environment, ultimately, would develop them into traits and talents, and reveal whether the character, born with her in the cradle, would be able to cope with them and control them.

There was good blood on her mother's side. But it was either remote or left-handed.

Her great-grandmother, at seventeen, eloped from a Seminary for Young Ladies, with a visiting instructor who taught drawing, penmanship, and piano; and died in utter poverty.

Her grandmother, celebrated for her beauty, sang in comic opera, and hastily married the low comedian in consequence of a careless romance with a college youth.

That carelessness resulted in her mother, who became

3

a child-actress of great beauty but little talent. Her father and mother retired from business and lived on what she earned. Usually that is the beginning of the end. Such folk don't last long. Drugs and drink ended their act. The low comedian went first. His wife's exit followed shortly. Not much chance for the child-actress.

At eighteen, Ellie's mother, now playing listlessly in vaudeville, met Harry Lessing, a racing man. And married him just in time. He never knew the difference. But that was the only incident in her strangely listless, gentle, and subdued career that ever troubled Ellie's mother. Probably because she had fallen in love with her husband.

Ellie Lessing's tenth birthday fell upon the day that the World War began—August fourth, 1914.

Convulsions rocked nations; assorted crowns tumbled; queens shed tiaras; cities crumbled; nations perished; millions on millions died.

But the Borough of the Bronx continued to grow and flourish. So did Ellie Lessing.

Afterward she recollected little of the World War except that the apartment was cold and sugar became scarce.

However, she did remember a dark November afternoon when she saw a regiment marching on the Grand Concourse—remembered particularly their band which she followed along with other school children. That had been her first profound æsthetic sensation; her first deep sentimental emotion—the sombre thunder of their marching music through the gloom of a looming storm. . . .

Those long masses of men surging up out of the November murk; lengthening lines vanishing into muggy obscurity. . . . Scarcely a dull sparkle on their rifles and band instruments; only the flag, startlingly fair in the gloom. Only that single accent; and the rending crash of their music—these were about all that Eleanor Lessing remembered of the World War. . . .

She continued to grow. So did the Borough of the Bronx. So did the four other Boroughs of the monster city. But the Bronx grew faster, lustier, vaster, becoming almost overnight an ungainly, independent creature of itself—a sprawling thing all limbs and no head—a wilderness of jerry-built or well-built homes, apartments, churches, cinemas; and of schools swarming with children.

The Grand Concourse with its quadruple rows of trees —basswood and maple—and its three wide roadways, was now almost completely palisaded for miles with new apartment houses, brick, limestone, stucco, concrete, each with its strip of grass, or flowery court, or foundation planting of evergreens, or privet hedge.

Millions and millions of new window panes sparkled in the sun along the endless avenue stretching southward from Fordham to the Harlem into the gullet of the huge city on Manhattan Island.

Where yesterday were rocks, vacant land, grassy bluffs, patches of woodland, bill-boards, dump-heaps, now ran street after street of bright new buildings. Far to the south-west the tower of High Bridge rose like a misty minaret. Northward lay the fountains and forests of the great public parks—Bronx Park, Botanical Gardens, Van Courtlandt, Pelham. To the east stretched Westchester and the Sound.

In a brand new apartment house on the west side of the Concourse Ellie Lessing lived, grew, flourished, and had her being.

At ten she was a thin child with a mass of light, burnished hair, a warm white skin, vivid lips, and grey-green eyes that slanted a trifle, and seemed to have flecks of gold in the iris.

Harry Lessing, being a racing man, was seldom at home except when Belmont and Aqueduct and other neighbouring race-tracks required his professional attention.

He was a good-looking, stout, highly coloured, carefully groomed, and very common man. Mother and child were happy to have him at home, for he was always taking them to the track, to theatres, pictures, restaurants—always bringing them gifts. A great comrade to Ellie, romping, chatting, joking, playing with her in the comfortable apartment on the Concourse. Loving her much.

As for the slim, eager, clever, pleasure-loving little thing of ten, she remained indefatigable in her activities; in school, out-doors, at home. She learned quickly, with little effort. She could play rag on the piano, and the sentimental music of the day, by ear.

She was a mimic; had a lovely little singing voice, became a clever actress in her school entertainments; danced exquisitely by sheer instinct, was deft with her fingers, quick, resourceful.

She was not discriminating. As long as she was doing something it seemed to make little difference to her what it was as long as she had a good time.

She poked her delicate, *retroussé* nose into everything; she was the pack-leader in school and on the street among

her fellows; but she had no particularly mischievous rec-
ord. There seemed to be neither malice nor meanness about
the child, and hers was a very tender heart, for all her
cleverness and scatter-brained activities.

She used to come home on Saturdays and holidays,
dirty and dishevelled, from Bronx Park or Botanical Gardens where she had romped all day with her pack, running through path and thicket, swimming in the river,
sticky from lollipop and hokey-pokey and saturated with
lemonade.

If Harry Lessing happened to be at home he romped
with her some more and put her through all her tricks. He
was clever in a smart, nimble way, and always kind, horsy,
and jaunty.

But he loved his wife, Helen, who looked like a lovely
and delicate Russian princess with her pale, oval, Madonna features and smooth golden hair framing them—
and enough grey in the hair, now, to make it very pale
gold.

She was very exquisite to look at, but brainless. Had
only commonplaces for conversation; a gentle, good,
stupid chorus girl with the face, figure, and serene bearing of a delicate, exotic aristocrat.

She taught the Decalogue to Ellie; made all the child's
clothes; cared for her creature comforts; warned her of
bad companions in her gentle, obvious way; made her husband comfortable when he was at home—passed her serene, colourless days in this manner, loving him and her
daughter.

The Lessings had little company. Helen had possessed
neither talent nor liking for the stage, and had never

made any friends among stage folk. What happened to her during her career there never left any scar, any impression on her, pleasant or tragic. She seldom thought of it, and never either with pleasure, regret, amusement or remorse.

She had met Harry Lessing at the races. After a brief courtship he had married her and asked no questions then or afterward. From that time real life began for Helen Lessing, and had continued chastely, serenely, accented only by the birth of Ellie, and the periodical returns of her husband from the racing circuit.

Harry Lessing sometimes came back with empty pockets. He was none the less gay and affectionate, romping with Ellie and putting her through her paces and taking them both to restaurants and shows or spending lamplit evenings beside his wife, talking of distant lands, of strange race-tracks, and of bonny horses and great races won and lost.

Helen talked little because she had little to say.

But she looked the pale, frail patrician where she sat sewing in the lamplight; and Harry looked the handsome, florid gent beside her; and Ellie, tinkling the piano, resembled one of those lovely little English children one sees depicted in *Punch,* and whose parents surely must be thoroughbreds to produce such progeny. And there you are.

There was no culture in the Lessing home; none in the public school where Ellie was being educated. Besides, things of the mind rarely appeal to a child of eleven. Two things only, thus far in her career—the superbly sombre music of that regiment the winter before; the Lorelei statue near 161st Street.

The child's reaction was a distinct shock of pleasure when she first beheld the sculptured group. Of art she knew nothing, good or bad.

But, like the thrilling diapason of that military music, the sculptured marble profoundly moved the child. In the depths of her, unknown emotions awoke, stirred blindly, subsided. What evoked them she knew no more than the sparrows that hopped about the sculptured group. But the wistful pleasure of it never entirely faded from her mind.

When Ellie was thirteen she remembered hearing some talk between her father and mother concerning a business school for her—that it might be safer for her to learn secretarial work, or book-keeping, or stenography and typing.

It came to nothing and the child went to high school. That was in 1918. Influenza was epidemic throughout the world.

Harry Lessing came home from Belmont feeling "rotten." He developed pneumonia next day and lasted three days longer. That was Ellie Lessing's principal recollection of the end of the World War, because it ended her father, too.

Returning with her silent, black-veiled mother from the funeral, she heard the din of horns, whistles, bells, announcing the Armistice.

Brown, curled-up leaves were drifting from the trees along the Concourse; flower-beds were seedy and tarnished in the dull wintry light. They drove through the Park. Salvia, badly blighted, still opened bloody gashes through the endless borders. Beds of ragged cannas still dotted the sward. Scarcely a crimson petal remained on the blackening seed pods. Everywhere maples stretched naked branches; oaks, still in leaf, reddened and browned. Water fowl were very noisy on the lakes.

Ellie saw two spotted bucks fighting, their antlers interlocked. One was down on his knees, panting, and his tongue lolled out, sideways. Her heart bled for him.

On the Concourse there were more soldiers than usual among the wayfarers. Motors full of yelling youths rushed north and south. Noisy groups passed with horns, rattles, bells, and flags.

Ellie and her mother went into their abode and, after resting for a little while in silence, took up the household burdens of the evening in kitchen, pantry, and diningroom, aided by the stolid negress cook and maid-of-allwork.

The world had got on without a great many millions of its recent inhabitants. It was now starting on, again, without Harry Lessing.

"Mom?"

"What is it?" asked Helen in her gentle, colourless voice.

"I suppose Dad must be in heaven by this time?"

"Yes."

"I hope he's comfortable there," said the child.

"God will make him comfortable."

"Mom?"

"Yes."

"I don't suppose there are any race-tracks there. Or horses?"

"No."

"Do you think Dad will miss them?"

"No. . . . He's—turned into—something different——"
She lifted her napkin and held it against her face. After a while she got up from the table and went into their bedroom, motioning the child to remain and finish her dinner.

Ellie tried to eat her prunes, but presently got up and went in to her mother who was lying on the bed in the lamplight.

She held out one hand to the child. Her voice was full of tears but distinct:

"He never spoke an unkind word to me. . . . He never asked a question. . . . Just took me as he found me. . . . I wasn't so much when he married me. . . . I hope he knows h-how I feel. . . . I hope—hope he has horses, too, if he wants them. I don't know why God wouldn't let him have some. What harm could there be in a little racing? You don't have to bet. . . . But your father didn't harm anybody by making a living. And it was the horses he liked most of all——"

She made a piteous gesture in the lamplight:

"I should think God would let him have a few horses if he wants them. . . ."

Ellie lay down on the bed beside her.

"If," she murmured, "heaven is a place where people are happy, I am very sure that God will let Dad have horses if he wants them."

For a long while they clung together, in silence. Finally the child got up, went to the window and looked down into the street from which arose the roaring tumult of Armistice Night.

"Mom, darling?"

"Yes."

"I think I'll go out and see what they're doing. Would it be wicked—so soon after burying Dad?"

"No. . . . Put your thick coat on. And be in by half-past nine."

"I promise, Mom!"

She went to her mother and hugged and kissed her; then hastened out to the closet where her coat and hat hung, struggled into them, and ran downstairs, eager, excited, her face still wet with tears.

CHAPTER III

FROM an early age Ellie Lessing's heart had been intermittently involved. Various beaux in turn possessed it.

Her first was at the age of ten. A little Jewish boy in school became her favourite playmate and her first escort.

He was a frail, gentlemanly little fellow. He used to walk home with her from school. School gossip was their sole topic. A rose he once gave her, the only sentimental episode.

At thirteen she had had a succession of school beaux, always leaders, rough, noisy, tireless youngsters who succeeded one another in her favour through some unusual feat of agility or strength. She "went" with each in turn.

There was no sentimentality—or, if any threatened, it was jested to death as "mush." But the child heard some crude language and primitive humour. It all passed over her head, not even arousing her curiosity to comprehend it.

At fourteen, however, she had an unwholesome experience with older companions. She told her mother. Infuriated and tearful by turns, she demanded, "Why?"

The trite, gentle, comforting commonplaces of her mother left her no wiser—left her unsatisfied, and merely aroused an adolescent curiosity quite healthy in itself. To satisfy it she hung around whispering groups and listened in.

Girls of her age, or older, viciously enlightened her.

Also shocked her. The information she gleaned was usually grossly distorted; sometimes utterly false. However, it extinguished further curiosity and hurt her sex pride.

Also it convinced her that sex matters could have no bearing on romance—the only sort of romance she knew —which was to admire a boy and be his girl and go about with him quite happily and with no "mush."

She had a furious fight the first time she was kissed. Rage was the principal emotion. However, later, she became less violent when she realized that petting parties were considered to be part of the programme—part of the modern interpretation of the oldest game in the world.

The game was to flirt, jest, tease, provoke, challenge, defend herself, and turn savage if the youth presumed. Got "fresh" was the nomenclature in her circles. But of all her doings she kept her mother informed. And was mechanically cautioned in return.

When she was sixteen she went to a business school. Harry Lessing had not left enough to keep them going. Her mother needed help. Was needing it more and more. So Ellie learned stenography and typing as easily as she learned everything. These activities left her plenty of time for afternoon and evening diversions with the "gang"— the majority of them attending high school, now.

So, pending the day when she should be prepared to take a position, she gave her spare hours to play, craving amusement as do all healthy youngsters.

Her sphere of operations stretched from Bronx Park to the jaws of the Metropolis. Sometimes, with a "fella" she trusted, she even penetrated the city as far south as 110th Street—the objective a movie.

That was as far south as she ever had journeyed. She had never seen Fifth Avenue, or Broadway, or Wall Street; never had seen the East River bridges or Brooklyn, or Governor's Island. Hundreds of thousands have lived and died in the Borough of the Bronx, who never saw Central Park.

Ellie's city, and her world, lay north of the Harlem. Pelham Park gave her salt water; the only rural scenes she knew were thereabouts. As for the rest, the Borough was her metropolis; the Concourse her Grand Boulevard and Piccadilly combined. Manhattan Island was a foreign country to her. Brooklyn a legend. What more could anybody desire than this vast, teeming, homelike metropolis called the Bronx? What more had foreign cities like New York and Brooklyn to offer?

She was nearly seventeen when she was ready to take a position—and discovered that positions were not plentiful in the Bronx.

Ellie did not advertise, for economical reasons. The large, near-sighted Jewess, Miss Rosenblatt, who ran the school for stenography, promised to "keep her in mind" and "recommend her." But, so far, nothing had come of it, although several Jewish girls, less proficient than Ellie, had been "recommended" and had secured jobs.

Her mother had not been well that winter; had taken to lying on the sofa a great deal. It was unease and weariness more than pain—a disinclination for food—or rather for the taste of food.

For a long while she had worried in her gentle way over using any of the small capital which Harry

Lessing had left. It was steadily dwindling; and so was the income. But, lately, she had become apathetic concerning ways and means: seemed interested only listlessly in Ellie's preparations to contribute toward their support. So the girl imagined there was no hurry; made no effort; left it to the near-sighted woman who had plenty of young girls of her own kind to "recommend."

At seventeen Ellie Lessing's bright hair was bobbed in a boyish cut. She had a shapely head. Her throat and the nape of her neck were lovely. Her slightly slanting, greenish eyes flecked with gold gave her a clever look. There was humour in those eyes. A few faint freckles on her nose; her oval face, high cheeked; her determined chin; her straight figure and long, capable fingers, all seemed to indicate decision, efficiency and shrewdness, which the vivid mouth denied, hinting of a heart neither shrewd nor cold. Valiant, perhaps, but tender.

Yet, save for the mouth, it was a clever, intelligent face, with a certain smartness to it in the English sense of "smart"—to be noticed particularly in profile. A definite profile, chiselled, charming yet tinged with impudence, youthful yet decisive.

"A snappy skirt," boys said of her.

Also it was generally admitted that she "had a bean with something inside it."

She came in from market one noon, her arms laden with materials for dinner. The hall-way echoed with her gay, clear voice:

"O-hoo! Mom!"

Her mother was still in bed. Ellie entered with her bundles:

"Are you sick, Mom?"

Helen turned a delicate, bloodless face to her daughter.

"Not very," she said. "I don't want any dinner. I'll just lie quiet. Tell Smilax."

"Oh, Mom, let me fix you something nice——"

Helen slowly shook her head.

"Was the Doc here again?" asked Ellie.

"Yes."

"What did he say it is?"

"He doesn't think it's dangerous. . . . It's a—a sort of growth——"

"Oh, *Mom!*——" in a sort of vague horror.

Helen went on: "It's not the dangerous kind. He is going to cure it. Most women have them. It—it makes me feel—heavy—and tired."

"Mom, darling, it *isn't* dangerous, is it? Does the Doc say it isn't?"

"Yes. Take your groceries in to Smilax. I'll have a cup of tea; that's all——"

"I brought you some fruit!"

"It tastes bad. Everything tastes bad to me. I don't want to eat. Tell Smilax to get your dinner."

Ellie went into the kitchen where the large, soft-bodied, yellow negress was shuffling about in a soiled apron, mobcap, and dirty red slippers.

"Mom doesn't want any dinner," said the girl, spilling her packages on to a table. "There's two chops and some green peas and a little fruit. I'm darned hungry, too——"

She went to the gas range, lifted the lid of a stew-pan:

"Gosh, that broth smells good, Smilax!"

"Ain' yoh Ma eatin' no dinner?" drawled Smilax.

"She'll have some tea in bed. I'll fix it——"

While she was busy with canister and tea-pot, the negress lazily opened the parcels.

"Ole Doc done come again dis mawnin'," she remarked. " 'N' bimebye 'nudder Doc come, too."

"Two doctors?" repeated Ellie uneasily.

"Yaas. I brung 'em water an' towels, I did. . . . Yoh Ma had a zamination."

"An examination?"

"Yaas. New Doc he toted a valise. I peeked in it. All full o' contraptions lak he wuz fixin' to carve yoh Ma into bits——"

"Smilax!" cried the girl. "What did they do to Mom?" She set the tea-pot on the range and came over to Smilax.

"I dunno. I ain' seen whut dey wuz a-doin'. Jess fussin' roun' de bed, an' a-walkin' sof' an' a-talkin' sof' in de hall. Me, I'se scared yoh Mah gwine be powerful sick——"

"Dr. McCarty is a good doctor. He says Mom isn't very sick. I guess a doctor knows more than you do!" said Ellie in a frightened voice.

"Me, I ain' botherin' no Docs, 'n' I don't want no fussin' dat-a-way," returned the negress sullenly. "No, suh. If I'se sick, I'se sick; 'n' I goes to my bed, an' I gets in an' lays low lak I wuz asleep. No Doc ain' gotta tell *me* when I'm poly. I knows I am, 'n' I keep my dollah in my stockin'. No, suh! When I got a misery I knows I got a misery, 'n' I ain' spendin' no money to ask no Doc is I sick——"

"You've got to be cured, haven't you?" demanded Ellie.

"I cures myse'f."

"How?"

"I don't eat nothin'. I jess picks a ham-bone, 'n' maybe a crumb o' pie. An' when I'se feelin' pow'ful hungry I gets out o' bed, 'n' I knows I'se cured——" She cast an odd glance at Ellie, half sullen, half sly, wholly African.

"Yaas, suh," she muttered, " 'n' I got sump'n I shove unda my pillow."

"What is it, Smilax?"

"Sump'n in a yaller calico bag, honey."

"*What?*"

"Oh, nuthin' . . ."

"Is it a charm?"

Smilax admitted that it was.

Her theory was that most illness was caused by somebody secretly working a "goofa jack" on you.

A bag of yellow calico containing specifics could be purchased for five dollars in the Black Belt. She advised Ellie to buy one and slip it under her mother's pillow.

The child nodded, took up the tea-tray and left Smilax languidly preparing dinner.

Helen drank part of a cup of tea, then lay back on her pillows.

"Do you feel better, Mom?" asked Ellie.

"Yes, I'm just tired. I feel so heavy when I get up and walk. . . ."

"Do you have any pain?"

"No; no pain. . . . I just lie here——" her voice trailed. She closed her eyes.

When Ellie's dinner was ready she rose cautiously from

the side of the bed, untangling her fingers from her mother's.

"I'm not asleep," said Helen, opening her eyes.

"I guess my dinner's ready, Mom."

"Very well."

"Won't you let me bring you something?"

Helen shook her head.

When Ellie returned from the table her mother opened her eyes again.

"Shall I play the piano for you?" inquired the girl.

"No. . . . I'll lie quiet. . . . Are you going out?" she asked.

"It doesn't matter. Shall I read to you, or talk, or just sit by you——"

Helen smiled very faintly: "Where are you going?"

"Oh, Jimmy Lacy was going to drive us somewhere——"

"Drive who?"

"The gang—Jessie, Mae, Al Farish, Arthur Graves, and me."

"Where?"

"Coney Island. He's got a new flivver. . . . But I don't want to go——"

"Are you taking your bathing suit?"

"I was—I'd just as soon stay with you, Mom——"

"They're nice boys, aren't they?"

"They're all right. . . . But we'd be back late——"

"Your—father—and I used to take you to Coney when you were a baby and we lived near 125th Street. . . . There was a race-track at Sheepshead Bay, once. . . . He had friends living there. We had a shore dinner when we went. . . . You don't remember, do you, Ellie?"

"I didn't know I'd ever been to Coney Island."

"You were just a mite. I used to say, 'Harry, do you think she'll *ever* grow any?' He always laughed. Once you cried for a taste of beer which he was drinking. I gave you a little in a teaspoon. Oh, what a face you made!——"

The girl laughed and her mother smiled palely.

"No, darling. . . . Life is short. Go and play."

So Ellie Lessing rolled her one-piece bathing suit into a ball, stuffed it into a chintz bag which closed with a draw-string.

"You *are* better, aren't you, Mom, darling?"

"Yes, much better. . . . Do you need any money?"

"Not with those fellas. Do you think Jessie Farish, Mae Graves and I would stand for tight-wads?"

"You'd better take a dollar. It's in the purse on the piano. . . . Don't let those boys kiss you."

"Who? Jim Lacy? He can't; he's driving. Aw," she added, "I feel like I was kissing a cunning puppy-dog when he starts petting." Her clear, virginal laughter rang in the quiet room. . . . "Mom, did they have petting parties when you were a girl?"

"No."

"Didn't any fella ever kiss you before you knew Dad?"

The pallor of Helen's face was invaded by a delicate breath of rose.

"Isn't that Jimmy's horn honking?" she asked.

"I guess so. Let him wait. . . . Mom, darling, are you sure you don't want me to stay with you?"

She knelt down by the bed and put her slender arms around her mother.

"Mom—Mom, darling," she murmured.

But, after they kissed, Helen closed her eyes and turned her head away.

After a few minutes Ellie went out on tiptoe to the open window at the end of the hallway, and looked down into the street.

"O-hoo!" she called softly.

The gang hailed her impatiently.

CHAPTER IV

THE gang was unanimous for Manhattan Beach and a "swell" swim.

It being Jim Lacy's party, he parked his newly painted second-hand car; paid fifty cents apiece admission. The girls and youths separated, seeking their several segregated bath-houses.

The July day was hot but superb; the sands blazed with the violent colours of half a million people. Brilliant sunshades, gowns, bathing suits and caps turned beach, pier, and pool into gigantic floral effects.

Thousands of brown-skinned girls and youths on the athletic field were engaged in setting-up drill or passing the medicine ball or sprinting.

A band blared on the pier; landward and seaward promenades were thronged; the great concrete pool was abloom with gorgeous bathing suits and, far away on the left, high-divers and fancy-divers were plunging, like tropical kingfishers, and everywhere foam flashed and gaily coloured youths and maidens raced and chased and sported or thronged the great sweep of stone steps from the seawall to the pier. Multitudes, multitudes as far as the eye could reach; swarming throngs stretching away in chromatic chaos toward Brighton and the fairy spires and domes of Coney Island. Overhead a blinding white sun, eastward the blue Atlantic in immemorial motion. Sandy Hook vague as horizon smoke.

It was on this that Ellie emerged from her bath-house, a scarlet cap tied beneath her chin, a scarlet bathing suit of one piece moulding her slender body from hip to breast.

Mae Graves padded along beside her in blue; Jessie Farish was in yellow which suited her dark hair and skin.

The three youths were skylarking on the beach, awaiting them. And as, at that time, Ellie was Jimmy Lacy's girl, that red-headed youth seized her and dragged her toward the water. Where she presently managed to duck him, amid yells from the others, then plunged under and swam swiftly toward the distant diving pier.

They all thrashed out after her, but Ellie's slim limbs flashed in the sun far ahead.

She was first to climb out on the raft; first to mount the pier, step out on the spring-board, and dive backward, cleaving the water vertically—a perfect effort.

It was wonderful. She proclaimed it to the others. Far more thrilling than Pelham.

She proposed having a look at the ocean—not the beach but outside the rocks along the sea-wall.

Her arm rested lightly within Jimmy Lacy's as they sauntered along toward the concrete promenade. She was a little taller than he; her slender, prettily rounded arms and legs were already tanned to a creamy tint from the season's Pelham experiences.

She held her clean-cut, clever little head high; her grey-green eyes slanted happily or humorously upon the gang, upon passers-by, upon the sparkling world around her. With imperceptible and leisurely dexterity she savoured her chewing-gum.

"You want to make up your minds," said Lacy, addressing the gang; "—is it Coney and hot dogs or a square meal and a dance at Villy's?"

"The square meal for mine," said Ellie. "I'm fed up on hot dog."

Mae liked Luna Park, but Jessie Farish seemed inclined to dance at Villy's.

The three couples came out along the great sea-parapet and looked down at the weed-covered rocks of the breakwater where the limpid sea curled and washed and rocked.

"Come on, Jim," said Ellie briefly, and climbed over and down and was into the ocean with a wriggling dive. Seaward she drove her slender shape until a life guard, resting on his oars far out, warned her shoreward.

For a while she held on to the bow of his boat, looking back at the distant shore where the gang were disporting themselves more prudently. However, Jimmy's head appeared half-way between boat and shore, making for her.

She said over her shoulder to the life guard: "He isn't good enough for that. I've gotta look after that kid——"

She let go, swam strongly to meet Jimmy. He turned when she approached and struck out shoreward.

"You all right?" she asked.

"I guesso——" he gasped.

She swam beside him, her slanting sidelong glance on him.

After a few moments: "You're a darned fool," she said; "rest on me."

"Is—it—all right——"

"Certainly," she said scornfully.

She began to tow him along.

"You poor sap," she said, "don't you know how far you can swim? What did I tell you at Pelham Park?"

Thus, towing, admonishing, she helped her young man in. Off the breakwater she freed herself and let him come ashore alone and with apparent self-respect.

"Gosh," said his sister from the terrace above, "—you're some swimmer, Jim."

Arthur Graves also voiced wonder and approval at Jimmy's progress in aquatic prowess.

Ellie landed demurely and climbed up. But the gang knew about her skill in the water and took it for granted.

They descended the concrete steps and sat down in couples to sun and gossip and watch the gay throngs in the pool below.

Jim Lacy, with Ellie, was glum. Hurt pride operated within him to cripple both self-assertion and sentiment; and he had no other topics of conversation; no mental reservoir.

The girl was aware of it, mischievously, not maliciously. She was a pretty thing to look at; she undid her scarlet skull-cap, ruffled her bright bobbed hair, stretched her dainty, naked feet to the sun and smiled upon Jimmy.

"Aw," he said. "I wasn't as pumped as you think. I coulda got back all right."

"I'll remember that next time," she said, still smiling.

"Damn it," he muttered, "every guy isn't a fish."

"Who's picking on you, anyway?" she demanded.

"Well, you sit there grinning——"

"Can't I smile?"

"What you smiling at?"

"I don't know. It's nice here. God!—and to think I've never been here—except when I was a baby! . . . I don't know that I ought to have come to-day——"

"Why not?"

"Mom's sick."

"Isn't she better?"

"I guesso. She's tired all the time. She just lies there. . . . She's been feeling like that since last winter. . . . I don't know—God! it kinda scares me sometimes——"

"What does the Doc tell you?"

"It's a—a growth."

"A—what?"

"A growth. He says most women have them. . . . I'm not going to talk about it to *you*——"

She sprang up, looked at the pool: "I'm going in again. Coming?"

"Aw, have a heart, Ellie——"

"Aren't you rested?"

"Sure. But let's sit and talk——"

"No!"

As he made no offer to rise, she turned up her nose at him, walked a few paces toward Jessie Farish and Arthur Graves. They also seemed to prefer gossip and a sun bath. Jessie's hand lay in Arthur's.

"Mush!" remarked Ellie with a shrug; pulled on her red cap and tied it; cast a disdainful glance at her fella and at the two pair of indolents, and, poising, took a header into the pool.

Some time later she found herself on the raft amid some dozens of dripping swimmers.

After she had dived several times she climbed up to

the diving-pier, seated herself on the edge, and looked across the lagoon toward her distant comrades. Finally she made them out.

They were still sunning in couples. As for Jim, he lay flat on his back in the sun, his red hair gleaming. Apparently her fella slept.

Ellie watched the high diving, admiring the experts. There was one man who sauntered out, took careless measure of the water below, launched himself backward, turned over three times, and struck vertically. He did it two or three times. He was a cleanly built, nice-looking fellow of thirty, perhaps. Several of the fancy divers came over to speak to him. Finally, as though urged, he threw away his cigarette and once more performed the stunt for them.

When he reappeared and pulled himself up from the water, he seated himself near Ellie. As he was lighting another cigarette from a waterproof case, his lifted glance met Ellie's. His smile was involuntary. She smiled too. There was no effort on either side.

"Would you like a cigarette?" he asked.

"Thank you—yes."

He lighted it for her, still smiling.

"You dive well," she said.

"Oh, that? I'll teach you, if you like."

"Shall we finish our cigarettes first?"

"By all means," he said.

Smoking amiably together she cast a slightly mischievous glance toward the distant, recumbent form of her fella.

"You seem always to be smiling," remarked the young man beside her.

She laughed: "Some things *are* funny, you know."

"Do you take life as a joke?"

"Well, not as a joke, exactly——"

They both laughed.

"I suppose," he said, "you are not alone down here."

"No; there are six of us."

"There always are," he remarked.

At that they laughed again.

"Are *you* here alone?" she ventured.

"Yes."

"What a shame!——" Their ready laughter rang out again.

She looked out over the lagoon; made a swift sweeping gesture with her arm: "All these pretty girls! Do you see them?"

"I do."

"And yet you are *alone?*"

"Not at the moment."

"But I'm going when I finish my cigarette."

He said nothing.

"You'll be alone then. . . . You'll be all alone. . . . Are you sorry?"

"Yes, I am."

"Are you going to be lonely?"

"I begin to believe I shall be," he said, smiling at her. "You know you're *very* pretty," he added.

"You don't think so."

"I'll try not to. It'll make it easier for me——"

Her quick laughter pealed. Presently she threw away the cigarette.

"You said you'd show me," she reminded him, and sprang lightly to her feet.

He rose at once.

Walking slowly together toward a spring-board where few people were gathered, he carefully and very clearly explained the theory of the triple back-somersault and dive.

Twice he did it for her.

Finally she launched her slim body upward and outward, went hurtling toward the water, struck with sufficient accuracy, and presently appeared swimming back to the pier, radiant under the noisy applause from dozens of gathered swimmers.

She climbed up beside her instructor, excited, triumphant, eager to do even better.

She made dive after dive, always improving, always climbing back to him to challenge his approval.

"I'll practise that," she said, "at Pelham, if there's a good enough place. And thank you for teaching me——"

She held out her hand and he took it. They had moved back and apart from the crowd.

"I suppose you are going to leave me cold," he said gaily.

"I've got to——"

"I suppose you have, if you're with a party."

There was a pause; she withdrew her hand; turned and gazed across the lagoon. The gang still sunned. Jimmy was now lying on his belly, his cheek resting on folded arms.

"Gosh," she said with unconscious emphasis. "I'd like to stay here. . . . But I'd better get a wiggle on." She looked up at him out of her clever grey-green eyes: "I don't suppose I'll see you again."

"Do you come here much?"

"No; it's my first time."

"I come Saturdays," he remarked. . . . "And Sundays."

There ensued another pause. The girl's restless eyes sought her distant comrades, discovered them, roved elsewhere.

"Perhaps you'll be down next Saturday," he said.

She looked up, inclined to laugh: "You never can tell. . . . Anyway, I'm going now——" She started to offer him her hand again; thought better of it and went overboard.

CHAPTER V

A T Villy's they ate soft clams, green corn, and drank near-beer. A negro jazz band droned, thumped and squealed on the wide, screened verandas. The parking space was crowded with automobiles; every table was taken.

Ellie, being considered Jim Lacy's girl, danced exclusively with him in the beginning. But in such combinations a time arrives when girls swap beaux and beaux trade girls. She danced with Albert Farish once, and once with Arthur Graves, returning to the table to consume more food after every dance.

The floor was too crowded for comfort, but nobody minded. It was a noisy, smelly, hot place, filled with incessant uproar of jazz and seashore gaiety, where tables and chairs were jammed too closely, and perspiring couples laboured for space to dance in.

Toward ten o'clock Jim Lacy ordered silver-fizzes. When they were served he produced from his hip pocket the material necessary to complete them. He dosed each fizz very liberally with synthetic gin, but it seemed only to add a slightly aromatic flavour to the iced beverage, and, after the first sip, no caution was observed in allaying thirst.

The distant popping and whizz-banging from Coney

Island, and the glare of rockets in the calm, dark sky, drew away enough people to relieve the jam on the dancing floor.

"How about it, Ellie?" asked Lacy, "—do we go over to Coney, or stay put?"

But instinct and passion for the dance was in every fibre of the girl. Her tireless body and restless feet needed no other stimulant, yet both were beginning to feel the tingling of the silver-fizz, now. She tired out Lacy. Besides, he wanted something more to eat.

"You old poke!" she cried. "You always want to eat. If you don't dance you'll have to find another girl. I'm not going to stick around watching you feed yourself——"

"Aw," he said, "gimme a chance. Go on and drink your fizz——"

"I want to dance!"

"Well, ask Arthur——"

"He's dancing with Jessie, and Bert is dancing with Mae. *You're* still eating!"

"Sure, I am," he said, starting on a broiled lobster.

"Is that all you care about my wishes?" she demanded.

"My God, what's the matter with you——"

"I told you. I want to dance!"

"You always had crazy feet."

"Yes, and legs, and the rest of me. Are you going to dance?"

"I'm busy."

"Pig."

She emptied her fizz-glass, turned a flushed face to the throng. On the other side of the dancing floor, alone at a table, she saw a man whose face seemed familiar. His amused glance met hers. For a moment she was in doubt, then no longer in doubt.

She gave him a delightful smile. He was very nice to look at in his clothes. The crisp, brown hair which she had seen all wet and plastered, was now combed; the nearly naked bronze body now covered with a fashionable and very becoming suit of thin white serge. She greatly approved the altered appearance, the twist of his tie——

"Jim?"—without looking at him.

"Wait a while——"

"There's a friend of mine over there. Is it all right with you if I dance with him while you're eating your lobster?"

"Which guy?" He suspended operations on the claw he was dissecting and followed her glance. . . . "Who's he?"

"A fella I met. . . . Is it all right with you if I dance with him once?"

"You're not hog-tied."

"No, but I'm pig-tied," she retorted.

"Do as you like," he said sullenly. "You always do, anyhow."

"Do we dance? Last call!"

"Not now—no."

"Then I'm going to dance with him."

She glanced across the floor at her late diving-master, and gave him an almost imperceptible nod. The young man seemed to understand it for he rose and came straight across to where she was sitting. It was then she realized that she didn't even know his name.

But he seemed to have his wits about him; he said, politely:

"It's very nice to be remembered. I was afraid you had forgotten you ever had met anybody named Westall."

Ellie, excited by the silver-fizz, thrilled to her first adventure.

"Oh, Mr. Westall," she said, "I want you to meet Mr. Lacy."

Lacy got up: "Pleased to know you," he said without cordiality; and resumed the lobster.

"Do sit down, Mr. Westall—unless you'd rather dance?" inquired the girl.

Westall looked politely at Lacy, who said, "Cert'nly." So he took her out and swung into the circling current of dancers.

After a few moments their eyes met and they laughed.

"It was awfully nice of you, but risky, wasn't it?" he asked.

"Yes. I thought I was in dutch with Jimmy when I remembered that I didn't even know your name. . . . You dance well."

"So do you. Wonderfully."

"You're the best ever," said the girl, blissfully. . . . "You make me feel like I was part of you. . . . Gee, I never danced with a fella like you. . . . Any step you like. I don't care. I'm your other leg."

He laughed: "You're both my legs, and the rest of me. You're easily the best I ever danced with. . . . Are you professional?"

"Who? Me? Now you're getting funny. . . . What's the rest of your name?"

"John."

"John Westall? You'd better know mine, hadn't you?"

They laughed.

"In case of inquiry by friends," she added.

They laughed again.

"My name's Ellie Lessing. What shall we call each other? Mr. and Miss are safer for a while, I guess."

"Yes, for the first two or three times——"

They laughed and laughed.

"Are you coming down next Saturday, Ellie?"

"You never can tell. . . . Besides, I'm going with Mr. Lacy."

"Are you engaged to him?"

"No," she laughed. "I've never been engaged. But you know what I mean——"

"What do you mean?"

"Why, when a girl goes with a fella—well——"

"She can leave him flat if she wants to? Is that the idea?"

She enjoyed the idea: "Sure, she can. . . . I don't have to go with him. . . . Only to-day—I ought not to have done this to him—because it's his flivver and his party. . . . Well, I haven't done anything, have I?"—the fresh young face upturned to his, flushed, mischievous, and her grey-green eyes brilliant with laughter.

They waited for the gust of hand-clapping to force another encore. When it came she smiled, sighed, and her long, smooth fingers tightened around his.

"I better not dance with you again," she whispered. "He's got red hair. You just say good-bye to me when we get back to the table."

"Until next time."

The girl looked up quickly, then turned her head. They

danced, following the current around the ring of tables. Lacy was still picking lobster claws as they passed. His face was not very friendly.

"He's got a mad on," whispered the girl. "I ought not to have done this. . . . But I'm glad I did. . . . Are you going to be down here Saturday?"

"Yes; are you?"

"All right."

"You pretty thing," he whispered.

She laughed, glanced at him, turned her cheek perversely.

"I'm treating Jimmy like a dog," she said. "That's not the worst of it, either. I'd *rather* be with you."

"You're so sweet——"

"No; it isn't right. Not when a fella takes you out. God, I'm behaving something rotten. . . . You'll be here next Saturday, won't you?"

"Yes, at the pool——"

"Give me a ring in the morning. Can you remember my number?"

"Yes."

She gave it to him, hurriedly, repeating it.

"And I want to tell you," she said fiercely, "——whatever you think, you're the first man who ever picked me up. . . . If it was a pick-up. Was it?"

"I don't—I shouldn't say so——"

"*I* picked *you* up, didn't I? I *did!* Well, I wasn't thinking of it that way."

"I wasn't, either," he said.

She seemed relieved. The music ceased at that moment.

"Don't forget," she whispered. His parting clasp reassured her. They walked over to the table. The other two couples were there. Jimmy gave them a sombre look as Westall was introduced all around.

He lingered a moment in amiable chat, then took his leave, pleasantly.

"Who's the guy?" demanded Arthur Graves.

"Oh, just a fella I met," said Ellie carelessly. And, to Lacy: "What time is it? We gotta get home to-night."

CHAPTER VI

I T was one o'clock in the morning when Ellie let herself
into the flat with her mother's latch-key.

A light burned in the hall. There was a light in her
mother's room, also.

The girl went cautiously to the threshold and saw her
mother lying on the bed, her face, with closed eyes,
ghastly white in the full glow of the night lamp.

"Mom?" she called cautiously. Helen opened her eyes.
Ellie went to the bedside:

"It's one o'clock. I couldn't get back any earlier. It took
two hours in the flivver."

Her mother looked at her with the vague, glazed gaze
of a sleeper not fully awakened.

"I had a dandy time," said the girl, seating herself on
the bed's edge. "I learned a fancy dive. I talked to a
strange fella. Was it all right? He acted like a perfect
gentleman. Was it all right, Mom?"

In Helen's white face, gradually the sunken eyes were
becoming intent on her daughter—like the eyes of a deaf
person striving to understand.

"I told him I'd meet him next Saturday—and to give
me a ring. He's a dandy dancer, Mom. He's kinda old—
I guess about twenty-seven or thirty. He's a swell dresser,
at that. . . . Well, I don't just know how we came to
speak. . . . Then he showed me how to do a fancy dive.

. . . Gee! it's a swell stunt! Some dive. . . . His name is John Westall. . . . He didn't act up a bit—fresh like. But Jimmy's mad. . . . Let him! I don't care, either. There are plenty of fellas. . . . If I wanted to. . . . Mom, are you sleepy?"

Her mother's eyes remained intent on her child. She seemed to make an effort to say something, but there was only a quiver of the features.

"Darling! What's the matter?" asked Ellie. "You act dopy."

"Very—tired," murmured Helen.

"You're sleepy. I'll turn out the light." She put her arms around her mother and kissed her; and Helen's arms clung to the girl's neck.

"Sleep soundly, Mom, darling," murmured the girl. Then she turned out the lamp; felt her way to her own room, began to undress in the dark, still excited by her day of pleasure, still thrilled by her first adventure.

In her mind she kept repeating: "He is the best-looking thing—the best-looking—I had a dandy time. . . . I guess he'll give me a ring. . . . I guess so. . . . He's kinda old for a girl to go with. . . . But I'd have a dandy time with him. . . . I guess he's got a girl. He could have all he wanted. . . . But he liked me. I *know*. He liked to dance with me——" She slipped out of her underclothes and flung the last garment from her. "He seemed to like it, teaching me to dive. . . . The only thing is, if he doesn't forget to ring me up. . . . He said it like he meant it. . . . It's a long time to next Saturday. . . ." Naked, she searched in the dark for her night-gown and pulled it on.

She was on her knees now, her bobbed head in both hands. The routine bedside prayer—remembering her dead father and hoping he was happy in heaven; asking health for her mother; asking daily bread; giving thanks for the day ended; and a yawning Amen. . . . And, after another yawn, a sleepy postscript:

"Oh, Lord, I hope he'll remember to give me a ring next Saturday. . . . I hope he sleeps soundly to-night and—and doesn't forget what fun we had when he wakes up to-morrow. . . . Amen——"

Smilax awoke the girl at nine to say that breakfast was on the table and that there were two doctors and a trained nurse in her mother's room.

Ellie, very sleepy, scarcely understood. However, she got out of bed and turned on the bath, still only half awake.

Scrubbing in hot water and sponging with cold brought her to her senses. In slippers and bath-robe she went into the dining-room and ate her toast, oatmeal, and egg. Her face was very pink; her bobbed hair tousled.

"What did the Doc say?" she inquired. But Smilax remained sombre and uncommunicative.

Twice, while breakfasting, the strange trained nurse passed through the dining-room to the kitchen.

She was a stout blonde woman, all in white, and she gave Ellie a look of curiosity out of two very pale eyes.

"What's she doing here?" asked Ellie of Smilax. "What's she doing in the kitchen?"

"I ain't asked nobody nothin'," grunted the negress.

"Is Mom any worse?"

"You ask them Docs. They ain't gwine tell me nothin'."

Ellie finished her breakfast, went to her bedroom and dressed. When she entered her mother's room the physicians had gone, and the stout, white-clad nurse sat by an open window, reading.

Ellie tiptoed to the bed; looked down at her mother.

"Your mother is asleep," remarked the nurse. Ellie went over to the window:

"Is she worse?"

"She's comfortable."

"What is the matter with my mother?" whispered the girl.

"Hasn't Dr. McCarty told you?"

"He said she has a growth, but it isn't a bad kind of growth. . . . Not dangerous. . . . He said that nearly all women have that kind of growth. . . . He told me so."

"Oh!"

"It isn't the bad kind, is it," whispered the girl.

"You don't have to whisper," said the nurse; "she won't wake."

"He—he told me the truth, I suppose, about the growth, didn't he?" demanded Ellie.

"What? Oh, certainly."

"Well, when do you think my mother will be well again?"

The stout woman shook her head: "I couldn't answer such questions, Miss Lessing."

"Why not?"

"I'm not a physician. You must talk to Dr. McCarty or Dr. Stein. They'll tell you what they have to tell."

"Can't you even tell me whether my mother is any better?"

"She is comfortable. Dr. McCarty left medicine for her."

"For pain?"

"Yes, I suppose so."

"To make her sleep?"

"I—yes."

"Is that why you're here—to give it to her?"

"Yes, and to make her comfortable."

"What ought she to have to eat?" asked the girl.

"Anything she wishes."

Ellie sat down and gazed at her mother.

Helen slept most of the day. At long intervals she awoke to a sort of frightened consciousness, trembling, incoherent of speech, clinging convulsively to Ellie; finally to relapse again into restless drowsiness after the nurse had given her medicine and changed her pillows.

She ate only a little broth; seemed thirsty when conscious.

Ellie did not go out-doors that day. For supper she thought her mother might like an *omelette soufflée,* and cooked it for her; but Helen turned her head away murmuring unintelligible things—lay with face averted and pallid fingers, restless, trembling, muttering on her pillows.

Miss Wylie took a nap that afternoon on the sofa in Ellie's room while Ellie sat by the window or beside the bed, fanning her mother or clearing the room of flies.

"I don't see why my mother doesn't wake up if she is getting better," she said when Miss Wylie came on duty. The nurse made no reply.

After dinner she said to Ellie: "Why don't you go out and take a walk?"

"Isn't Dr. McCarty coming?"

"Not till morning."

But Ellie had no desire to leave her mother.

Jimmy Lacy telephoned about eight:

"Hello, kid! How about a joy-ride?"

"I don't feel like it."

"You got a date?" he asked suspiciously.

"No."

"What you doin'?"

"Sitting here with Mom."

"Sure," he said sarcastically, "that's like you. You're going somewhere with that guy you got fresh with last night."

"What of it?" asked the girl coldly.

"Oh, so you're goin' out with him, are you——"

"No. But what of it if I was?"

"Plenty! You can't do that to me——"

"Do what?"

"Go with another guy when you're goin' with me!"

"Aw, shut up your red head," she retorted disdainfully. "If you don't like what I do, stay away."

He was very mad; he began to talk loudly and angrily. She hung up in his ear.

Presently back he came with a ring that incensed her. She said, calmly:

"Don't get fresh and try to bully me. It won't get you anywhere!"

"All right!" he shouted, "I'm off you from now——"

"Stay off, then. It suits me——"

"—Leaving me cold for *that* guy! Yaas. You did! And give me a dirty look when I tried to kiss you——"

"Mush never went with me. I've told you plenty of times——"

"You're a cold cut of chicken, you are! What d'yeh think a fella goes with a skirt for?"

"Cut it out," she said, "if you wanta be friends with me, Jimmy. I'm fed up on your pulling me around and your hands all over me, and always figuring out how you'll get me to kiss you. I'm fed up fighting you and telling you to quit every time I ride in your darned old flivver. Now, get me right; I'm off that stuff. And if you can't act the way I want, you better get another girl!"

"You fixin' to can me for that fancy guy?" he demanded, fiercely.

That exasperated her. But she said in a controlled voice.

"What I do is none of your damn business. . . . And don't you ring me up again. Mom's sick—and I'm sick of this argument. Act like a gentleman and I'll be friendly. But if you talk rough and act up you can kiss yourself good-bye right now!"

She hung up and went into her bedroom. For nearly an hour she sat there on the side of the bed, motionless. At last, with a deep breath, she rose and walked into her mother's room.

Helen lay in the restless slumber which seemed to be characteristic of her illness. Ellie drew a chair to the bedside and took her mother's hand in both of hers; and sat so until midnight, listening to the noises in the street.

In the morning Dr. McCarty had a brief talk with Ellie, and the girl learned then that her mother was very, very ill; that the "growth" did not behave like a "benign" growth; that an operation was not possible; that other treatment was being given; that the outlook was serious.

The girl was frightened, but seemed incapable of comprehending that such a thing as death threatened. She was scared and dazed, and unable to grasp the possibility of her mother dying.

"But you are going to help Mom, aren't you?" she demanded of the doctor.

"Yes—help her," he said soothingly.

CHAPTER VII

ALL that week her mother remained in a strange, drowsy state, often restless, sometimes awaking with a frightened cry, reaching out trembling arms for Ellie. At such moments the girl sat on the bed locked in her mother's convulsive embrace, until, gradually, drowsiness invaded the sick woman and she sank back to her pillows once more.

Helen was no longer clear in her mind. That had become evident. She never spoke at all save in intervals of sudden fright, and then incoherently, seeming to be aroused from stupor by some sudden access of terror or of pain. But these nightmares became rarer; and, now toward the end of the week, they no longer occurred. Her mind seemed to clear, also; and, with consciousness, a lovely serenity came into her face and voice.

One morning Helen opened her gentle eyes—no longer wide with fear or dilated with pain—and gazed peacefully upon her daughter, smiled at the nurse, at the sunshine where a potted flower which Ellie had bought made a brilliant mass on the window ledge.

"How pretty," she whispered.

The nurse moistened her lips and gave her a spoonful of water.

Ellie, just finishing midday dinner, heard her mother's voice. The next moment she was bending over her, tremulous with joy and inexpressible relief.

"Mom, darling," she whispered, "you are beginning to get well at last! I heard your voice. Oh, Mom, I am so happy!"

Helen smiled drowsily; her lips parted; she said in a soft, distinct voice:

"It's all right. . . . All right. . . . my little daughter. . . . All is so quiet, now . . . and the sunlight seems . . . pleasant. . . ." She lay smiling with closed eyes for a while.

Presently she opened them and looked up at the nurse who gave her more water in a spoon.

Ellie put her lips to the nurse's ear: "She's getting well," she whispered excitedly.

"You'd better go out and take a walk," said Miss Wylie. "You haven't been out of the house since last Saturday. That's a week to-day."

"My mother is better," whispered the girl with a radiant look at the bed. "She is getting well, Miss Wylie."

"You have become very pale and thin," said the nurse. "You should spend the afternoon walking in the sunshine."

Ellie gazed at her mother. Helen had fallen asleep. She seemed very frail and white and looked no older than her daughter, save for the silvery light on her pale gold hair which the nurse had braided.

The girl drew a long, deep breath of happy relief. "All right," she murmured, "I'll go out. . . ." Suddenly her eyes filled and her lip quivered. "I was so—so afraid of Death," she faltered, "—so afraid I'd *see* it!—see my mother—die. . . . Now that it's all over I can tell you how I felt, Miss Wylie—I've been so afraid! . . . I

didn't see my father die; I *couldn't*. . . . And if Mom
had, I—I couldn't have stood it—to see her—die——"

"You are very nervous and tired," said Miss Wylie
quietly. "You must walk in the sunshine this afternoon
and come back strong and calm and composed."

Ellie gave her mother another blissful look, nodded,
and went into her bedroom.

The blessed relief from uncertainty, surcease from fear,
left her rather limp for a few moments. And there had
been something else on her mind, too; something which
had persisted even amid terror; a memory; an undercur-
rent of consciousness that the day was Saturday.

But her telephone had not rung. And it was now nearly
two o'clock in the afternoon. He had not called her up.

What to do about it she didn't know. She did not want
to go out with the chance that he might telephone her. Yet
she needed air and sunshine—felt the want of it after this
week of suspense spent indoors.

As she stood there, hesitating, her wistful glance fell
on the telephone directory.

At the thought, pride checked her with a faint blush.
Nevertheless—what else was she to do? Anyway, she'd
look him up, and consider——

There were only three Westalls in the directory; only
one John Westall.

She went to the telephone, trying to think whether it
would be a "fresh" thing to do. He said he'd give her a
ring—or, rather, she had asked him to. Her cheeks were
hot at the idea that he had not troubled to keep his word.

After a minute's hesitation she called the number of
his office; and at the same instant she remembered that

business places were likely to close on Saturday afternoons during summer.

"There's nobody there now," she thought. Then she heard his voice, crisply impatient:

"Westall Construction!"

The suddenness of it scared her silent.

"Hello!" he said sharply. "Who is it?"

"I—I'm Ellie Lessing——"

"*Who?*"

"M-Miss Lessing. . . . Do you remember——"

"*Oh!* . . ." She heard him laugh. "Hello, Miss Lessing," he said in an amused voice, "how are you?"

"I'm very well," she said; "—are you?"

"Perfectly, thank you. I suppose you thought I'd forgotten to give you a ring?"

"I didn't know——"

"I remembered. Only my partner is ill and I have had to remain here and give up my Saturday swim this week."

"Then you are not going to Manhattan Beach?"

"Not until three or half-past, anyway. That's why I didn't call you; didn't want to spoil your day——"

"Oh, it wouldn't have," she cried. "I couldn't have gone, anyway. Only—I've been waiting for you to give me a ring——"

"I'm sorry. I didn't call because I wasn't sure I could get off at all. Will you come down this afternoon, then?"

"I can't. I must be home by supper-time. My mother is quite ill."

"Oh! I'm sorry——"

"But she is better; she is getting well. The nurse thinks

I should take a walk in the sunshine. I haven't been out of the house since last Saturday."

"You poor girl! Certainly you should go out. Where are you going?"

"I think I'll take a long walk in Bronx Park. I—you wouldn't care to—to do that, would you?——" She laughed in sudden trepidation, confused, sorry that she had courted this man's polite excuses—laid herself open to his refusal.

But he said in that gaily amused voice which she began to find both agreeable and stimulating:

"Why not?" he said. "You can take your diving lesson next Saturday."

"Yes, I will. But I know you'd rather go to the beach this afternoon."

"No; I'd rather take a walk with you."

"But I'll have to leave you at six. I'm just telling you in case you wanted me to go somewhere and dance——"

He laughed: "I've a car. Shall I stop for you?"

"Oh, thank you."

"At three-thirty?"

"I'll be ready. I can't ask you up because my mother is ill. Would you mind ringing our bell, and I'll come right down. And thank you so much——"

"Three-thirty?"

"Yes. Good-bye."

CHAPTER VIII

ELLIE stole to the door, looked at her sleeping mother, smiled happily at the nurse, tiptoed back to her bedroom, seated herself before the looking-glass of her little white enamelled dressing-table.

She had an hour and more, and meant to employ every second of it.

First she used cold cream, thoroughly. From this massage her fresh young skin emerged ready for the powder it did not require. But her grey-green eyes were fixed upon two faint freckles near the nose, and these fascinating adornments she effaced without mercy.

She never had plucked her eyebrows—two fine, thin, straight-growing lines of deep golden brown—but she used a pencil on them now, carefully, deliberately.

On temples and cheek-bones she used something labelled *Rose Byzantine,* which left a faint flush there. Her eyelashes, which were silky, thick and long, she knew enough to let alone. But her brilliant mouth she "improved" into a cupid's bow—a shape not as lovely as its own, but very fashionable.

Now, with her iron, she fell to crisping and curling the burnished bobbed hair which naturally was full of charming little twists and waves and bright tendrils.

That took some time. After her hair suited her she

dressed in a light summer sport suit, sheer stockings that showed the smooth skin through; little suede shoes.

Now, with the precision born of practice, she pulled the close little hat over her short curls and settled it with one deft jerk.

Her wrist-watch gave her half an hour for her nails. She spread out the collection of instruments, polishes, liquids, and fell to. Her hands and feet were very lovely. She knew it, and kept them well.

When she finished, and was minutely enhancing the facial make-up to a natural and distractingly pretty harmony, the door-bell rang.

She took one last, earnest look at herself in the glass, rose and ran to the window and looked out. Then she hastened to her mother's door, went in and lightly kissed the sleeper's hair, looked at Miss Wylie with a breathless smile, and stole away down three flights of hot, smelly stairs.

"How do you do?" she cried; "I am so pleased to see you," and offered her gloved hand.

"That's a lovely car," she added, "and I'm so glad to get out of the house. It certainly is sweet of you, Mr. Westall——" She rested her hand on his arm and sprang into the seat. He got in on the other side, took the wheel; the golden-grey sports car slid away up the Grand Concourse.

"Well," he said, "this is very jolly, seeing you again."

"I think so, too. That was a great lesson you gave me. I hope I don't forget next time I try."

"You're a born swimmer," he said. He smiled: "And I'll say you can dance, too——"

"So can you. Wasn't that dance the best ever?"

"How did your young man take it, later?" he asked, mischievously.

"Oh, dear. I'm certainly in dutch with him——"

"That's too bad. I was afraid he didn't like it——"

"Let him get over his grouch," she said. "And I don't care if he doesn't."

"But that won't do. You mustn't let me butt into——"

"You didn't butt in. Anyway, I asked you——"

"Yes——"

"I wanted you to. Don't let's talk about it. . . . Did you think I was fresh to call you up?"

"Not at all," he said, laughing.

"Well—it was your office. Of course I wouldn't have rung up your home."

That amused him still more: "Why not?"

She gave him a youthfully sophisticated glance and a dainty shrug:

"Not me," she said. "You might be married."

"Ah," he said, "I see. Well, a girl ought to be careful."

"Certainly . . . You're old enough to be married."

"Indeed, I am," he said, gravely.

She made a gesture: "So I took no chances. . . . Not that there's anything wrong about *me,* you understand——"

"I do. But you've got to watch a married man."

"You've said it. . . . I can take care of myself anyway."

"You've learned how," he nodded.

"Girls have to. . . . I've been out with married men. They're mostly the same. But I wouldn't go with one, steady. You gotta fight 'em all the time. . . . And if I was their kind I wouldn't do a thing like that to any man's wife. . . . No, not if he was the last man left in America. . . . It isn't worth it, anyhow, going out with married men. What does it amount to?—a swell dinner, a show, supper, a dance—and they're always trying to get you away somewhere alone where you've got to keep fighting them—ah, it's no good bothering with parties like that—these travelling men looking for trouble—and all they want is to get you—like the cheap bunch they are——"

He said: "You don't look quite old enough to have had so much experience."

"I haven't had much. But you know how it is; some girls will ask you to make up a party. That's the way. A lot of girls I know think it's smart to fool with married men and get what's in it—candy and stockings and all like that—and then leave them cold. . . . Well, I've done it, too. But it makes me kinda sick——" She pulled a wry face, then glanced at Westall with a deliciously impudent air:

"Like if you are a married man," she explained. "I grab a diving lesson, two or three dances, and a joy-ride off you, and when you try to kiss me I tell you I'm through."

"Well, but you haven't grabbed very much," he pointed out, laughing. "Couldn't you do better than that before you left me cold, Ellie?"

"You mean graft some stockings and things?"

"Certainly. And perhaps a fur coat and a bar pin."

She turned and looked at him, and her grey-green eyes were hard and intelligent.

"Some girls," she said, "can get away with murder,

without giving up. . . . I don't think I could. . . . I know a girl who got a lot of things, that way. . . . Without giving up. . . . Well, I don't need a bar pin bad enough to stand for everything—I mean almost everything. . . . No, it makes me sick. I don't see how girls do it. I'd be ashamed—taking things. . . . I don't mind fooling a married man. Stockings, candy, all right. But graft?—not *me!*"

"I see," said Westall, much interested; "bar pins and fur coats are graft."

"Certainly. It's like stealing."

"You couldn't take them without pay; and you have no intention of paying," concluded Westall.

Ellie laughed her youthful, scornful laugh: "I guess not! . . . And I'll tell you some more; I won't be a married man's darling and I won't be a young man's slave. He's got to make good money, the guy I hitch with. . . . I know girls—the mushy kind—that fall for good looks and twenty dollars a week. And what they get is a two-room flat and a washtub and a baby! Not *me!*" she added scornfully.

"Well," he said, "what *are* you going to do, Ellie?"

"Stay put." She smiled at him. "I never was man-crazy, anyway. When I take a position I'll be all right."

"Haven't you a position?"

"Not yet. I guess I better advertise and quit waiting for Miss Rosenblatt to find me a job. . . . I'll tell you why," she added, leaning a little toward him with engaging confidence. "I am running the flat, now that my mother is ill, and I'm worried stiff over the bills. . . . Mom explained about our money before she was too sick to attend to things. We can't go on like this. I've got to get busy."

He nodded: "Everybody, men and women, rich or poor, ought to have jobs."

She turned and stared at him: "What does a rich girl want of a job?"

"Everybody ought to be self-supporting. Everybody ought to have a job of some kind."

"Why?" she demanded.

"There would be fewer divorces—for one reason. The man or woman who hasn't anything to do is a public and private nuisance. And the richer they are, the bigger nuisance they become."

"I'll tell you," she cried, "that if I were rich I'd never take a job."

He smiled: "What would you do with your time, Ellie?"

"I'd have a dandy time."

"How?"

"I'd have a car and a house and more clothes and jewels than I needed! I'd go to shows; I'd dance. I'd go around the world."

"And then?"

"You mean I'd get tired of doing all this?"

"You certainly would. You'd want a change."

"Well, I'd study."

"Aha!" he exclaimed, "what would you study?"

"I don't know. Piano. Stage dancing. . . . And I like statues."

"Statues?"

"You know what I mean? Statues. Like that Lorelei

fountain. Gosh, I'd like to learn how to make a statue. If I were rich I'd learn how. I'd make statues."

"You'd like to study sculpture?"

"Well, I guess that is what I mean. I don't suppose a girl could learn. . . . But I can pinch a man's head out of a wad of chewing-gum. You can laugh, but it looks like a man's head. . . . Once I bought a little plaster statue from a Wop. It was Venus—you know?—she didn't have clothes on her. So I copied her."

"In clay?"

"No. Is that what they use? No; I made a naked girl like her out of dough. Now, you're laughing again!——"

"No, I'm interested."

But she turned shy and silent and they drove on along quadruple rows of trees, past 175th Street and Eastburn Avenue, past Valentine Avenue at 188th Street, on past Fordham Road and the Poe Cottage at Kingsbridge Road; and had swung around St. George's Crescent before she spoke again:

"You'd be surprised," she remarked abruptly.

"How, Ellie?"

"If I made enough money to learn how to make statues."

He glanced at her.

"If you have a chance," he said, "and enough ambition to study, I don't know why you shouldn't make statues. . . . Or anything else."

"You don't really believe I could!"

"Why not?"

"I'm not well educated. I can't go even to high school; I've got to work."

"Do you want an education?"

"I don't know. . . . Yes."

"If you want one badly enough you'll manage to get it."

She said, absently: "I've never thought about it much." . . . She added, suddenly: "I'll tell you one thing; I'd like to use the words you use. I know the difference between how you speak and the way I speak. But—what the devil can you learn in primary?"

They were crossing the viaduct, now, near which Westall must park his car if they were going to do any walking.

"How do you feel about it?" he asked.

"Oh, yes, please let us walk. I really do need it."

So the car was parked and side by side they walked forward into the Botanical Gardens.

CHAPTER IX

EVERYWHERE in garden, greenhouse, grove, and among rolling meadows, the "plain people" were holiday-making in the fine summer weather.

Parties of dishevelled children, running wild, sped along gravel paths bordered by flower-masses in heavy bloom. Little girls raced about at random with shrill cries; gangs of small boys hastened across meadows, appearing to know where they were going and why. Family parties trundled babies. Middle class owned the landscape; wallowed in it; misused, brutalized it. Like dogs, feeling good, rolling on flowers.

They littered lawns with greasy papers; fed themselves out of paper boxes; crowded, animal-like, around drinking fountains awaiting their turns to wet their muzzles; nursed and chastised infants; sweated, spat, belched, sprawled on the grass, belly-full, gaping stupidly at the blue sky.

A sour herd smell tainted the breeze where the solid substance of the Nation, unconfined, was taking its pleasure in its own natural way.

Ellie, moving lightly beside Westall, a cool, lithe shape in her summer frock, indicated the conservatories with a careless gesture:

"When I was a kid they looked like crystal castles to me. I used to run wild around here—run my legs off. . . . A crowd of crazy kids—no sense—just running and yelling all day long. . . . The grass feels good to your feet, doesn't it? It smells sweet too."

"Yes," he said amiably, "it has a swell smell."

After a moment she looked up at him, cleverly suspicious, and detected malice in his gravity.

"A swell smell," she repeated; "that wasn't the way to say it. I talk slang too much. The trouble is I don't know the kind of word you know. . . . I wish to God I had somebody to call the turn on me when I talk wrong."

"Do you want *me* to?"

"Would you—every time I make a bum break?"

"If you like."

"I'd be darned grateful," she said with an enchanting smile.

They walked out across the undulating meadows bordered by clumps of evergreens, crossed the drive and the hard-wood ridge, and came out into a rich, sunny little valley where a tiny brook ran.

Everywhere in the blue air dragon-flies glittered and darted; butterflies sped through sunshine, hovered and flopped among flowers; trees and thickets were vibrant with bird music.

"Let's get away from all these stinking people," she suggested, turning up her nose. "I like the wild, shady part where the river runs. Do you?"

"It sounds agreeable."

"You know where the woods are, don't you?"

"No."

"Don't you know the park?" she asked, surprised.

"I don't," he admitted. "Show me your woods and wild river."

She took him to the end of the meadow; down a stony wood-path edging a heavy growth of hemlock; over a stone bridge, then down beside the amber waters of a little woodland stream. Along this path they walked where ancient trees towered—huge hemlocks, pines, then sycamores, maples, oaks, and giant tulip trees.

Sunshine filtered through the cool, still groves where wood-thrushes were singing—where the pert chatter of golden-winged woodpeckers rang out from tall elms; where rose-breasted grosbeaks sang and robins chattered, and golden orioles fluted from somewhere amid high branches. Ripple, ripple went the little river under leafy boughs, over rock and shoal. Except the mellow voice of the Bronx and the bird-songs, there was no other sound save, sometimes, the feathery whirr of some distant automobile on an unseen highway—save for the breezy stirring of summer foliage on lofty boughs—the chirring of a squirrel—the scuffle of some bird in the underbrush.

Everywhere butterflies were flying—green-clouded swallowtails on velvet wings, lovers ever of moist woodlands. The golden melodies of thrushes filled all the woods, calling, answering incessantly from the demi-light of still glades. In spots of white fire the sun's rays touched the water.

The girl seated herself on a bank of wild grasses and invited him with a glance. Then she slipped off one shoe, extracted a pebble, replaced it.

"Here's where I used to come all alone and sit sometimes . . . and look at the water. . . . Kids are queer. They do a lot of dreaming sometimes."

"About what?" he asked.

"Gosh—I don't know. I used to like to sit here by myself and just look and listen. . . . I felt like I was in church——"

"—Felt as *though*," he corrected her, smilingly.

"Oh, *thank* you!" she exclaimed, gratefully; "I felt *as though* I was——"

"—*Were*, Ellie."

"Thank you, Mr. Westall! Is this the way, then?—'I felt as *though* I *were* in church'?"

"That's correct," he nodded, amused at her gratitude.

She said: "It's darned kind of you, but I am afraid it's a lot of trouble——"

"I'm going to send you a book or two on correct English. . . . If you'll promise to study a little."

"Oh, I will! But *you* don't have to buy books for me——"

"Books," he remarked gravely, "are not like bar pins and fur coats——"

Her quick laughter echoed at that. However, she gave him a rather searching look:

"If you're married," she said, "you don't act like—act *as though* you are." . . . He laughed. But her eyes still questioned.

"Do you really want to know?" he asked.

"If you think it's all right to tell me. . . . But I'm not the nosey kind——"

"You mean 'curious,'" he remarked.

"Thank you so much. . . . No, I'm not curious,"—she hesitated, "—that's a lie, too. I *am* curious! If a girl says she isn't she's a liar. I'd certainly like to know whether you *are* married. . . . But you don't have to tell me——"

"Why don't I have to?"

"—As long as you act the way you act—like a gentle-man——"

"You're such a funny combination."

"Why?"—defiantly.

"Theoretically sophisticated, and practically innocent."

Her eyebrows bent inward. Effort to follow unaccustomed words. But she was clever enough not only to penetrate his meaning but also to remember the words for future use.

"You keep a watchful eye on me," he advised her with pretended gravity, "and if ever you catch me giving you a fur coat or a bar pin, you start and run for home as tight as you know how——"

They were laughing, now, without restraint; and when his features finally sobered again, hers still were bright with all the accumulated gaiety of this summer afternoon.

"Well, I'm not afraid of you," she decided. "If you've got a wife and kids at home you can do the worrying. . . . Do you really want to send me those books?"

"I do."

"All right. I'll study like the devil. . . . Gosh, there's so much to know——" She caught him by the arm: "Oh, look at that red bird!" she whispered. A scarlet tanager lit in a tree across the creek, and sat, preening, brilliant as a glowing coal.

He told her the name of the bird. As she seemed interested he mentioned the names of other birds which from time to time came within their vision. It appeared that already she had learned in primary school a little about the commoner birds and insects and trees.

"I tell you," she repeated in an annoyed voice, "there is so much to know that it makes me feel like a fool. If I was—*were*—rich I'd hand myself an education. Ignorance don't get you anywhere——"

"*Doesn't* get you anywhere," he corrected her pleasantly.

She shrugged: "Oh, hell," she remarked, "what's the use!" She sprang to her feet, and when he rose, she slipped her arm through his—an unpremeditated confidence. Perhaps something germinating, instinctive toward support.

They sauntered on along the Bronx. Once he pointed out to her a big snapping turtle basking on some bleached driftwood. Once she paused, unashamed, to watch some naked boys sporting in the river where grassy banks lead down through clumps of willow and aspen.

Moving on, presently, she said: "Kids are pretty. . . . If I ever learned how to make a statue I'd copy one of those little boys. They're so cute. . . . That Venus statue I bought off that Wop——"

"—Bought *from* that *Italian*," he interrupted, and grinned at her.

"You're so sweet to me, Mr. Westall!" she exclaimed gratefully. "I was going to say that all the statues he sold seemed to be naked. Why is that, I wonder?"

He told her about the Greek worship of the ideal human figure. Mentioned Praxiteles.

"I like clothes on them, too," she confided, "—the Greek kind of clothes, I mean. That Lorelei fountain is sw—is pretty. God—what a lovely shape! She's got a drapery over part of her. . . . Once I took some dough when Smilax was baking—that's our nigger—and I tried to remember how the Lorelei looked, and I made me a statue. . . . Smilax baked it, afterward, and I ate it."

"I'll send you some plastolene for you to play with," he promised. He was obliged to explain what is plastolene. Ellie appeared enchanted; then, doubtful, glanced askance at him out of slanting, clever eyes.

"Well?" he inquired, aware of the intermittent scrutiny.

"I'm just wondering," she said carelessly; "—you don't have to buy me all those things. Why do you? As soon as I mention something, you say you'll send me a sample——"

He laughed: "You haven't mentioned a fur coat, yet,——" watching her cleverly chiselled profile. She turned and gave him a hardy look and straight.

"At that," she said, "I might. What would you do if I started that line with you?"

"Do? What could I do except send you a sample?" he replied.

"You would? A sample fur coat?"

"What else could I do?" he repeated mischievously.

"You know what they cost?" she demanded.

"I think so."

"And you'd send me one?"

"I suppose so."

"Why?" incredulously.

"Well, if you wanted it——"

"Why?" she repeated with emphasis, watching him out of unbelieving eyes. "There'd be nothing in it for *you!* . . . And I'll tell you another thing; even if you're not married, I'm not the kind of girl *you'd* go with. I'm not well enough educated. Besides——"

"Well?"

She reddened, then laughed: "I'm only eighteen. You wouldn't like me, anyway. . . . I wonder why you came out here to take a walk with me!"

"I wonder, too," he said, laughing.

"I guess," she concluded in her hard, bright manner, "you thought you'd take a chance with me."

"So that's your conclusion?"

"Why didn't you go to the beach, then?"

He admitted, gravely, that his behaviour was a mystery to him. But she saw laughter in his eyes.

"Well," she retorted, "you don't have to tell me anything—if you want to make a mystery of yourself. All the same, I don't see why you are spending the afternoon with me."

"What do you care," he asked, "what my reason may be as long as I don't bother you?"

"How, bother?"

"Pull you about; kiss you."

She said with a hard, young laugh: "If you're married you'll sure try to start that line some time. If you're not,"—she shrugged her shoulders—"I guess you don't like me enough to want a girl like me. . . . I guess you can get any girl you want to go with you." The naïve tribute to his attractions both touched and amused Westall.

"I'll be frank," he said. "I don't quite know why I am spending Saturday afternoon in the Bronx with you,

Ellie. You're nice to look at—exceedingly pretty—and you're interesting."

"How am I?"—in surprise and incredulity.

"I haven't tried to analyse your charm," he admitted, smilingly, "—but that's the right word—*charm*—and you have it. I suppose I was conscious of it when we swam and danced last Saturday. . . . Anyway, I am here with you instead of at the beach. How can we account for it?"

After a few moments' walking she looked up at him with a lovely childish expression:

"I *thought* you liked me a little—down there at Villy's."

She amused him immensely: "And, how about *you?*" he inquired.

"You mean, did I like *you?* Well, I'll say I was dying to dance with you. I guess I showed I wanted to, didn't I?"

He nodded.

She said: "I called you up, too, didn't I? Well, then."

"What do you find likeable about me?" He had become curious concerning the mental and emotional processes of this young middle-class girl with her lovely, overpainted face, her pretty figure, and her jumbled stock of innocence and sophistication so naïvely unconcealed.

"Well—I guess you know. You're good-looking." She gave him one of her clever, hardy glances. . . . "And the way you swim and dance makes you popular with me. . . . And I like the way you talk. . . . I want to tell you something——"

As she hesitated he said: "Go ahead!"

"I don't know how to explain. . . . Going this way

with you—well, it peps me up. . . . Exciting. You make
me want to start something. . . . I'm on tiptoe with
you. . . . You know what I mean? I want to kick into
something. . . . The way you feel when you hear a good
jazz band. . . . Ambitious. . . . Do you get me? Well,
going with you makes me want to get busy. . . . Snap
into it. . . . Damn it all, I don't know how to tell
you——" She ended in disgust at her lack of vocabulary.

"You mean," he suggested, "that I seem to stimulate
you mentally."

"Oh, God!" She sighed, "How easy! You've sure got
to know your own language. *Stimulate, mentally!* Why
the dickens can't I talk that way! . . . Will you send
me those books? Will you, please, Mr. Westall?"

He promised. They turned and started to retrace their
path; and she took his arm again with a defiant confidence
in him and in herself—unwarranted, now that she was
ready to accept things from him.

A little uneasy, she presently reverted to the matter:
"How many things are you going to give me? Books and
plastolene?"

"That was the idea, I believe."

She retained his arm as they came out on the meadows,
moving lightly beside him with a lithe, springy stride
across the clover, her clever face bent as though noting
every step they took.

Without looking up she said: "Life's a queer thing.
Just meeting that way at the beach . . . and here we
are. You've been so nice. . . . When I think of Mom's
getting well I'll always think of the park and our walk.
. . . Gee, it would be funny——"

She checked herself.

"What would be funny?"

"Oh, nothing. . . . Sometimes I don't get you. . . . A girl doesn't exactly know how to take a man like you."

He turned and looked at her, amused. She walked on beside him with head lowered as though counting each step across the clover.

After a little while she glanced at her wrist-watch.

"Oh!" she exclaimed in genuine sorrow, "I've got to go home. Isn't that the limit?"

All the way back along the pretty little brook she lamented the termination of the afternoon:

"I've had a dandy time," she said. "I wish we could go somewhere. I mean to dance—if you'd take me. But maybe you've got a date——"

"No," he said with a smile, "but you couldn't go, anyway."

"I know it. My mother is sick——"

"*Ill*," he remarked, tersely.

"Thank you so much. . . . *Ill*. . . . Yes, but she is getting well. . . . That's why I can't go out with you to-night. My mother is *ill*."

As they came out of the grassy valley, traversed the groves, crossed the drive and walked toward the flower-beds by the conservatories, she dropped his arm.

"I know enough not to do that in public," she remarked. "Only rubes take arms and hold hands." And added with a smile of dazzling malice: "Besides, if you're married you've got to be careful. Suppose we run into your wife?"

"Probably," he said, "she'd think you very pretty."

"And what would she do to me?" inquired the girl with her hard, clever smile disguising the slight shock of discovery that she had to do with a married man after all. Yet, she had been convinced of this, or, rather, afraid of it, from the first.

"So you *are* married," she added carelessly.

"I haven't said so."

"You said your wife would think me—pretty——"

"I assumed that, *if* I had a wife, and *if* we met her, *probably* she would think that." His amusement disconcerted the girl.

"If you continue to worry," he added, "I'll be tempted to tease you."

"I'm not afraid of you," she returned in a cool voice, tinged with sullenness. "Even if you liked me I don't have to go with you."

He said, greatly amused: "Of course you don't. You are under no obligations to see me again."

"Yes, I am."

"What obligations?" he demanded, surprised.

"Books and p-plastolene. And this joy-ride. . . . And our walk. . . . And your telling me when I make mistakes in English. . . . And all your kindness. . . . The only trouble is—is—I don't want to get in dutch with—with any man's wife."

He was too much amused to speak.

After a while: "I'll tell you," she said abruptly, "that a girl who is straight can't afford to get in dutch with a married man. . . . Not that I don't like you. . . . You know better."

He made no reply.

Presently: "I'll tell you another thing," she said with nervous animation; "if I took a chance going with you and knowing you're married, you'd certainly start something. You'd think you had a right to. . . . Wouldn't you?"

He laughed so gaily that her rather fierce expression altered.

"It would be jolly if we had a swim and a dance together next Saturday," he said. "I hadn't thought of trying anything more reckless with you."

Her face slowly glowed. Finally, when the bright colour died:

"I *want* to meet you. . . . If you say it's all right, I'll be at the beach."

"Quite all right. . . . Shall I stop for you with the car?"

"You'd better not come upstairs. Just ring our bell. . . . The devil of it is, I've been out with married men before, and I swore I'd never go again. . . . But the married men I've met are different. . . . Not like you. . . ." She looked up at him, unconscious of the distress in her face: "You don't seem li—*as if*—you are married. . . . I often wonder why married men like other women. . . . I'd die if my husband went with other women. . . . Aren't you—sorry—for your wife?"

"Not very."

"Why not?" she asked sharply.

He laughed at her.

After a pause: "Is there any danger of my running into her whenever I'm out with you?"

He laughed: "Had you intended to spend very much time with me, Ellie?"

The girl blushed scarlet; looked sharply away from him until, presently, she felt the pressure of his gloved hand on hers.

"I was just joking," he said. "You mustn't take me too seriously. I'm always likely to be joking."

She recovered her coolness and poise: "I was, too. I didn't expect to go with you, anyway. . . . Only a few times. . . . At the beach this summer. . . . We're pretty near home," she added.

He nodded, slowed down a little.

"Call me up when you're not too busy," he suggested, pleasantly.

"All right. . . . And I've had a great day. It's been so nice of you. . . . It's been *wonderful!* . . . What with Mom getting well . . . and our walk, and all——"

They drew up at her apartment house. Both got out.

Hat in hand, and in his pleasant manner, Westall thanked her for coming and was glad her mother was better, and hoped to swim with her next Saturday.

She paused in the doorway to watch him drive away. Then, glancing at her wrist-watch, she ran gaily up the three flights of stairs, fitted the key, entered with a happy mind and excited heart.

Miss Wylie stepped noiselessly out of the shadows; took her slim, gloved hand; led her aside into her own bedroom.

"Dear," she said gently, "Dr. McCarty has just left. . . . He wishes me to tell you something. . . . You must try to be very brave——" She put both arms around the girl: "I want you to summon all the courage you have——"

About eleven o'clock that night Helen was made ready to receive her daughter. She looked incredibly young—no older than Ellie.

Grief had stunned the child. An astonishment infinitely stupefying paralysed emotion when at last she was taken in to see her mother, and scarcely recognized her, so young Helen looked—so exquisitely white and still.

Death had not only robbed her but had cheated her, taking what was dear and warm and familiar and leaving a silent, youthful stranger on the bed with delicate folded hands——

It was her sudden and awful loneliness that overwhelmed the girl——

"Mom! It isn't *you!* My God—my God, where are you!——"

CHAPTER X

THERE were a dozen people at the funeral, Mae and
Arthur Graves, Jessie and Albert Farish, Jim Lacy
—all Ellie's friends. Smilax, in white shoes, sheer white
stockings, and white lisle thread gloves, was present with
her daughter, Rosie, aged fifteen, a pretty, light golden-
tinted coloured girl of disputed paternal descent. Then
there was Miss Wylie, Dr. McCarty, the Honourable
Tom Barrett, ex-Assemblyman, the Lessing family's law-
yer. There were present, also, two of Harry Lessing's
sporting friends—Jake Favor, a sleepy-looking, silent,
expensively dressed young man who wore heavy, handsome rings and a black pearl; and George Considine,
large at the waist-band, ruddy, double-chinned, minutely
groomed from his clipped grey hair and grey moustache
to the tan-coloured spats on his polished tan shoes.

Many elaborate floral pieces banked the casket. An extra automobile was necessary to carry them to the cemetery—crosses of Madonna lilies, white tuberose and car-
nation pillows, crowns, wreaths—every device known to
necrology.

The Honourable Thomas Barrett escorted Ellie, dazed,
confused and nearly suffocated by her veil; supported her,
patted her black-gloved hand when advisable.

In his florid, kindly manner, pedantically emphatic by
reason of much public speaking, he assured her that her

father had been "a grrand man," and that her mother had been "a lay-dy—leastways that was her r-repu-tayshun."

The Lessings had been Lutherans, if anything. That was the service. The weak-eyed minister spoke with a German accent; had excellent though stilted manners. Smilax and her golden-tinted daughter were Baptists; all the others Catholics. Everybody was considerate and polite to everybody else.

The hearse was the shiny latest in automobile construction.

It was a long, hot, dusty drive in hired automobiles to the cemetery. The return journey under a blazing July sun seemed interminable.

Dr. McCarty, the Honourable Tom Barrett, and George Considine ascended to the Lessing apartment with Ellie, where Smilax and Rosie had remained after the service to prepare a one o'clock dinner.

Ellie went into her mother's room. The desolate, sunlit silence terrified her. She knelt by the bed, cried noiselessly for a while, then got up and went into her own bedroom to take off the hot black emblems of mourning and bathe her swollen eyes and lips.

She came into the dining-room when Rosie summoned her. It appeared that Dr. McCarty was in a hurry. He hastened to finish his steak and potatoes. George Considine produced a flask, and the three men mixed a very little water with their Irish whisky, looked solemnly at Ellie, and drained their glasses with slight shudders, as though the duty were not entirely agreeable.

As Dr. McCarty was going, Ellie started to rise, but he gently forced her back:

"Judge Barrett wants to talk to you after dinner. I'll stop in this evening. Cheer up, Ellie; God needed your mother. She's on her way to your father, now. She's all right——" He kissed her pallid cheek: "—She'll be safe and happy now, God bless her——" He kissed the child again: "—Don't worry; we'll stand by you——" He seized his hat and went out in a hurry, still recommending her in a loud voice to cheer up.

Ellie held her handkerchief to her eyes for a while, then resumed her steak and potatoes.

Tom Barrett, "Judge" by courtesy, made conversation. George Considine poured out two more drinks and a thimbleful in half a glass of water for Ellie.

"It won't harm you," he said.

She tasted it, docilely, complained of the taste, comparing it to medicine, but sipped it at intervals during dinner.

"Judge," said Considine, "how about a little snifter?"

"Why not?" returned the "Judge," gravely; "that's one of the reasons that God grows grain."

He and Barrett lighted cigars. He said to Barrett: "I never saw Harry Lessing smoke anything but cigarettes. You remember?"

Barrett nodded.

After a silence: "He was all white," remarked Considine; "they don't make 'em any whiter. . . ." To Ellie: "Your father was all to the good. By God, there wasn't a crooked hair on his head. Am I right, Tom?"

"You said something. . . . All racing men will say that much for Harry Lessing. He played square with men; square with his wife. That's going some."

"You said it. . . . How about a chaser?" inquired Mr. Considine seriously.

They nodded to each other solemnly; to Ellie; drank; resumed cigars and attitudes of grave decorum.

Presently George Considine poured out two more drinks, swallowed his, shoved the silver flask into his pistol pocket, rose.

"Ellie," he said, "when you're lonely, come and stay with me. I've got a floor on top of my house. Judge Barrett will tell you——"

He held out a carefully cared for, highly coloured hand:

"Your father and mother were my friends. That means you, too."

"Thank you, Mr. Considine."

He shook her hand gravely; shook hands with Tom Barrett; took his pearl-grey hat, and walked away with that peculiarly heavy and impressive dignity of the full-waisted and well-preserved.

When Judge Barrett had gone over Helen's papers with Ellie the girl's situation became clear enough. When all debts were settled there would remain nothing except the income from the trust fund established by Harry Lessing. Twelve hundred dollars a year.

"I'll look for a position to-morrow," said Ellie.

"Take your time. George Considine and I can let you have——"

"No. I *want* a position. I need to be busy. You're very kind, Judge Barrett, but I must occupy my mind and start to support myself. Will you see about subletting this apartment?"

"I'll attend to that. You want to sell your furniture?"

"I'll keep enough to furnish one room."

"You tie tags on what you want, Ellie. When you find a place I'll have it sent there. . . . Why don't you stay with George Considine until you can look around——"

"No; I'll find a room. I'd better do it now—get it over with——" She blotted her brimming eyes with the black-edged handkerchief. "I can't stay here alone," she said desolately. "I *can't!* I want to go somewhere alone. . . . It's all ended, now. . . . Everything is ended here—since Mom left me——"

"All right, Ellie; all right," he said soothingly. "You do just what you want to do. I'll fix up things for you. You stop in to see me at my office to-morrow——"

They stood up; he put one arm around her and patted her shoulders:

"You're a good girl, Ellie. You come to me when anything worries you. . . . There, there, you'll feel better when you have a good sleep——"

All that afternoon she lay on her bed, sleeping and weeping alternately, unable to comprehend—to reconcile herself to what had happened.

About six o'clock she fell into a deeper sleep. Smilax sent Rosie to ask her what she wished for supper, but Rosie hesitated to arouse her.

About nine o'clock Ellie awoke in darkness and sat up, frightened.

There was a light in the dining-room, and she called out to Smilax, and stumbled to her feet.

Rosie appeared from the kitchen to say that her mother had gone home and that she was remaining to give Ellie some supper.

There was a cup of tea for her, and an omelette. The pretty coloured girl hovered around Ellie at table, friendly, soft-voiced, deft in service.

"Ma said for me to stay to-night if you feel lonely," she informed Ellie. "I can sleep on your sofa and get breakfast in the mornin'."

Ellie nodded: "I'd be very glad to have you, Rosie——" She choked, bowed her bobbed head in her hands.

Rosie hovered over her; ventured to touch her——caress her hot temples, her hair.

After a little while Ellie stood up, drying her eyes on her napkin, and Rosie began to remove the dishes to the kitchen.

About ten o'clock Ellie went into the kitchen and found all in order and Rosie seated there, awaiting her pleasure.

"I think I'll go to bed," said Ellie. "If you're going to fix yourself a place on the sofa I'd better show you where the bed clothes are——"

They went to the linen closet, got out what was necessary. Ellie watched her arranging the sofa, a trifle uncertain about this coloured girl using her mother's bed-linen. But Rosie looked so clean and wholesome, and her pretty person seemed so well cared for that Ellie was satisfied.

When her sofa-bed was made she turned down the sheets on Ellie's bed, and, smiling in her shy, friendly way, began to undress Ellie with all the natural skill of a capable maid.

There is no woman alive who doesn't naturally lend herself to such ministrations. No maid ever before had laid a finger on Ellie Lessing; but she abandoned herself to Rosie as though accustomed to having her stockings drawn off.

"I'd like to be a lady's maid," said Rosie. "I'd like to work for you, Miss Ellie."

Ellie smiled faintly: "When I'm rich I'll want you."

Rosie, kneeling to gather the shoes and stockings, looked up earnestly: "I hope you won't forget me?"

"I won't."

"I know how to make you comfortable. . . . You going to take a hot bath, Miss Ellie?"

"Are you going to turn on the water?"

"Yes, if you want——"

"Make it very hot. I want to sleep. I've *got* to sleep——" Tears rushed to her eyes as she let fall her underclothes, held out her arms blindly for the bath-robe which Rosie held and belted around her.

After her bath she felt better; lay on her pillow watching Rosie undress, reassured by the girl's extreme neatness of clothing and cleanliness of person.

"I'd like to make a statue of you—just that way, Rosie," she said, "—if I knew how——"

Rosie's dazzling smile transfigured her.

"You've got an awfully pretty figure," said Ellie. "I wish I knew how. . . . I'd like to make a statue of you, naked, teaching a parrot to talk—you know?—this way——" She held up one finger as though admonishing

an imaginary parrot balanced on the other wrist. "Do you
know what I'd call my statue?"

"I don't know, Miss Ellie——"

"I'd call it 'Africa.' I know what I mean by that, too——"
with an odd flash of insight—"I wouldn't mean just because you are a coloured girl and came from Africa—or
your ancestors did. . . . You haven't got a night-gown,
have you? I'll lend you one"—she pointed "—there, in
that second drawer. What pretty little feet you have! . . .
I never before saw a coloured girl undressed. . . . Well,
I'll get a job first, and then maybe I'll be able to learn how
to make a statue. . . . In primary school we made things
out of modelling clay. . . . I learned how to make an ap-
ple, a pear and a peach. That's all they taught us. . . ."
She yawned, lying on her pillow.

"Shall I turn off the light, Miss Ellie?" inquired Rosie.

"Yes, I'm sleepy——" She yawned again; and again
after the little bedroom was wrapped in darkness.

"If I'm frightened by dreams," she murmured, "I'll
call out to you, and you must turn on the light."

"I'll get right up and come to you, Miss Ellie."

"Good night," she said drowsily.

She fell asleep in a few moments.

Rosie lay awake listening to her breathing.

CHAPTER XI

BY the end of the week Ellie Lessing had concluded that either Miss Rosenblatt couldn't help her to a position or wouldn't take the trouble to help her.

July was a bad month anyway for stenographers and typists. The weather had grown hot; business became slack; people were irritable.

She accomplished something, however; she found an unfurnished room on West 86th Street. There was an architect on one floor, a piano teacher on another, a beauty parlour on the first floor, and a real-estate office in the basement. Her floor, the top, had a sort of pent-house. It was now divided into two very large, square rooms with two kitchenettes and two baths connecting. An actress occupied the front room. Ellie's quarters faced south, overlooking the rear of the houses on West 85th Street, and a stretch of sagging wooden fences and shabby backyards, ailanthus trees, and cats.

The end of the month was approaching; her Bronx Borough apartment already had been sublet to a prosperous Italian fruit-dealer and his family of seven; and where they all were to sleep only an Italian fruit-dealer could guess.

What furniture Ellie desired to keep she used to furnish her new quarters—her own bed of white enamel, the bureau, dresser and one chair; her mother's chintz lounge

and arm-chair; her chintz and lace curtains; the piano and
stool; a large chenille rug; two coloured engravings of
famous race horses, Ormond and Man-o'-War; framed,
tinted crayons of her father and mother; a few books,
mostly about horses; a trunk, a suit-case, a rocking chair
in which Harry Lessing used to sit in velvet slippers and
read the *Sporting Life;* and a small Japanese centre table.

On this table were collected an "art lamp"; the fifty-
cent plaster statue of Venus; the two books on how to
speak correct English, presented by Mr. Westall; and a
large tin box, unopened, containing plastolene—also Mr.
Westall's offering.

These, and bed-linen, table linen, towels, a refrigerator,
dishes, cooking utensils for the kitchenette, and her own
personal effects were all that Ellie retained from the an-
cestral flat.

Judge Barrett sent the rest of the furniture to a local
auction room. It brought very little after fees and cartage
were deducted.

Twice Ellie went down to 125th Street to the Judge's
office, where her bills and other financial matters were
being straightened out. The Judge put everything through
in a hurry because the racing season was about to begin at
Saratoga, and he and George Considine had never missed
an opening day in thirty years.

"Come on up with us," he said to Ellie; "we'll stake you
to a good time. You'll meet a lot of your father's friends."

"I'd like to," she said wistfully, "but I've got to hustle.
I want to start *doing* something. It's lonely—to sit and
do nothing."

"Sure, Ellie. Go to it if you feel like that. . . . Say—

under your hat—is there anything between you and that
Lacy lad? It came to my ears that——"

"Who—Jimmy?" she demanded.

"Yeh."

"No," she said shortly.

"Oh. . . . Oh, all right. His father, old Tim Lacy, is a
friend o' mine. . . . He's well heeled. I'll say Tim is rich.
The boy gets it all, and the garage business——"

"Nothing like that," said the girl, crisply.

The Judge smiled: "Well, don't be snapping me up like
that! If you'd rather work than marry a rich man's son,
that's your affair——"

"I would! I *want* to work. . . . I don't want any——"

"Any what?"

"Babies!"

"In God's name suit yourself then!" laughed Tom Barrett. Ellie laughed, too.

"No babies," she repeated. She swung her silk reticule
and looked brightly at Tom Barrett: "If I get a job I'll
have enough to live on," she said. "I want no man's
bread."

"Oh. No man's bread! Is that so? Well, then, you'll
not be marrying at all. Is that it?"

"I'm not saying so."

"Well, if you won't marry good money and a good
lad——"

"I'd rather marry brains."

"God save us, listen to the child! Isn't it brains that
make money? Isn't it brains that keep it? Young Lacy's
no fool——"

"I mean brains that—that are educated. Brains that

think and study and know all kinds of things—I know what I mean. . . . I know the kind of man I mean. . . . Only—well, that kind don't—*doesn't*—marry uneducated girls. . . . I don't care, either. I don't have to marry. I don't want to. . . . Will they send me a cheque for a hundred dollars on August first?"

"They will, darling, or I'll twist their necks."

Ellie thanked him, kissed his shaven cheek, and went back to the dismantled flat where, already, the Italian family's furniture was being moved in. She stood for a few moments in the empty room where Helen had died; then she went slowly into her own bedroom, also empty except for the telephone which was to be transferred in her name to her new quarters—a luxury she had ventured.

In this empty, carpetless, uncurtained room she had first spoken to John Westall over the wire. Once, only, this had happened. Now she was going to try it again.

She called his office. A strange voice answered. She gave her name, learned that Mr. Westall was busy at another wire; waited.

After a long while: "Hello, Ellie!" came his voice very gaily. "Did you call me up to remind me that we are going to have a swim to-morrow?"

"No. . . . I can't go."

"Oh, I'm sorry."

"I'm sorry, too."

There was a pause; then his voice: "Are you well? And has your mother recovered?"

"Mother died."

"Oh," he exclaimed in a shocked voice, "I'm so terribly sorry for you——"

"—The day we went to the Bronx," added the girl.
. . . "When I got home mother was dead. . . . I was
with you. She died all alone."

"You poor girl. Is there anything I can do in any
way——"

"Thank you for the books and for the plastolene. I
haven't read them or opened the tin box. . . . Well, I
thought I'd call you up."

"But isn't there anything I can do——"

"No, thank you. . . . I've moved to a room on West
86th Street. Shall I give you my address?"

"I'll write it down—one moment. . . . Go ahead, Ellie——"

She gave him her address and telephone number.

"I'll be busy getting settled and hunting up a job," she
explained. . . . "Perhaps a week from to-morrow we
could—see each other—if you feel that way, too——"

"I'm so sorry," he said; "I have to make a business trip
to Montana. I am leaving Sunday—day after to-morrow.
. . . Really, I'm sorry——"

"How long will you be away?"

"Several weeks. . . . I can't tell, now, how long I
shall be away. . . . I'm awfully sorry not to see
you——"

"So am I," she said. "Are you going to the beach to-
morrow? I suppose you are."

"Yes, I think I'll go."

"If you get back in time, will you give me a ring? I'll
be in my new dump."

He said he would; spoke again, sympathetically, concerning her bereavement, hoped she would face things with courage.

She said: "I seem to have courage. Or whatever it is that makes you go on—keep on going. . . . God knows why and where. . . . Is that courage?"

"It is indeed."

"Oh! . . . I'll read those books while you're away. . . . As soon as I can find a job I'll see what I can do about learning how to speak correctly. . . . Also, I'd like to learn how to make statues. . . . Am I keeping you, Mr. Westall?"

"Not at all. I'm interested."

She sighed: "Well, I haven't anything more to say to you—or, perhaps, there's so much to say that my small stock of words has given out. . . . Death is the most awful thing in the world, isn't it? . . . I must be very hard-hearted to want to go on living and improving myself when she isn't here to see me. I—suppose I don't yet realize what has happened. . . . It's terrible here in our old apartment—all empty and dusty and bare except the kitchen where the new family is moving in. . . . They seem to have a lot of copper pots and pans. . . . Well, I'll not keep you any longer. . . . Good-bye, Mr. Westall. Please don't forget to call me up when you get back from the beach——"

"I won't go to the beach if I can be of any help to you——"

"You're so sweet to me! No, there isn't anything, Mr. Westall. I've done everything. . . . Shall I tell you what I've done? Or have you time to listen——"

"Certainly I have."

"Well, then, I did the whole thing myself—I mean fixing up my new room. I laid the carpet and hung the curtains and pictures and arranged all the furniture, and showed them where to put my piano and the bed.

"It's all done, now. I've a gas range in a two by four kitchenette, and my own bath. All I had to buy was dust cloths, a cedar-mop, a carpet sweeper, and a feather duster. Gosh, how everything costs, though. A dollar doesn't get anything. I don't care. I've got enough to live on, and when I find a job I'll be all right. . . . I'm not going to wait for a stenographer's job, either; I'm going to take whatever I can get." Her voice became lower and confidential: "—I'll tell you why, Mr. Westall, shall I?"

"By all means."

"Then I'll tell you; I want to make enough to have a teacher learn me——"

"*Teach,* not learn," he interrupted sharply.

"Oh, thank you so much! I want somebody to *teach* me how to make statues——"

"You want to be taught how to model in clay or wax. That art is the art of sculpture. You would like to be a sculptress. Isn't that it?"

"Y-yes. . . . Shouldn't I say that I want to learn how to make statues?"

"No."

"I should say that I wish to be taught the art of sculpture——"

He laughed: "No, just say that you wish to learn how to model in clay—take lessons in modelling."

"Thank you, Mr. Westall. It's such a pleasure to have you tell me. . . . Now, I really mustn't keep you any longer. . . . So now I'm going back to my new dump. . . . And I do hope you'll call me up to-morrow night. . . . *Good*-bye, Mr. Westall——"

She slept in the "new dump" that night. In the morning she awoke in tears, dreaming of her mother.

It was very hot in her room. A cold bath helped. She got her breakfast in the kitchenette—toast, cereal, fruit, tea.

When she had made up her young features with the inevitable cosmetic abominations—transformed her lovely mouth into a featureless cupid's bow, pencilled eyebrows, rouged, powdered, scented, curled—she got into her thin black gown and little crêpe hat, took her reticule with its list of help-wanted, cut from yesterday's paper, and started down the steep stairway.

The architect lived and planned and draughted and had his being on the floor below hers. Whenever he heard anybody on the stairs he came out to see who it was. He came out now and stared at Ellie, who gave him an insolent look and passed on.

The piano professor was in boisterous action on the next floor, hammering the keyboard with dexterous digits.

Ellie continued on downstairs to the first-floor landing. The dingy vestibule doors were open; a slatternly negress was sweeping out the Beauty Parlour. Business had not yet begun. The empty shop reeked of cosmetics.

Outside on the brownstone stoop Ellie looked up at the gilded sign:

BEAUTY PARLOUR

FELICE

All kinds of bobbing $1
Marcel waving
Permanent waving
Hair colouring
Manicuring
Chiropody

But what interested her was a white placard below this sign on which was scrawled: "Girl Wanted."

She drew from her reticule the clippings containing advertisements for help wanted, and considered them. Only a very few business houses needed stenographers and typists in mid-summer. Probably there were hundreds of applicants for each position. She was almost afraid to go down town, leaving behind her this opportunity for employment here on her own threshold.

As she hesitated, a neat, short, stout woman came up the stoop, gave her a baffling look out of shallow, yellowish eyes, passed her, and entered the beauty shop.

To Ellie's whispered inquiry the slatternly negress informed her that the woman who had just entered was Madam Felice.

On impulse Ellie re-entered the hallway and came face to face with Madam Felice on the threshold of the Beauty Parlour. The woman somehow reminded Ellie of a yellow cat—her cheek-bones, light reddish-yellow hair, and shallow eyes, crystalline intent.

"Good morning," said Madam Felice. "Have you come about the position?"

"I noticed your sign——"

"You understand the business?"—her yellowish eyes appraising the girl from head to foot, person and clothing.

Ellie explained that stenography and typing were her business, but that, being out of a position, she thought she'd try something else.

"If you want a high-class girl, I think I'm that; and I learn things quickly," she added.

"I need a skilled operator," returned Madam Felice, staring at her.

"You'll have one by the middle of the week," remarked Ellie coolly.

"You think it's that easy to learn our business?"

"I do. I take care of my own hair and skin and nails, and I know how it's done," returned the girl, calmly confident. She walked into the shop, glanced around, inspected one of the separate compartments, picked up several jars and flasks and examined the labels.

"We don't teach the business," observed Madam Felice, watching her.

Ellie shrugged: "You don't have to. I only need to watch you operate *once*."

"Oh! Just like that!" said the woman.

Something between a smile and a sneer quivered on Madam's thin lips. But the girl's personal attractiveness, clever features, and self-confidence were having their effect.

"What is your name?"

"Eleanor Lessing."

"Married?"

"Not that you'd notice."

"I tell you what I'll do," said Madam Felice. "You can

start in as lady's assistant—if you think you can pick up the business so darned easy——"

"What do I do?"

"Fetch and carry and help. There's five of us. My husband, Dr. Crouch, is the chiropodist. You'll take off his patients' stockings and shoes and put 'em on again.

"Angelo's the barber. He does bobbing, colouring, and marcel waving. He and me does permanent waves. You assist us when we want you."

"All right."

"Then there's Miss Stella," continued Madam, "—and Miss Grayce. Miss Stella does manicuring. Miss Grayce and me does facial treatments and massage." She gave Ellie another of her odd, intent looks. Something between a smile and a sneer was always twitching at her squatty feline features:

"If you're as smart as you say you are, Miss Lessing, you'll pick up the business like you tell me you can. I'll believe you when you show me."

"What do I start on?"

"Ten, per. And you can start right now."

Ellie reddened: "Ten a week?"

"And half the tips you get——"

"All right."

"—And you gotta wear a cap and apron, too!" added Madam. Her yellow eyes were malicious, now, but her smile became almost audible—like a purr.

The bright flush still lingered on Ellie's cheeks as she pulled off her hat, shook out her short curls:

"Can you lend me a cap and apron for to-day?" she asked. "I haven't any of my own."

Madam produced both from a drawer. They were frail, lacy affairs. Ellie put them on before a pier-glass. Her cheeks were burning again at the insignia of domestic servitude.

"You can hang your hat and bag in that closet," purred Madam Felice; and watched the girl cross the room, her shrewd eyes a pair of limpid yellow slits.

Two young women came in a moment later. Madam made the introductions: "Miss Stella, meet Miss Eleanor; Miss Grayce, Miss Eleanor, our new assistant."

Miss Stella's features were so obscured by cosmetics that it was difficult to judge what they really resembled under a shock of henna hair.

Miss Grayce, equally masked with rouge and powder, reeked with a suffocating perfume.

Angelo, a lively little man with frizzy golden-brown hair and tiny moustache, came gaily in, all smiles and bows; and Ellie smiled in sympathy when introduced to him. He had such kind eyes. He shook her extended hand deferentially, bowed from the waist, and went off at a lively trot to change into white clothing.

The first client arrived shortly afterward—a Mrs. Hymen Mendelbaum—to be facially improved—if possible—and have her bristly eyebrows and moustache plucked. Madam Felice took her in charge in one of the compartments. Presently the stench of a depilatory filled the shop.

A cloak-model—a Miss Rae Schoenberg—appeared in a hurry for a manicure.

Ellie fetched the crystal bowl of tepid water and two towels for Miss Stella. Madam Felice needed her, also.

And about the same time a West Side flapper came in to be bobbed; and Ellie took her to the barber's chair, and there invested her with a bib and fresh cotton slip.

Angelo appeared, smiled his thanks, bowed politely to the flapper.

"Hello, Angelo!" she drawled. "Gimme a clip like the last one——" extracting a cigarette from her wrist-bag, which Angelo lighted for her. It was scented.

Catching a glimpse of Madam peeping around the corner: "Hello, Felice!" she said, "is the Doc in? I got a bum foot, sore as hell. Gee, I thought I'd pass out, dancing last night——"

Dr. Crouch came bustling in—a short, stocky man with puffy eyes, thick, wet-looking lips from which sagged the remains of a cigar.

He greeted everybody amiably but bluntly; looked hard at Ellie, and, when he caught her eye, smiled his thick-lipped smile; and went on into his office. From whence, presently, he emerged, very neat in a white duck mess jacket; looked a little too steadily at Ellie; retired again until the flapper had been bobbed. Shampoo and tonic left her thick, brown hair damp and straight and shiny. Angelo curled it into two crescent-points over the ears and cheek-bones.

"Is the Doc ready for me?" she drawled, lighting another cigarette.

Ellie went to inquire.

"Bring her in, my dear," said the "Doctor," suavely.

So Ellie piloted Miss Meyer in. Knelt down and drew off her stockings and shoes, carelessly conscious all the time of the bold, thick-lipped smile of Dr. Crouch.

"Thank you, my dear," he said, patting Ellie's shoulder as she passed toward the door.

"That," thought the girl coolly, "is where I've trouble coming to me."

When she returned to the outer shop a number of clients were being treated; the place was heavy with scent of pastes, powders, tonics, and the acrid stink of depilatories and of singed human hair.

They kept her busy enough waiting on them all,—operators and clients—pulling off shoes and stockings and putting them on again for Dr. Crouch's clients; fetching and carrying for Madam, for Miss Grayce, for Miss Stella; receiving newcomers; ushering out the beautified, and dropping into her frilly apron pockets the tips offered her. And all the while her clever eyes and ears were alert to grasp the general idea of this new business—observe the manner and custom of its conduct; watch procedure and practice; note and remember details.

Ellie never had to be told the same thing twice. One careful reading of labels on pot, bottle, tube, box, flask, fixed in her memory the names and contents. Once she saw how and when these substances were employed, she knew how to use them herself. Besides, the girl had experimented enough upon herself with cosmetics, washes, salves, to be fairly familiar with this sort of thing.

At a quarter before twelve Miss Stella, glancing out of the window, whispered in Ellie's ear: "Here comes that damn Becker woman, and I got a date for lunch. Could you take her? She likes her nails pointed and the cuticle trimmed. Can you fix her up?"

"I guess so," said Ellie, "—if Madam will stand for it——"

"I'm going to make a sneak anyway; I'm so empty I got a belly-ache," muttered Miss Stella and she slunk away to the cloak-room, pulled on her hat, crept swiftly out of the front door as Mrs. Becker waddled into the shop.

"Miss Stella has gone for the day; it's nearly noon," said Ellie to Madam Felice; "—I'll take Mrs. Becker."

Madam darted an odd look at her: "All right. Take off your cap and apron." She went into the shop and said to Mrs. Becker: "Miss Stella has went for the day. We close at twelve, Saturdays. Miss Eleanor could take you. She's a new girl——"

Mrs. Becker fretfully demurred; became irritated and scornful when Ellie was indicated in her black gown of mourning.

"Try her," urged Madam. "She hasn't had time to get her white uniform yet, but she's an expert."

Mrs. Becker, hostile, fearful for her fat hands, yielded them nervously to Ellie's delicate, long fingers.

Presently reassured, she relaxed, and her prominent eyes behind thick-lensed glasses, insolently inspected and appraised the clothes and person of the girl bending over her hand.

Satisfied, Mrs. Becker became voluble about a visit to the Catskills which she was about to undertake with husband and five children.

When she had been manicured she gave Ellie ten cents for a tip and went out all smiles.

The others were finishing their jobs. Madam Felice, watching Ellie, came over to where she stood.

"You can go now," she said.

Ellie got her hat. Going, she said to Madam: "I'll be ready to take anybody Monday morning. . . . At twenty, per, and tips. . . . Shall I buy white uniforms?"

The woman's smile was always a sneer, too: "You don't hate yourself, Miss Eleanor, do you?"

"I'll work for ten next week," repeated the girl. "Week after I'll need twenty, and all my tips."

"To-morrow's another day," remarked Madam.

"Yes, and high-class girls pull trade. . . ." She counted out her tips; gave half to Madam: "—It's all right if you won't want me after next week——"

"I didn't say so. You're doing the talking. Will you be here Monday?"

"All right. Think it over in time for me to get something in white goods——" She took her hat and wrist-bag and went away up the stairs to her own quarters, where she prepared herself some tea, bread, and a chop.

She took a full hour to wash her teeth, tint up, re-count her tips.

"Darned grafter," she said aloud, dropping the small change into her wrist-bag purse.

CHAPTER XII

SHE had gone out that afternoon to explore and enjoy the unknown down-town of that vast metropolitan area in which she had been born.

It being Saturday, shops were closed; Fifth Avenue without attraction; so she decided to make for Broadway by way of Central Park.

To cross this unfamiliar park was not as simple an undertaking as she supposed, but after an hour or so she found herself on the East Side of it, and very near the Metropolitan Museum.

She did not know what the vast, silvery-grey building was, but, seeing a stream of people going in, followed them, quite unconscious that Fate stood awaiting her in the cool, grey demi-light of the vaulted lobby.

The first object that met her gaze was the bronze Bacchante. Suddenly she became aware of sculptured figures everywhere.

"Oh, God," she breathed, "this place is full of statues!"

For a few moments she remained rooted to the pavement, then, hypnotized by the Bacchante, stole toward the impudent, frisking jade.

And now, under Ellie's excited eyes, opened a wide stone corridor to the right, revealing the snowy marbles of Rodin . . . *The Hand of God.*

Trembling, she approached, her vivid lips parted, her gold-green eyes ablaze.

By four o'clock she was dead tired. Surfeited mind and senses refused further function; replete, rejected nourishment. The great halls swam under her dazed gaze. Her neck hurt; the back of her head felt sore.

Her last consciousness of beauty had been Stewardson's *The Bather*—a white flame amid a bewildering blaze of colour. . . .

She went out, slowly, to the great portico in the sunshine of late afternoon; rested her aching head against a cool stone column:

"Oh, my God," she murmured to herself, staring at nothing where the glittering rush of traffic on Fifth Avenue sped north and south in two curb-wide torrents.

Recrossing the Park, she rested for a while on a bench near the Esplanade west of the Casino, where beds of gayest flowers were banked below a strangely carved terrace of greenish stone. Below, a winged angel floated over splashing fountains. Beyond, swans sailed on a glassy lake where scores of rowboats moved to and fro disturbing the reflections of green trees and grassy shores.

Lawns, esplanades, asphalt walks, were thronged; everywhere amid flowering shrubbery the gabble of the foreign born, and the smells of them, and their litter of newspapers and paper boxes over sward and terrace—dirty democracy, abusing hospitality, turning liberty into swinish licence, and tolerated by the Great American Ass—himself as slovenly, ignorant, uncouth as the wandering wastrels he entertained.

It seemed a very long way to Central Park West. She was very tired and dusty when she came to 86th Street and started to climb the four steep flights of stairs. All she wanted to do was to get her clothes off and lie down.

She had kicked aside both shoes and pulled her black gown off over her head; and was seated on her bed looking at her stockinged feet. . . . That was all she remembered until, in darkness, she sat up, startled, the clamour of the telephone confusing her.

She reached for the telephone in the obscurity; for a moment or two circumstance and environment were not clear to her mind, nor was the man's voice over the telephone.

"Oh," she said, "it's *you!* . . . I fell asleep. It's very dark here. Will you please hold the wire a minute?"

She got up, felt around for the switch, lighted her lamp, stood dazzled, rubbing her eyes and cheeks with both hands.

Then at the telephone again: "I fell asleep," she repeated. "What time is it? Nine-thirty! The dickens!"

She heard him laughing.

"Where are you?" she demanded; "in town? . . . When did you get back from the beach? . . . Did you have a good swim? The water must have been fine! . . . It's so sweet of you to remember to call me up. . . . Are you really going away to-morrow? . . . I'm so sorry. . . . When am I going to see you again, Mr. Westall?"

"When do you want to?"

"Am I not going to see you before you leave?" she asked, wistfully.

"I could run up for a few minutes this evening and say good-bye to you——"

"Here?"

"Unless you'd rather meet me somewhere else———"

"It's all right for you to come here," she said. "I don't feel much like dressing and going out. Gee, I'm tired! . . . My feet and the back of my neck———!"

"I didn't think you ever got tired," he said.

"I never was before—*this* way. I've been looking at sta— at *sculpture*—and my back and legs ache. . . . I'm going to take a red-hot bath. . . . You'll excuse a negligée, won't you? Gee, I could dance all night and never feel this way. I had a devil of a headache when I come in———"

"*Came* in—for Heaven's sake!———"

"Thank you so much! *Came* in—when I *came* in. . . . What time will you be here?"

"How long will you be dressing?"

"I'm going in to turn on the bath, *now!* . . . Come up in half an hour. . . . I'll be *so* glad to see you. . . . G'bye!"

CHAPTER XIII

R ELAXED from a hot bath, in her frilly negligée of white and lilac, she seated herself before her little mirror and examined her young face washed clean of cosmetics.

Somebody in the Beauty Parlour had told her that freckles were coming into fashion in Paris—that, lacking natural ones, even artificial freckles had become *à la mode*.

She scrutinized the two or three faint marks near her delicate nose, undecided.

A make-up calculated to dazzle this man was her intention. Would he have heard that freckles were fashionable?

Still hesitating, she detached the stopper from a tiny vial of scent, touched her long forefinger to the liquid, passed it over the white skin of her breast.

As she did so the door-bell below rang.

"The devil!" she murmured; but went swiftly to the door and pulled the cord.

Listening on the landing she heard somebody enter and start to climb upward. On the third landing she leaned over the banisters:

"Mr. Westall?" she called cautiously.

"Hello, Ellie!"

He appeared, slightly out of breath, shook hands, was ushered in.

"You live high," he remarked, smiling at her.

"High living suits me," she said gaily. She took his hat and stick and laid them on her bed. Seating herself on the sofa she made room for him, too.

"You're looking exceedingly well," he said.

"You're spoofing! I haven't even made up——" She turned to her dresser and reached for the lip-stick.

"Your mouth is made up, isn't it?" he inquired.

"No; that's natural——"

"Why not leave it alone?"

"You *like* it that way?"

"Yes, I do."

"You like *these,* too?"—she leaned closer and placed a finger-tip on a freckle.

He laughed: "They're becoming. . . . I suppose you don't think so——"

"I don't know. . . . A girl feels funny without make-up. . . . All right, then, if you'd rather have me like this."

Regarding him smilingly out of her clever, slanting eyes, she clasped her hands under one knee and leaned back against the cushions.

"Shall I tell you about everything?" she asked.

"Always, Ellie."

"Gee, you've let yourself in for some job if I'm to tell you everything I do. . . ." She considered him in her frank, interested way, and with no more than natural coquetry. She noticed his dinner jacket and tie and pumps, and thought him attractive. "All right," she said. "I'll tell you——" Her expression altered; she was remembering the circumstances of their last afternoon together.

After a few moments she spoke of her mother with self-control, confidently aware of his sympathy.

Then, after a silence, the girl mentioned her present circumstances; the necessity for economy;—told him about the new job in the Beauty Parlour—described Madam Felice, the "Doctor," Angelo—her agile mind all cleverness, now, imitating all the people in sparkling mimicry of voice and gesture—and Westall was laughing, now; and she in gay excitement of impersonation:

"That damn corn-doctor!"—she laughed—"you could grease a frying pan with those lips of his!—and always reaching to get his fingers on me—with his, 'Yes, my dear; come here, my dear'—all that bunk!—as if a blind baby couldn't get his number!——"

She was on her slim, slippered feet, now; lightly:

"Here's the woman whose nails I did—she gave me ten cents, and I stayed after closing hour at that!——" She waddled a step or two; peered at her finger-tips in a near-sighted, shrewd way:—"Vell, I tink you done very good, Miss Eleanor—most as good as Miss Stella"—fumbling in an imaginary wrist-bag and offering a phantom dime—"The nerve of her! Ten cents! . . . Well, I made over five dollars in tips and they let me keep half——"

She stood smiling at him, limbering up her slender, supple body by flexing arms and spine:

"Gee, I feel better. Do you want to hear what I did this afternoon?——" She re-seated herself beside him; memory of the day's discovery began to excite her again:

"I've got a swell place to go now, when I want to look at—at sculpture. Pictures, too. All kinds of art things. All you want to look at——"

"You've discovered the Metropolitan Museum," he suggested, amused at her eager young face.

"Imagine! Me eighteen and never heard of it until this afternoon! . . . You've been there, haven't you?"

"Oh, yes."

"Do you remember *The Hand of God?*"

"Rodin?"

"I guess so. . . . Isn't it beautiful? Gee, that's the swellest thing I ever saw. . . . And there was a tiny baby, ten weeks old, done in marble; and a marble girl—God, I can't remember—it's got me groggy like a three-ring show!——" She clasped her knee again with her long, smooth, nervous fingers, balancing and rocking as she continued her recollections of those enchanted hours. Under the bright bobbed hair, cheeks and vivid lips glowed with a new warmth, the while her clear, clever eyes alternately played over him or were lost in brief reverie of pleasure.

"I tell you," she said, "—to look at those things seemed to pep me up; made me want to try, too. It's funny—all the grand ideas that come into your head—and you get excited—you get wild. . . . I don't know how to tell you, but—but those things hurt—they were so beautiful—you don't get me, do you?——"

"I think so," he said.

Her gold-grey eyes rested on him for a moment; became remote, fixed on the lovely phantoms of her mind.

He had an opportunity to study her, now, so detached her mind and unconscious of observation.

He thought that, at the moment, she scarcely looked what she was—an uneducated, common girl of no antecedents, versed only in the precocious wisdom and cunning of vulgar sophistication.

Her person, he thought, quite lovely in its supple, healthy youth; and her limbs and throat were the dainty features of aristocracy. . . . Indeed, her head and profile were almost beautiful, even in close analysis. . . . Strange how some of these children of the lower middle class are born so flexible and sound and graceful! . . . Even her small, narrow foot. . . . And those long, snowy fingers so exquisitely interlaced.

No, she didn't belong in a Beauty Parlour—until she opened her pretty lips. . . . *Then* she belonged there very certainly. And at Manhattan, and at Villy's, and in a Bronx flat—and here, on West 86th Street. . . . Still— still the glimpses the girl unconsciously permitted of her naked mind were something else to consider before consigning her to her class and the Beauty Parlour. . . .

"Gee," she remarked, abruptly emerging from her reverie, "I got to eat. I haven't had any supper!"

"What!" he exclaimed.

"I fell asleep. And what with all that sculpture, and *you,* I didn't have time to get me anything——"

"Well, then, I'll take you out," he said, smiling at her.

"No, I don't want to dress. Will you excuse me if I get something?"

"Why, certainly."

"There's some canned soup, and there's cold ham. I'll fix some potatoes, too—" She indicated the kitchenette. "Come and talk to me while I'm fixing it—" She hesitated; then, shyly: "—I've got plenty for two, Mr. Westall. Will you join me?"

"Yes," he said, "I'd like to."

They had hot tomato soup, cold ham, toast, potatoes fried with shredded onions, some stale Danish pastry, and two glasses of iced tea. They ate in her combined bed-room and sitting-room—the girl entirely aware of the intimacy of it all; stimulated by it; slightly excited; not the least disconcerted on account of the simplicity of her hospitality.

"Well," she said, smiling at Westall, "as my Dad used to say—'God bless what we eat and forgive what we spit out——'" She laughed, audaciously, at her own vulgarity.

In that mischievous laugh was perverse defiance of superior respectability. And, in it, too, unconsciously, that immemorial feminine resentment of man.

She sipped her iced tea and looked at him gaily, her grey-gold eyes greenish with malice.

"When I was a kid," she remarked, "I said things so terrible that Dad used to wash my mouth with soapy water! Ugh! I can taste it yet when I remember. . . . I suppose you were a very good little boy."

"A perfect little gentleman——"

They both considered that extremely funny. Everything this evening was combining to please and stimulate her —the Museum, this man, the intimacy of the situation— all these were keying her up to a sort of happy excitability.

The girl had become restlessly vivacious, agreeably nervous, inclined to laugh at the slightest provocation— sought occasions, in fact. And partly this was reaction from grief, so recent, yet, to youth, already so far away. And partly it was youth and sex and all the superficial phenomena of unawakened emotions.

Happy self-confidence warmed her, even incited her, to meaningless provocation. She experienced an indefinite and happy sort of apprehension in the possibility of the situation. . . . She knew how to take care of herself! . . . But enterprise was natural to men. . . . Presumption characteristic of the male as she had encountered him in her career of eighteen years.

Now her clever, grey-green sophisticated glance met his, and she experienced the tiny, agreeable thrill of recognized trouble impending.

She said: "Do you think it's all right?"

"What?"

"For a married man to take supper with a young girl this way?"

"You conclude that I am married?"

"Certainly you are. I know the signs. They're all over you."

He laughed.

"Do you think it's right?" she insisted.

"It's been all right so far," he remarked.

"Do you expect me to believe you are always going to be as tame as this?"

"Don't you want to believe it?"

"Y-yes. Of course. But I don't believe it. You're *too* tame to be true."

"When do you expect me to turn wild?"

"I don't know . . . but they always do act wild—sooner or later."

"In the meanwhile," he suggested, "we are touchingly safe and secure."

The girl laughed; but she didn't quite like that, and didn't know just why. Unconsciously her instinct was resenting something about this man—his pretended immunity, perhaps.

An unconsidered defiance was on her lips—"If I wanted to——" she began; and stopped.

"Wanted to do what?"

"You're only a man, anyway——"

"A *married* man, according to you——"

"They're worse. . . . Maybe you're not married, you haven't tried to start anything——"

"Well, I'd better begin, then——"

"If you do I'll *know* you're married."

"And if I don't?"

"*You* will. . . . Even if you've got a girl. That's the way with men. Didn't Myra Klein slip it to me that Jimmy Lacy was hugging and kissing her while he was going with me? . . . Not that I begrudged him. . . . And he acted jealous at that—you remember down to Villy's——"

"Down *at* Villy's."

"Thank you; down *at* Villy's. The cheek of him—petting Myra on the side and calling me down for dancing with you. Men!—My God, what girl can dope them out? . . . Yes, *you*, too! What do I know about *you?* . . . I admit I don't get you. What's your line, anyway?"

"*Line?*"

"Yes."

"I build dams and water-works."

"I don't mean that. . . . But why do you go with me. . . . With a girl like *me?*"

"But I don't."

"No; we don't go with each other li—*as* I used to go with other fellas——"

"*Men,* not fellas—not even *fellows.*"

"Thank you. . . . No, there hasn't been time for us to get to go with each other——"

"Good Heavens, Ellie!—'get to go with each other!' You don't 'go' with a man. If a man's attentive to you, you *see* more or less of him—you are *with* him more or less. Why don't you read the books I sent you?"

"I haven't had much time. . . . I've read some. . . . Do I speak so bad I sicken you?"

"Sometimes you do."

She blushed painfully but tried to smile: "Probably," she said—not considering her words—"that's why you don't bother with me."

"I *do* bother with you. . . . And your grammar, too."

"I mean—that's why you don't bother to go—to 'see more or less of' me."

He began to laugh: "Haven't I seen you whenever there was any occasion?"

Suddenly her nervous excitability became effrontery; she gave him a flushed, breathless look. "I'll tell you what I mean if you're so dumb you don't understand!—I mean that you wouldn't want such a girl as I am for *your* girl. . . . Because I'm ignorant and uneducated!"

His smile of mischievous amusement altered. There was a short silence; then:

"Were you considering the possibility of a serious affair with *me*, Ellie?"

"Serious?" She reddened again: "I should say *not*," she returned disdainfully, "—if you mean do I think you'll ever marry me!"

"Well, what have you in your mind, then?"

She was still pink and scornful: "*I* don't want to marry, either. Do you think I'd bother with *that*—until I have to? . . . Maybe not then, either. . . . But I—every girl—likes to go—likes to *see* 'more or less' of some fel—some *man*—oh, hell, you got my tongue twisted something fierce!"

Exasperated, she sprang to her feet and began to walk about; halted with her back to him to cool her cheeks in both hands.

"You know," she said, without turning, "you don't have to trouble yourself to see me unless you want to."

"I know that."

"All right; remember it."

She walked to the piano; seated herself; ignoring him with lowered head; and ran over the keys—prelude to *"What Shall I Do?"*—presently sang it, clear voiced, defiant.

When at length she lifted her eyes to him his expression was so friendly and unembarrassed that her nervousness subsided a little.

"Aren't you disgusted with me?" she inquired, beginning a rag. Her long, nimble fingers played it brilliantly to an end. Then again she looked up, inquiringly.

"When I return from the West," he said, "we must try to see each other when convenient."

"Do you *want* to?"

"I do."

"I do, too. . . . *Why* do you want to—when I'm such a total loss? I can't see that there's anything in it for you. . . . Just talking to an uneducated girl——"

"You'll be educating yourself. That's interesting to watch. Don't you know you're extremely interesting anyway?"

"Me?"

He had risen, taken his hat and stick from the bed, and was walking slowly toward the piano. He said:

"Probably I have a better time with you than you do with me."

"No, you don't. I *like* you. I'd—*see* 'more or less' of you, if you wanted me. . . . A girl likes to feel there's some *one* man——"

She sat on the piano stool looking up at him, her fingers linked on her lap.

"Every girl has some man," she said. "It's natural for a girl to like *some* man, isn't it? . . . Somebody to think about. . . . He's company, even when you're alone."

She rose: "Must you be going?" she asked with unfeigned regret.

They walked to the door together.

"—But you seem to think I'm married," he said mischievously. She laid her hand in the hand he extended, looked away in silence.

"Do you want to take that chance?" he insisted.

"I'd have to, I suppose."

"What! After all you've said to me about——"

"Well, you wouldn't marry me, anyway. . . . I'm

never going to marry, anyway. I—I'm not interested in the kind of men who'd want to marry me. . . . I'm always thinking about you——" She looked up at him; her face became suffused with delicate colour.

"Suppose," he said, "you try being my girl for a while and see how you like it?"

"Do you *want* me?"

"I do."

"All right. . . ."

He passed his left arm around the soft column of her neck and kissed her; and she encircled his body with both arms, abandoning her lips to him. . . . She clung tightly for a while. Once or twice she laid her face against his shoulder.

After a few moments: "I've been lonely for Mom. . . . Your arms feel so good. . . . When you come back you'll take me where we can dance, won't you?"

"I certainly will."

". . . Lay down your hat and cane—just for a little while?"

They sat on the chintz sofa, her long, smooth, childish hands in his:

"I promise to study those books and educate myself," she said. . . . "I know you don't like it when I swear and use slang. I'll cut it out. . . . And you needn't worry about men while you're away."

"You reassure me," he said with much seriousness.

"I wouldn't double-cross you," she returned earnestly; "I wouldn't put one over on you. One at a time for me. When I'm through with a man I quit before I start anything else."

"That is honourable," he commented, controlling his amusement.

"I *am* on the square. . . ." She drew a deep breath, smiled at him, pressed his hands between hers: "I'm dam—I mean I'm very glad that I'm your girl," she murmured. "Gee, it's a relief!—" She breathed deeply again, her happy, flushed gaze on him.

They remained so for a minute or two, then he was obliged to take his departure—matters of preparation for his journey on the morrow.

She went to the door with him again, returned his kiss and embrace with youthful recklessness—yet without nervousness or passion—the hot candour of affection, free utterly of deeper emotion—or any trace of subtler experience.

"I shall be so glad to see you," she said. That was all of her valedictory.

When the street door closed below she closed her own door. She was very much excited, and very happy. She sped over to the piano and rattled out rag after rag until her next-door neighbour rapped sharply on the partition.

So she flung herself on the bed and lay flat, arms extended, looking at the ceiling with wide-awake eyes.

She had been in love many times. Never as overwhelmingly as this. That there was no permanency, no future for her love affairs, neither disturbed her nor even occurred to her. Nor did it now, for this newest love affair.

"I do love him," she said to herself, "—I do—I *do!*"

After a while she said her prayers.

CHAPTER XIV

SEVERAL times Ellie Lessing had encountered her neighbour, the actress who divided with her the top floor of the house on West 86th Street.

She was tall, dark-haired, dark-eyed, and young. As these encounters continued, they exchanged nods and an amiable commonplace or two when they met on stairs or landing.

One Saturday afternoon the house was filled with smoke and the corridors and landings with excited tenants. But it was only an ash-can afire in the basement.

A common anxiety had brought Ellie and her neighbour to the landing.

The girl said to her: "If this house ever does get afire I shall go through the scuttle to the roof. That would be our only chance."

"Where is the scuttle?" inquired Ellie.

The dark-eyed girl showed her a door on the landing, opened it, and revealed a ladder leading to the roof. She said:

"It's a good thing to be near the scuttle—although sometimes robbers get in that way, too. . . . Are you ever nervous, Miss Lessing?"

Ellie laughed: "I haven't any pearls to make me nervous."

Her neighbour laughed, also: "I haven't either. But

one reads of so many hold-ups—girls who live alone——"

They had stopped outside her door. "Won't you come in?" she said with a friendly smile. "We could have tea." They entered together.

The room had a studio light, and a partition dividing it from the bathroom and kitchenettes. Curtains, furniture, rugs attracted Ellie. There was an unfamiliar but mellow richness about the place that charmed her. Her first contact with antiquity and the bloom of old-time beauty.

Ignorant of the meaning and value of the objects surrounding her, she was merely conscious of the charm of the place—the restful quiet of it.

She said politely to her hostess: "You are Miss Nieland, aren't you? I noticed the name over your bell in the vestibule."

She nodded: "Leda Nieland."

"I'm Eleanor—Ellie Lessing. . . . I was so ashamed that time you had to knock on the wall when I was pounding the piano——"

Leda Nieland laughed: "I didn't like to do it, but I had such a headache! I hope you'll forgive me."

"You must always rap on the partition when I'm too noisy. . . . What a perfectly lovely place you have! It's so charming, so different——"

"It isn't mine," said Leda; "all these antiques belong to a man I know. This is his studio. He's been studying in Paris, and he lets me have the place while he's absent. The deuce of it is, he's coming back soon."

"Oh," exclaimed Ellie, "will you have to go?"

"Certainly—unless I bunk in with him," returned Leda,

laughing. . . . "I am going to get you some tea——"
She disappeared behind the partition.

Ellie, her hands linked behind her back, made a light-footed tour of the place. She had had vague notions concerning antique furniture; supposed it consisted of decrepit curiosities; never associated any idea of beauty and utility with antiquity.

The carving on the chairs, on chests; the deep, sombrely vivid pile of the rugs under foot; the brocaded hangings of wine-red and silver; the dusky pictures with their azure, rose, and shadowy flesh-tints; the hanging lamps of silver; the old marbles—all these fascinated the girl. A burning desire invaded her to know something about them.

There was one very lovely naked girl done in fairer marble than the rest, who seemed to have wings. On closer inspection Ellie discovered that the wings belonged to a swan; and swan and girl seemed to be inextricably involved.

Her hostess came in with the tea-tray and set it on a beautiful old table. They took tea and little cakes together, evidently inclined toward the budding acquaintance.

"You are on the stage?" ventured Ellie.

"Yes. There's nothing doing now, of course. But Max Mayer sent for me yesterday and promised me something in September. . . . You're not in the profession, are you?"

"No. . . . My mother was."

"Oh," said Leda with increased interest, "probably you'll drift into it, then."

"Maybe. . . . That is such a beautiful sculpture—that

one!"—stretching out her hand—as much a gesture of caress as of indication.

"Leda and her swan," nodded Leda, smiling.

"Is it a story?"

"One of those scandals in Greek mythology. . . . You know it, don't you?"

"No, I don't."

Leda demurely sipped her tea as she related the tale.

"It's a crazy story," said Ellie, "but the sculpture is so beautiful it makes you—makes you *ache!*"

"I'll tell you a secret," said Leda. "Shall I?"

"I'll never tell it!"

"The man who owns this studio did that. And—and *I* posed for the *Leda!*"

"How wonderful! . . . But you didn't pose like *that,* did you?"

"I had to. I needed the money. Lord, but I was scared. . . . Well, I was just as badly scared when I was in the Follies. . . . You get used to it. If you're well made and pretty you don't mind it; you rather like the thrill of it. . . . Only it's one thing to have a thousand people looking at you. . . . It *is* different—with just one man in a studio. However"—she shrugged and looked laughingly at Ellie—" a girl can get used to anything. I've found it so. . . . What's your line?"

"Nothing yet. . . . I'm working in the Beauty Parlour downstairs."

"Do you like it?"

"Well, I've got to work."

Leda offered her a cigarette, lighted it and another for herself, poured more tea.

"Are you on your own?" she asked.

Ellie nodded absently, her eyes on the sculptured Lady of the Swan. Leda pulled another chair toward her, rested her feet on it, and reclined at her ease, blowing rings of smoke toward the ceiling.

"I've got to move," she said, "and I don't know where the dickens I'm going. You never can settle down in this profession. . . . They might give me a good part in a No. 2 Company if our show goes over. . . . Of course nobody wants the road. . . . But you've got to travel it more or less."

"Isn't it interesting to see the world?" asked Ellie.

"Not the way we see it. No, there's nothing in the show business unless you can remain in New York."

Ellie had supposed that all travel was education. Leda laughed:

"Is that your line—education?"

"I'd like to know something. . . . Behave like I—*as if* I had an education."

Leda regarded her with amused interest. She said:

"If a girl hasn't had an education before she goes to work she isn't likely to get one afterward."

"She can study," said Ellie. . . . "I'm starting."

"Well, of course, if you're as determined as that——" She smiled at Ellie: "—You *look* clever——"

"I am. . . . But I'm ignorant. . . . A man I know showed me up."

"Is that the way he tried to make himself popular with you?" laughed Leda.

"He made himself so popular," returned Ellie, "that I'm studying like the dickens."

"Studying what?"

"English. . . . My own language. . . . How to use words. . . . What not to say. . . . I'm trying to learn to speak as he does." There was a slight flush in the girl's face; her greyish-gold eyes had become softly brilliant.

Leda said: "To be with educated people is one way to learn."

"Is that the way you learned?"

"No; I went to a convent school in St. Louis. . . . But it was the refinement and education of the Sisters that counted most. . . . We women are monkeys for imitation. We're impressionable and quick. We're easily coloured and moulded by the people we're with. . . . More than men are. . . . In the shows I've played the kind of men we meet usually are a common bunch of mutts. We don't bother with them. But the men we meet outside the profession, usually, are educated. . . . That's how lots of girls learn anything. . . . That way, and the drilling in the parts they get. . . . If a girl in the profession really wants to give a good imitation of refinement, she can learn how if she has any brains at all."

Ellie said, slowly: "I don't want to give an *imitation*. I want to *be* educated."

Leda's expression became serious and sympathetic: "If you feel that way you'll become what you want to be. . . . It's a pity you can't go to college——"

"I haven't even been through high school, damn it!" said Ellie fiercely. "But I've doped out what I'm going to do when I can afford it: I'm going to night schools. I'm going to take French at the Strelitz Institute—an hour three times a week. I'm going to take a course by correspondence in history, literature, and art. I cut out an ad. in a magazine that guarantees you a thorough college education if you follow the course. . . . As soon as I am making enough money I'm going to start."

Leda lay watching her, fascinated by the nervous animation and vivid vitality of the girl—by the clever charm of her face—the beauty of her outflung hand swept toward the marble Leda beyond:

"I want to do such things as that!" she said. "I suppose you think I'm ridiculous. Maybe I'm crazy to think I can—make—sculpture——"

She sprang up and began to walk about the room in her lithe, light-footed way:

"—Now, all at once," she said, "—ever since I met the man I told you about—something inside me has started. . . . It's like something burning, sometimes. . . . I've got to do something—and I don't know how to do anything. . . . And I realize, now, something always has been burning inside me. . . . I can dance till I drop, but it doesn't satisfy me. . . . It drives me frantic sometimes—that was one of the times when I pounded the piano. . . . After you rapped on the wall I did setting-up exercises and toe-dancing and stunts—just to take it out of me. . . . But I *know* what I need. . . . I need to do stunts with my mind, too; and with my hands as well as with my feet and body. . . . I want to learn sculpture, and I'm going to if it takes every nickel I make!"

There was a silence. Her flushed face began to cool. She came toward Leda, already reacting, already ashamed.

"I'm afraid you think me a cheap talker," she said. . . . "But I wasn't trying to brag. . . . It's terrible to want to do so much and not know how to do anything. It's a lonely, desperate feeling—I was so bottled up with ideas that I guess I just blew up into words!——"

Leda laughed and laughed.

"You're full of *something*," she said.

"Tea and cakes, probably——" in self-disgust.

"Ambition, my dear. . . . That's what gets away with things if you have enough persistence; if you don't weaken. . . . The trouble with us is, some man comes along. . . . They're always coming along. . . . Men! . . . To take your time. . . . Always going to do something for you. . . . Help you on in your profession. . . . Yes, if you'll sit pretty. . . . If you'll be their baby doll."

They both laughed.

"Not me," said Ellie; "nothing like that."

Leda said: "Not that I condemn a girl. . . . Life's a bum deal unless you're well heeled."

But there was intolerance and scorn in Ellie's clever features.

"My God," she said, "isn't it bad enough to marry without starting something worse—tangling yourself all up—and every chance he'll quit you if there's a baby! . . . Quit you cold! I've known girls——"

She shrugged her supple shoulders, then looked up at Leda. They both laughed.

"I'm going back to that damn English grammar," remarked Ellie. . . . "I hope you'll come and see me—Leda——"

They approached, joined hands and kissed.

"I'm glad you're next door to me," added Ellie.

"What are you doing a week from Sunday?"

"Nothing. . . . Studying."

"Will you come to lunch?"

"I'd love to."

"I'll see you before then," said Leda. She kissed Ellie again; "—you're so sweet," she said.

CHAPTER XV

AT the end of the first week she had said to Madam Felice:

"Do you want me to go on?"

It was after hours. Everybody had gone except the "Doctor," who was fussing and whistling in his room.

Madam's yellow gaze, crystalline, uncertain, appraised her, watched every shade of the girl's expression. Then her smile appeared, ingratiating, insincere:

"What salary did you think you ought to get, Miss Eleanor?"

"Twenty-five and tips."

"Why, we couldn't pay you that——"

"Why not? I can do anything the others do. I can do what *you* do. Give me another week and I'll do Angelo's job. And the Doctor's, too!"

"You're a beginner."

"There's nothing to this beauty business," retorted Ellie, scornfully. "It's three-quarters bunk. Anybody who's quick and clever with their fingers can fill any job in this shop. . . . But it's all right—if you don't want me——"

"I'll give you fifteen and tips——"

"I can get twenty-one as a telephone operator."

"I'll give you twenty," said Madam Felice, staring at her. "And tips."

"Twenty this week. Twenty-five next—with tips."

Madam's baffled gaze was becoming malicious.

"We don't have to have you——"

"And I don't have to stay, you know——"

"You think jobs are as plenty as that?"

"High-class girls are not plenty, either——"

The "Doctor" appeared dressed for the street: "Hey!" he said in his jocular, leering manner, "you two girls quit your fightin'!" He came up between them, put an arm around each.

"I heard the argument you put up. If a high-class girl can pull trade she'll be worth the twenty-five."

"If you want to pay her that, all right," said Madam, always watching the girl.

The "Doctor" burst into one of his noisy laughs which never seemed quite genuine: "I don't want to pay anybody anything!" he said jovially, "but I gotta or quit business! Now, you girls kiss and make up and I'll do the worryin'——"

"I won't stay if Madam isn't satisfied——"

"If you don't kiss and make up I'll kiss you both——"

"Quit pulling me," retorted Madam; and Ellie also twisted out of his embrace.

Ellie opened the door and started upstairs. The "Doctor" called after her: "My wife says O.K. and come Monday!"

Ellie halted and looked back. Madam nodded.

As she climbed upward to her room she remembered what Miss Stella had told her about the "Doctor": "—He's sump'n turrible after the girls!—always pinchin' you on the sly and rubbin' up against you——"

"The cheap skate," she thought, remembering his jocular familiarities and inclination to get too near her.

But she knew how to take care of herself. Besides, her salary was worth some personal inconvenience. She ought to clear fifty dollars a week. Two hundred a month.

The first week netted her sixty-one dollars and thirty cents. Nearly every client she served not only became a customer, but brought others.

Already she was able to give any treatment required. She remembered the idiosyncrasies of each customer. Her cleverness, nice manners, the charm of her person, her long, smooth, capable fingers, her daintiness, all created a demand for her.

There was, too, in her touch something physically grateful—soothing yet exquisitely stimulating. She was deft, swift, gentle, sympathetic. No gossip yet a good listener.

At odd moments she watched Angelo and his apparatus for permanent waving; assisted him sometimes. She was capable, resourceful, competent, already haughtily disliked by Miss Grayce; endured by Madam who often watched her out of yellow, treacherously uncertain eyes; adored by the thin manicure, Miss Stella; and pursued by the "Doctor's" jocular familiarities in public and his sly, lewd behaviour and annoying solicitations in private.

On one occasion she quietly told him to "go to hell"—at which he pretended to laugh immoderately. Once, when Madam was absent, he got her into his office on some pretence, and pinched her thigh; and she slapped his face so hard that the crack echoed through the shop outside.

She waited until her cheeks had cooled, eyeing him carelessly the while, yet alert to repeat the punishment; then she walked into the shop so calmly that the curious gaze of Miss Grayce, Miss Stella, and Angelo discovered in her features and demeanour nothing to account for the sudden and suggestive sound which had so startled them.

She told Miss Stella about it: "He'll do it again; he's one of those crazy fools," she said contemptuously. "I'm going to hold down my job, anyway, if I have to knock his damn block off."

She had lunched with Leda, once. Was enormously interested in the girl's stories of the stage; the part that Max Mayer had given her in the Westchester Follies:— "My dear, I don't wear a rag in the *Diana's Hunting* number! Probably they'll pull the show, but I can't help it!——"

They lunched and gossiped the afternoon away, and kept the Victrola going; and always Ellie's clever, slightly slanting eyes were roaming among the old-time objects, or caressing with their tender regard some lovely classic bronze or modern marble.

As they parted, Leda to return to the hired hall where rehearsals were called for the afternoon, she said:

"I suppose I'll have to get out of this place pretty soon, now. Francis Tolland sailed yesterday on the *Cyclonic*."

"The man who let you have this studio?"

"Yes. . . . Francis Tolland. . . . I had a cable——" She laughed: " '—Dinner with you Saturday.' That's all he cabled. . . . He's an awfully nice boy. You come to dinner, too, Ellie. I'll ask another man. . . . I'll ask two

other men and another girl. I can manage six. We'll have
a party. . . . Why can't we open the door between the
two kitchenettes?"

"All right," said Ellie; "we can dance in my room.
. . . And I'll tell you this; I'm pretty much excited at
the idea of meeting a sculptor. . . . I never even saw
one——"

Leda thought that very funny.

"Francis isn't long-haired; he's just a nice boy—a
regular fellow. . . . You'd better look out or you'll fall
for him, my dear."

"Are you serious?"

"Well, he has a way with women——"

Ellie said: "There's a man I—see more or less of. He's
away——"

Leda's laughter rang out uncontrolled: "You're so
funny, dear! What's a beau to a girl when he's away?
. . . All the same, you needn't try to fall for Francis Tolland; I like him pretty well myself——"

"Oh!"

"—No, it isn't a real affair. . . . I don't know what it
is, exactly. . . . Nothing, I guess. . . . I don't care what
you do to Francis Tolland."

"I'm not going to do anything," said Ellie.

Leda shrugged her shoulders: "He's a nice boy. . . .
He's been darned decent to me. Women like him. You
will, too. . . . Well, I've got to go, dear——"

They exchanged their customary embrace.

"Honestly," repeated Leda, laughing, "I don't care
what you do to Francis. I wish you'd hand him a jolt. He
finds women too easy——"

She was off and down the stairs, gaily, with a light gesture of adieu. Ellie went into her room, seated herself, picked up one of her English books.

"Oh, Lord!" she sighed.

She had not heard from Westall since his departure. That was now three weeks ago. The only address he had left her was his office down-town. She had not written. She was unaccustomed to writing letters. Several times since his departure it occurred to her to write to him. It occurred to her now.

She had lilac-tinted note paper and envelopes. She had never used them except once in writing to "Judge" Barrett.

She missed Westall. There were days when she thought about him continually; wanted him back; longed to hear his voice; look at him. At such times she became very lonely and tender-hearted; and went over minutely in her mind the last phases—the last moments. . . . Caresses. . . . Her lips against his. Her excited mind and her heart so full—so hotly full of him. . . . His arm around her neck; hers around his body, strained to her in sudden overflow of warmth—reckless, ecstatic. . . .

She got her ink, her pen, and her lilac-tinted paper. She wrote:

MY DEAR,

Have you been too busy to write me?

This is the news of me: I am making between fifty and sixty dollars a week. Next week I shall go to the Strelitz School to study French, Monday, Wednesday and Friday evenings.

Also, I shall begin my Correspondence College education

in History and Literature. I have paid a quarter in advance
for the course.

I hope you are well. I shall be very glad when you return.
I want you *now,* very, very much.

The girl who lives next to me on my floor, I now know.
Her name is Leda Nieland and she is in the Westchester Follies. We have become friends.

These are all the things that have happened since you went
away.

I haven't seen any other men. I know plenty in the Bronx,
but don't feel like seeing them. That's strange, because I
like men, and am used to seeing more or less of them.

So I hope you'll come back soon.

I remain,

Lovingly,

ELLIE

After she had run out to the corner box and mailed
her letter she wondered whether he would find in it mistakes to criticize.

There was a book advertised in the evening paper:
*Etiquette for Everybody. How to speak, write, and be-
have correctly under all conditions and circumstances.*

It cost $5.00. Probably it was worth it because it was
written by Mrs. Celestia Gates, a very fashionable New
York woman of early 1900.

It turned out to be, for her, one of the most valuable
books the girl possessed. Every evening she pored over
its gilt-edged pages after she had studied her English
grammar. The contents of these books fascinated her.

October promised to be a busy month for Ellie, with
her business hours from nine to five—and including Sat-

urdays, too—which gave her only the lunch hour to prepare her French lesson. Because the evenings required a considerable part of her time to keep up with the correspondence courses in the histories of art, literature, and of civilization.

Sunday now remained her only day for relaxation. Her choice of pleasurable recreation for leisure moments was modelling in plastolene.

In an artist supply shop on Columbus Avenue she bought for two dollars a pamphlet instructing beginners how to model in clay or wax. Another five dollars purchased two or three modelling tools, a ruler, dividers, a spool of copper wire, a block of wood, pliers, hammer and nails, a file, and enough metal for an armature.

Never had she experienced such excitement as when in the seclusion of her own quarters she opened the several parcels, spread the contents over her centre table, and seated herself to read the $2 pamphlet of instructions in the third oldest art in the world.

That night, in consideration of a tip, the janitor affixed the armature to the heavy wooden block for her and bent it according to her directions.

Late into the evening she was busy with ruler, dividers, pliers, and copper wire, constructing according to Phidian proportions the bony frame of the conventional human figure.

About eleven she heard Leda Nieland come in, and she ran to her door and called her.

Leda entered very tired from a gruelling rehearsal, and stood looking at Ellie's work, the satchel containing her working clothes hanging from both gloved hands.

"Yes," she said, "that's about the way that Francis Tolland starts his work. . . . It looks all right to me, Ellie. . . . And that smelly stuff in the can is what he uses. . . . Who are you going to get as your model?"

"You, dear——" Ellie put both arms around her, persuasively.

Leda laughed: "I knew devilish well what you were up to. . . . You've got to have a model, I suppose. . . . All right, then—when I'm not too darned tired——"

"Sundays, darling!" pleaded Ellie, caressing her. "To-morrow will be Sunday——"

"If you'll promise to give me a hair treatment afterward——"

"I'll give you one now, you poor, tired kid!—and a wonderful massage!"

"Oh, gosh! I'd like that all right," sighed Leda. "That boob of a ballet master drilled the legs off us to-day. . . . I'm all in."

"I'll fix you up," said Ellie. "You'll sleep like the dickens and you'll wake up to-morrow feeling like a million dollars——"

"Feeling like posing for you, you mean!——"

"You will, won't you?"

Leda nodded. "I'm going to get into a hot tub," she said, turning away. "I feel as sore all over as a kicked pup——"

"You'll feel all right when I finish with you," said Ellie absently, fussing over the armature. . . . "I'll be with you in about ten minutes——"

"I'm sore in my mind, too," said Leda; "can you fix that up, too?"

"What's wrong?"

"Oh, I had another cable from Francis. He's changed his plans. He isn't sailing for another month. . . . The party is off."

Ellie was disappointed, too: "I thought perhaps he'd be willing to tell me a few things about sculpture——"

"Don't worry," said Leda, "he'll tell you a few things about everything when he arrives."

"A live one," nodded Ellie, carefully twisting a strand of wire with her pliers.

"I'll say he's alive. . . . Gosh, I'm sore! I'm sore at him, too—cabling he was coming like that! . . . Is that the way your young man behaves—sending you cables and then renigging——"

Ellie shrugged: "Mine doesn't even write."

"Well, I'd can him," remarked Leda.

"The trouble is I don't want to."

"That's the trouble with all of us," said Leda; "when they behave carelessly we don't want to can them. . . . Not until we're sure of them, anyway. . . . Oh, Lord, how lame I am! . . . Are you coming in?"

"You don't expect me to give you your bath, too, do you?"

"Ducky! *Would* you? Just as though I were a kiddie?"

Ellie laughed and laid away her pliers: "All right, darn it!—if you insist——"

CHAPTER XVI

ELLIE LESSING and Leda Nieland had a busy month of October. Every hour of Ellie's day and evening was employed; Leda's show, the Westchester Follies, tried out at Atlantic City, Danbury, Hartford, and came back pell-mell to open on Broadway.

Ellie secured two tickets through Leda; called up Judge Barrett; made him take her the first night.

"Great heavens!" he kept repeating, during the colourful and naked evening, "this is no show for a young girl!"

But Ellie retorted that he was old-fashioned, and vowed that the show was beautiful beyond criticism.

"Yeh?" grunted the Judge; "well, watch 'em pinch it; that's all."

Indeed, that seemed to be the question in the morning papers. Was a Christian public to stand for all this pagan nakedness?—assuming always that there were some Christians left in the metropolis.

Interviews with Max Mayer, who wept and protested that it was all for art; interviews with his Honour the Mayor, who said he hadn't seen the show, but would if necessary; interviews with exasperated clergymen, which bored everybody. In short, the show was launched for a run, and the town babbled about "that girl in *Diana's Hunting*—what's her name?—Nieland—Leda Nieland."

Wall Street unanimously approved her figure; Broadway
endorsed her "shape"; Max Mayer exercised his option
by tying her up with contracts certain to result in litiga-
tion; publicity men began to lie about her; photographers,
manufacturers of soaps, creams, lotions, corsets, bath-
tubs—all the familiar phenomena of success—announced
themselves as ready and anxious to put Leda Nieland on
the map. October was a great month in the girl's career.
Alternate applause and threats of arrest kept her in a
highly excited state; the instant hostility of the star and
of the majority of the headliners was scarcely calculated
to soothe her. But Max Mayer could be counted on to
extract every atom of publicity and every dollar out of
the situation. He had no hesitation in saying that Leda's
number was the making of the show; that it was ART!—
pure, chaste, guileless, beautiful; and that it was up to the
public to appreciate and revere it. And the Public did—
in the front row—or as near it as the speculators permitted.

For Leda Nieland, suddenly, everything in the world
had changed—except her salary.

Ellie took her, one Monday morning, to see "Judge"
Barrett, who gravely assured her that it was no crime
to break a contract if she were willing to let a jury decide
what the breakage would cost her.

"Ah," he added genially, "that's not the way to do
it, little lady. Max Mayer's a friend o' mine. Leave me
to talk to him after dinner some night. He's a square Jew
and a family man, and he'll never be grinding the face of
anny pretty orphan like you!"

"I've a mother in St. Louis——"

"The more reason, then! It's not Max Mayer who'll be hard on the sole support of a poor old mother! Lave me to talk to him once!——"

He shook hands, patted Leda's face, kissed Ellie goodbye, and escorted them to the door.

On their way home Leda said demurely: "My mother married again and is quite well off."

They both laughed unrestrainedly.

Sundays, and on other days when not playing or called for rehearsal or otherwise engaged, Leda posed for Ellie Lessing in her charming studio apartment.

Ellie's inspiration was grandiose; fearlessly ambitious. Her theme was *Diana's Hunting*—the moment in the really beautiful number where the goddess discovers that she has slain a young Dryad and not a deer with her arrow; and turns away in horror and grief from the dying creature at her feet.

Only a great sculptor could have done it. Ellie, in rapturous ignorance, did not hesitate; and the pretty fool rushed in where Rodin might have trod on tiptoe.

Excepting in school the girl never had handled plastic material. Her efforts with dough had completed her sculptural experience.

She did not hesitate now. Ignorant of materials; of ways and means; of composition, of proportion, of measurement, of construction—only excepting what she had read in the $2 pamphlet—she tucked up her sleeves to the arm-pits, dug a fistful of plastolene from the can, and started in.

Leda, who had been watching her with wonderment

and misgiving, giggled, and took the pose they had rehearsed and agreed upon.

Near by, on a stand, was an open box of bon-bons which she could reach.

"I'm sketching you; just blocking you in," remarked Ellie, sticking lumps and smears of plastolene all over the wired construction. . . . "I guess this is the way to start it. . . . I guess so——"

Leda reached for a bon-bon. While it was melting in her mouth she held her position and gossiped with the sculptress as well as the saccharine impediment in her mouth permitted.

"Gosh," she said, "it will be great if you ever learn to be a sculptress."

"I'll learn," returned Ellie, absently.

"Do you really feel that way about it?"

"I'm crazy about it. Why shouldn't I learn?"

"You're clever, of course——"

"Yes, I am. But that's nothing. Where does it get me if I don't work like the dickens? I don't know any more to-day than when I was ten and pinched little pigs out of soft bread! . . . That's all I'll be doing ten years from now if I don't work. Clever? Yes, for a kid of ten. . . . I'll tell you what woke me up. That man. Talking to him started me. My ignorance made me sick. Not *ill—sick!* . . . Did you ever read Mrs. Gates's book on Etiquette, Leda?"

Leda laughed. Ellie looked up at her, reddened: "You didn't need to read it, I suppose. Well, I needed to, darling."

"You know," said Leda, "what is adorable about you is your candour."

"No use kidding yourself, is there?"

"No. . . . You're right; I knew most of the conventional rules of social behaviour. . . . It's funny. I had so much that you hadn't. . . . Opportunities. . . . And look at me!—look at the darned thing now!—doing a number in one of Max Mayer's girl-shows! . . . After an expensive education. . . . With a cultivated mother, a well-to-do step-father, a luxurious home. . . . Me, on my own, showing myself to Broadway just about as God made me——"

"He made you very beautiful, Leda."

"Yes, but when I think of the Nielands—and many of them in holy orders——"

"They've had their life, haven't they? It's all right for you to live your own. . . . I mean to live mine as I darn please."

"Yes—look at the difference between us," returned Leda, laughingly,—"you, with only a primary school education, educating yourself; aspiring; ambitious; bettering yourself every day, every hour. . . . And look what I am —whose inspiration was Ethel Barrymore!"

"The critics say you're an artiste, and you are!"

"*I* know why I'm making a hit! And so does God, who's responsible."

"You're beautiful and artistic. I suppose you mean that men applaud your body! Well, damn them, they'd better! —they'll never see a more lovely example of God's art! . . . Are you getting tired, dear?"

So Sunday slipped away—with interval for tea—and many pauses for critical consultation concerning the proportions of the blocked-in human figure that Ellie was rapidly creating.

"You clever little thing," said Leda, "it looks *something* like me already. . . . I wish that darned Francis were here to help us."

"I'm just crazy to begin to model it and soften and smooth it," said Ellie, "but the book says not to—says you'll get into an awful smear if you don't keep it bold and rough—just keep on adding pinches of plastolene and finishing by degrees. . . . I'm dying to make it smooth—like your skin—and make it delicate and lovely. . . . Damn it, I know I'm going to have a terrible time with it——"

"Francis Tolland works the way you are working— just slapping on plastolene. . . . It just grows graceful and rounded and real under his fingers. . . . You have such beautiful fingers, Ellie—long and smooth. . . . A wonderful hand to touch you. . . . Darling, if I do all this for you—*all day long!*—will you give me a scalp treatment——"

"You bet. . . . Now, please turn the left shoulder a little more—no! the other way——"

CHAPTER XVII

IN Ellie Lessing's mail-box, the next morning, was a letter post-marked at some mountain town in Montana.

On the envelope was printed: "Return after five days to the John Westall Co., King Street, N. Y. City."

She had no opportunity to read it in the shop, so immediate and continual the demands on her from Madam and from a clientele which so quickly she had gathered around her and made her own.

After half the luncheon hour was over, however, she managed to escape to her room upstairs. He wrote:

DEAR ELLIE,

Yours was a nice letter. I am so glad things are going well with you.

I see no immediate prospect of my return to New York. We are expecting to build a dam and power plant on Cat Creek. You never heard of it, probably, nor did anybody else except people who, in these days, are perpetually hunting for water to give them power.

This Cat Creek dam, together with another project for the Coast, and still another which may require me to go to Persia by way of the Pacific, are some of the reasons why I am not likely to be in New York for some time to come.

So I am afraid there isn't much prospect of—as you so correctly put it—our seeing "more or less" of each other.

I'm sorry. You are a most amusing and interesting girl. I've enjoyed our odd friendship exceedingly, and I really feel much flattered that you picked me out as the man of whom you cared to see "more or less."

I've thought of you, missed you, wished to see you.

I do wish—when you feel inclined—you'd write to me through my King Street office. Wherever I am the letters will be sent me.

But, probably, what will happen will be this: you'll quite forget me. Some young man will come along presently. Perhaps when I return you'll be married.

I'd like to say one thing before I close: you have an unusual character; you have talent, capacity, ambition and courage. These are qualities that ought to make for success.

But, like beating wings unable to fly, talents uneducated are impotent.

All your cleverness, latent capacity, courage, ambition, never can lift you above the ordinary level unless you have been instructed *how* to use these talents, qualities, and traits. . . . Blindly beating wings! . . . Frantic, futile. . . . There is no short road to anything—except folly.

The world's chiefest woe is Ignorance. Upon it are based all sorrows, all evils, all failures. Ignorance is the great Destroyer. It breeds wars. It incubates pestilence. Out of it hatches all violence, intolerance, inhumanity—all of sin; absolutely all of evil.

But in its most horrible aspect it is an infanticide; it strangles at birth the frail children of the human mind—the fragile aspirants toward art and science born of immemorial imaginings—slain at birth or starved, crippled, distorted by Ignorance.

.   .   .   .   .

My dear, probably you're yawning. What I've written seems trite and stupid as I re-read it. But I shall let it stand.

And, one more matter, my dear; there is a villainous servant of Ignorance whose name is Poverty, and who aids his master to murder minds.

Like Leparello in *Don Juan*—an opera of Mozart which I

hope you are to hear one day—Poverty bedevils the victims of Ignorance, mocks at the vainly beating wings of aspiration, slyly cripples them, mutilates maliciously. . . . Lord! the noise of beating wings in the world, which never are destined to fly—never destined to lift the soul above earth's arid level!——

Ellie, if you are not asleep by this time, please attend to my sermon a little longer: you cannot take wing until you learn how; to learn costs more money than you can make in your beauty shop.

Now, I'd like to have you make up your mind what sort of career you desire, what course of education you require for it, about what would be your expenses, and what amount you would require in addition to your own income.

It would give me much pleasure to advance to you a reasonable fund for this purpose. You need never worry about accepting this money. Return it without interest, at your remotest convenience, if you like. But it would suit me better if you would accept it as a gift.

I shall look for a letter from you within the next two weeks.

With much affection,

Your "fella,"

JOHN WESTALL

The girl wept over the letter; but had to get rid of her tears and go back to the shop. In the corridor the "Doc," who had loitered to intercept her, brushed against her purposely and halted, leering, thick-lipped, ready for violent reaction. But the outrage only made her cry again and she went on toward the hair-colouring cabinet, staunching the tears with her uniform-apron.

Later Miss Stella whispered, "What'n'hell's gotcha, dearie?"

"Not a darn thing," returned Ellie; "I'm a fool."

"Doc been actin' up?"

"That worm? Oh, it isn't that. But—everything's coming my way, Stella, except one thing. . . . It's all so beautiful—I just spilled. . . . That's all. . . . That's all. . . ."

Miss Stella grinned: "Some fella—on a bet! Honest, now, dearie?"

Ellie nodded; swallowed hard: "He's a peach. I need him. I need him right now."

"Well, where is he?"

"Out West."

"A travellin' man?"

"No. . . . Oh, gosh! I wish he'd come back." She seated herself at Stella's table during the brief respite from work, and bowed her bobbed head between widespread fingers.

"You been goin' with him?" inquired Stella.

"No; I was just beginning to 'see more or less' of him. . . . He's a peach."

"Sure. They all are till they turn rotten. . . . God, it's a shame we ever should hook up with anything in pants. . . . But I guess you're like me, Ellie. I gotta be petted. I can't go too long without it. . . . You like it too, don't you?"

"Well, all boys fuss around—I am—affectionate, I guess. . . ."

"Well, if your fella don't come back and give you what you want, can him!"

Ellie shook her head, drearily.

"Is it a sure-fire, serious, church hook-up?" demanded Stella.

"Oh, no." . . .

"He isn't keepin' you, is he?"

"No," said Ellie, simply.

"What's he after?"

"Nothing, I guess. . . . I went after him."

"Gee, that's bad!——"

"I couldn't help it. He's a peach. . . . I knew there wasn't anything in it. . . . But, gosh!—if I could only talk to him——"

"*Talk?*"

"Yes. It's mostly talk with us."

"No action?"

Ellie blushed. "Only once—a little. . . . I wanted it."

"Say, is there anything the matter with your fella?" inquired Stella scornfully.

"Not a thing. . . . I might as well get used to doing without him. . . . I guess so." She picked up a nail-file, absently; twirled it. Madam Felice called her at that moment, and another client opened the door and waddled into the shop to have a triple chin made beautiful.

That night, after returning from her French lesson, Ellie wrote to Westall:

MY DEAR,

Your dear letter caused me joy and sorrow. I do want you so. But I don't want any money.

It's so sweet of you. And I was surprised that you should offer to help educate me.

I have plenty of money. I have a small income and I am making enough in the Beauty Parlour to pay for an education through the Correspondence College, and study French besides.

Aren't languages wonderful? And isn't English beautiful? I've often wondered who made the English language and all the adverbs and adjectives and cases and tenses and prepositions. And all the wonderful rules! Isn't it a *miracle?*

I tell you what worries me so much—to know how to use *will* and *shall* and *would* and *should;* and when to employ an adverb or an adjective. I have just learned when to use *so* and *as*—for instance—"He is *as* tall as she," and "He is not *so* tall as she."

Isn't it *interesting?* But the pronouns!—Oh, gosh!— when to use *her* and *she, I* and *me!*—good night! I tell you what I do; I memorize the rules; there is no other way for me. Some learn from hearing correct English spoken around them in their families and by their friends; and to speak correctly becomes a habit. But I can't count on that.

So I study my book of rules like the dickens and I remember them all the time I am studying my courses in English literature and history.

Now, about my sculpture: I am working on a group—I think it is called a *group*—of two female figures in the nude. I have no instruction except from a pamphlet which I bought. A girl friend of mine poses for me when she has time.

Well, I've had great sorrow and trouble with it. I know it isn't right, but I don't know why or how to make it right. I'm mad about it; it tears my heart, but I can't keep away from it. What you say in your letter about blindly beating wings!——

Oh, gosh! I know what you mean—the wild desire to do what you don't know how to do. You *know* you've got wings, but you just beat them in vain attempt to fly—just beat and flap and flop and remain where you are, broken, exhausted, raging.

Oh, you're so right about ignorance. Isn't it filthy! I guess it is the root of all wickedness and sorrow.

Well, I'm trying. Dear, it isn't any money I need. I have enough. I need to talk to you. . . . And also—I guess you know what I mean. . . . You are so sweet. . . .

I don't know where that damn Cat Creek is. How long are you going to stay away? . . . I suppose you'll think me crazy or bad, but I'd rather be with you, even if you are married. . . . Isn't that terrible of me?

But I'm going to be honest with you: it's lonely for a young girl who is used to men. I get lonely, sometimes. I never minded petting, much. But I never knew I liked it until that night you left. That's why it's lonesome for me, I suppose. . . . But I haven't been out with any men.

Now, I must thank you for your kind offer of assistance. I don't really need it, but it is so good of you to offer it.

Please, dear, come back to me when you can possibly do so.

Your friend and sweetheart,

ELLIE LESSING

CHAPTER XVIII

FRANCIS TOLLAND turned up unexpectedly about ten o'clock one evening.

Leda Nieland was at the theatre as usual; had no intimation that he was arriving. Ellie, in her own quarters, was working on her French.

Hearing somebody passing her partly open door toward Leda's studio, she rose and looked out into the corridor; and saw a dark, graceful young man, carrying a suit-case and fitting a key into the door.

A little startled she said: "Miss Nieland is not at home. What is it you wish?"

At that he turned around leisurely, made her an engaging bow, and came toward her.

"It's quite lawful," he said. "This is my own dump, you see."

His manners were easy; his smile, amiable, became, appreciative:

"You're Leda's new friend, Ellie Lessing."

"Oh; are you Mr. Tolland?"

"I am. Leda is at the theatre, I suppose?"

"Yes. . . ."

"All right; I'll just go in and stick around——"

He opened the door with his key, switched on the light:

"Same old dump. Just the way I left it——" He caught

sight of Ellie's "group" in plastolene: "Well, I'll be dogged!" he remarked.

"Oh," said Ellie, blushing brightly, "that belongs to me. I'll take it out——"

"Who's working here?" he demanded. He turned and caught her expression: "Oh, are *you* the sculptress? I hadn't heard *that* about you. . . .

"I don't know anything about sculpture——" There was a hot colour surging in her cheeks; she entered the studio and went toward the group.

"Did you model that?" he asked pleasantly.

"I tried to——"

"Where have you been studying?"

"Nowhere."

"You've taken lessons?"

"Out of a pamphlet——"

"Wait a moment, please——"

He walked over to the modeling stand; Ellie's hands fell away from the smeared oaken block.

He examined the work in his easy, graceful way, revolving it on the zinc pedestal.

"Without instruction?" he inquired again.

"I told you."

"Well, well. . . . Well, I'll be dogged!"

He looked at her in his gaily amiable way. There seemed always to be a natural caress in this man's manner and voice—not at all offensive—a sort of unfeigned personal interest.

"Why," he inquired, "haven't you had instruction?"

"I didn't know where to go. . . . Besides, except evenings and Sundays I am employed." He thought her enun-

ciation, and the evident care she gave to phrasing, stilted,
self-conscious, yet oddly attractive. Leda had written him
a little about this girl.

He laid his hand on the base of the group with caressing grace:

"You know," he said, "this happens to be my line,
too."

"Yes, I know." The reverence in her voice secretly
amused him, but he said very seriously: "If there's anything you think I might be able to tell you——"

Her flushed expression checked him.

"Oh, my Lord!" she said; "I don't know *anything!*"

He began to laugh. "Yes, you do!"

"What do I know?" incredulously.

"Well, come," he said in his easy, agreeable way, "do
you think this is very rotten—this standing figure?"

"I guess so. Isn't it?"

"No, it isn't. . . . And I'll tell you, it's rather hard
to believe you've had no instruction except out of a book."

"I can show you the book."

A subtle excitement was invading the girl. She hurried
to her own room and returned with the pamphlet purchased at an art shop.

"Well," he said, smiling, as he ran over the pages of
the meagre brochure, "you certainly have extracted something out of this stuff. . . . Is that how you learned to
fix up your armature and wiring? I see." . . . He looked
at the few tools lying on the modelling stand. . . . "I
see," he repeated. . . . "You use your hands, mostly";
and noticed her long, childishly smooth, yet capable fingers.

Ellie had seated herself on the arm of a carved chair. Her clever face with its slanting eyes was earnestly intent upon him. One hand balanced the slim, curved body; her pendent feet did not touch the floor.

"Am I detaining you?" he asked so frankly that the girl detected no guile in this sophisticated young man.

"Oh, no," she said, "—I am *so* interested!——"

He seated himself, offered her a cigarette which she accepted in her excitement.

"About your group there," he said, "—tell me, what is your theme? Isn't this Diana?"

She told him about Diana and the Dryad.

"*Your* idea?"

"Yes."

"It's interesting. Also, more important, it's *new!*"

"Yes, I invented it," she said. . . . "I don't know how I came to imagine it. . . . I thought of it one day while I was looking at your *Leda.*"

"That's flattering," he said; "do you like *Leda?*"

He turned and glanced at the group over his shoulder.

The girl said, speaking with grammatic care, yet evidently with controlled emotion: "I think it is the most beautiful sculpture I ever have seen, excepting, perhaps, *The Hand of God* in the Metropolitan Museum."

No sophistication is proof against such depths of sincerity. The girl's unusual beauty—if it could be called that—already had aroused in him a lively appreciation. And the stilted and quaint caution in her speech was singularly attractive. . . . Knowing somewhat of her through Leda's letters . . . a young girl working in a West Side Beauty Parlour, trying to educate herself.

"Well," he said, following the train of thought, "*I* had to be kicked through college."

"*What?*"

"I'm sorry. . . . I was thinking aloud." He smiled; reached up, took Ellie's group from its zinc pedestal, and balanced it on his knees: "Continue to use those flexible young fingers," he said; "they're your best tools. . . . Rather marvellously made tools. . . . Just continue to stick on pellets of plastolene. Use your dividers and your plumbline. Don't finish. . . . You'll get into a smooth, nasty, greasy, featureless mess——"

"Oh, I know," cried Ellie, "—I've done it on her left leg! . . . But I was impatient; I was crazy to make it as smooth as a real leg——"

"Don't. Go on with your bony and muscular construction and watch your proportions. Don't bother about the skin. It will grow of itself."

"Oh, *tell* me," she said in her delicious excitement, "—oh, *please!*——"

"Very well; here's the critique, then"—and he set the group on the floor; and the girl dropped on both knees beside it.

He talked in his easy way, using no cant phrases, no technical terms. She understood every word; even sometimes divined what he was going to say. Once or twice, from her facial expression or some nervous movement, he comprehended that already she had forestalled him. The intense cleverness of the girl was now plain enough. That, coupled to sincerity, was to be noticed in anybody. . . . Meant something. . . . Rather unusual, this—to be hatched out of a Beauty Parlour. . . .

The upshot of it was that she *must* have instruction. Some night class. Cooper Institute—somewhere.

"You think there is a chance that . . . " But her voice escaped control; broke in a childish grace-note.

"I don't know why you shouldn't hope to make it your profession some day," he said.

Recovering: "Gee!" she said with a shiver.

Leda walked in—the door left open—saw her on her knees; and Francis Tolland there.

"The dickens!" she exclaimed: "—and isn't that like you, Francis Tolland!—what's that suit-case over there——"

Tolland, by this time, was on his feet and bending over her in his easy way—had kissed her hands very lightly and pressed them warmly:

"I made up my mind to come back. . . . Sorry I forgot to cable again. . . . Leda, you're a headliner now, aren't you? . . . Show going strong? . . . Well, I'll be dogged!——"

All three seemed happy, approving things in general.

"You've been vamping Ellie Lessing," said Leda; "it's like you to lose no time—"

"She caught me house-breaking—"

"Well, what the deuce do you intend to do with your suit-case?"

"Bunk here."

"Wha—t?"

"Where do you expect me to go?"

Leda laughed: "No," she said, "I'm not fussy but I'll be dinged if you're going to sleep on that sofa to-night. All right; call me Victorian!" Becoming more emphatic as she realized the situation: "—I'm not going to let you turn me out, either. I need a week's notice. Should have had a month to find me a dump. . . . Look here, young man, you're too darned casual. . . . Really, Francis, it was very sweet of you to let me have your place, but you should have cabled——"

"You throw me out?"

"Well, ducky——"

"*Do* you?"

"Well, I'll be ding-dang-dinged if I'll let you sleep in the same room——"

"Prejudice! Artificial, outworn, ridiculous——"

"—*And* Victorian! Yes—yes, my dear. But the day hasn't dawned when I bunk in with you or any other man. Not *yet!* . . . Oh, Francis, don't be so damn modern. . . . And—shall we have a bite and a little teeny drink-let?"

As Ellie went with her to the kitchenette: "Leda," she said, "why not sleep with me to-night and let him stay?"

Leda found some eggs for poaching; started the range; slammed open the bread-box.

"Chip some ice," she said. . . . "All right then. I won't turn him out——"

CHAPTER XIX

FRANCIS TOLLAND continued to occupy his own quarters and Leda Nieland continued to share Ellie's.

For one thing she was too busy to hunt up another place. Also, Ellie wanted her, although the apartment was small, closet room limited, and the bed only a three-quarter affair.

Ellie's motives were, desire to be of service, affection for Leda, and intervals of loneliness. She would not let Leda share in the rent. Other living expenses, however, were halved between them.

Meanwhile, the little household went on as usual. Leda gave Ellie what time she could spare for the Diana; in return Ellie gave the girl "treatments" which she adored, and, with her long, clever fingers, exorcised weariness from mind and body and revitalized both.

So busy was Ellie Lessing in her beauty shop, and, in the evenings, with French at the Strelitz School, or absorbed in the history of art, literature and manners by correspondence, or poring over the volume by Mrs. Gates, that she had no time left to seek out any night class where the art of sculpture was taught.

There seemed to be no time for other amusement, either —no spare hour for a show or a dinner or a dance. Circumstances were limiting her; crowding the girl back upon herself and her own resources. . . . And toward her next-door neighbor, Francis Tolland. He always had time for her. He had time for anything, it seemed.

That young man, now, was solidly settled in his old quarters. He had carelessly resumed what appeared to be his usual mode and system of life. Which was to live leisurely. But, nevertheless, *live* every moment of life. He worked leisurely, unhurriedly; but it was real work. He amused himself as leisurely; kept outrageous hours when he chose, yet rose, always, at half-past seven. After such irregularities he was sallow of skin and dark under his eyes, but neither nervous nor visibly tired, and his mind seemed to be as clear and alert as ever.

"Some party," he'd admit to Leda, who usually stopped in to chat with him after her return from the theatre. "But a man can't live by plastolene alone. Got to have a little gaiety. . . . What's your friend, Ellie, up to?"

"Studying. Where were you last night?"

"There was a party."

"You don't want to tell me? Don't, then!"

She shrugged her shoulders, looked about her, slowly walked from one modelling stand to another inspecting the work. There were half a dozen of these stands; there were studies in wax, in plastolene, in clay—the latter swathed in wet cloths. One was a portrait bust—a Wall Street gentleman's wife—one of those vigorous, slashing things he did sometimes. Another was a sketch for a regimental memorial—a muscular, nude figure fighting a terrific rush of eagles—no doubt symbolizing Germany, Austria, *et al.*

Another was a delicate Tanagra-like dancing figure called *Modernism*—exquisite in its scant draperies.

"Who posed for this?" inquired Leda.

"A professional. I forget her name."

"From the Models' League?"

He nodded.

"Was she as lovely as this?"

"No; I glorified her. You like it?"

"Yes; it's lovely—infernally so. She's a young terror—a baby devil. . . . So are you."

"What! Well, I'll be dogged——"

"Have you seen Ellie to-day?"

"I have."

"Did you give her a criticism?"

"Several."

"How is she coming on?"

"Oh, she's plugging away," he said.

Leda seated herself. "I want you to tell me, Francis."

"About what?"

"Ellie."

"Well, you can't expect her to do anything wonderful quite yet——"

"I want your opinion in absolute confidence. Is that girl likely to do anything in art?"

"I don't know."

"Tell me honestly, has she talent?"

"Yes," he said impatiently, "but that's almost a handicap. Talent is common enough. It's up to her whether she does anything with it. Few do."

"Poor child," said Leda, thinking of the Beauty Shop.

Francis said: "She has talent, imagination, taste. She seems to have persistency. If she has she'll get on. . . . I can't say how far."

"Is that the best you can say about Ellie?"

"It's a lot to say. . . . All right, then, in strict confidence, she's unusually intelligent. She's tireless. Insatiable."

He got up and began to walk about: "I don't believe you can get anywhere without foundation—without doing the dirty drudgery first. Study means a certain elapsed time devoted to manual and mental practice. . . . I don't believe you can step in and hold up art like a bandit, and rob her of all the preliminaries you require in one lump sum, and go away and instantly be wealthy in both theory and practice."

"You think Ellie ought to have gone through all the academical preliminaries?"

"I do. . . . There *are* blue moons. And white blackbirds. Prodigies who take short cuts. Who learn, acquire, digest, and are prepared to practise overnight what takes normal talent months and years to assimilate. . . . I don't know such people by sight. They exist, but I've never encountered any."

"You don't think Ellie Lessing is one?" suggested Leda, thrilled.

"No, I don't. . . . But I'll say—you won't tell her, will you? It's no good for her to hear such things——"

"Promise."

"Well, then—that *Diana and the Dryad* of hers— I'll be quite frank, Leda; it rather floored me. . . . Things in it that were surprising. Things that seemed impossible for anybody to do without instruction. . . . I didn't quite believe her when she said she never had had any instruction. I know, now, it's true enough."

He resumed his pacing. Presently: "She hasn't been through the mill. She hasn't done the drudgery. She's a bandit: she holds up Art and takes all the savings she ought to have worked for. She begins in the middle. She lops off the years and starts abreast of others who've been at it—digging away at it—in schools and classes all this time——"

"Oh, Francis, *is* Ellie a genius?"

"What the devil is a genius? Somebody who has no end of cheek and persistency? What's genius? The valour of industrious ignorance?"

He came and seated himself on the other arm of Leda's chair.

"In confidence," he said coolly, "she's got me guessing. It isn't reasonable that she should do with plastolene some of the things she seems to know how to do untaught. She worries me."

"Does she seem to profit by your criticisms?"

"Profit? I don't know. Yes, I suppose so. . . . She's in the imitative stage. We all enter that stage. Few of us pass through and become ourselves. . . . She studies Rodin with a kind of mental ferocity. You can see it on Mondays in her work. She spent last Sunday morning at the Metropolitan. Monday morning she was working at daylight and that night she showed me a sketch in plastolene—a near-Rodin idea—she called it *Motherhood*—a nude group—a girl of ten—a thin, formless, delicate little slip of a thing; and Pan, shaggy, wrinkled, his horned head pillowed on her lap, snoring . . . yes, *visibly snoring,* Leda—relaxed, lop-eared, his pipes fallen from his thick parted lips upon his hairy breast!—I'll be dogged if it wasn't a remarkable performance. . . . It was all wrong, technically, of course, even for a sketch—

no construction, no proportion, not composed, not placed, not studied—*but* there were things in that, too. . . . That child, *mothering Pan!!*—that unformed, virginal little thing . . . and that old goat!—something about her —don't know—like a gutter-baby nursing a rag doll— don't you tell her a word of this. Don't ever let her get any idea she knows anything about modelling. She's cursed with cleverness. She's humble and prayerful in her cleverness. Let her remain so. . . . I don't know what she'll ever amount to."

Leda got up, put both hands on his shoulders.

"Help her, Francis. . . . And I want to say this also; Ellie thinks you're a very wonderful man. Don't let her think more than that about you. She adores you as a pupil reveres a master. Don't amuse yourself by awakening any other sentiment in her."

He began to laugh, carelessly:

"I'm not likely to try to start anything——"

"Yes, you are. But don't!"

"She's got a beau; she told me so," he insisted.

"What's a beau when you're lonely? And affectionate?"

"It's entirely intellectual, our liaison——"

"She's very pretty," interrupted Leda, "very appealing, touchingly interesting. Don't start anything, just to see if you can. Maybe you could; you're an enterprising young man; but don't take a chance. The combination of sculpture and sentiment is terribly upsetting to a girl——"

"It didn't upset *you*," he retorted.

"It nearly did. . . . Only I managed to realize that you are much too modern to play with. . . . Nice but irresponsible."

She slid from the arm of the chair to the floor and stood smiling at him:

"—Not perfectly safe," she added; "nothing permanent about you, Francis, except your art."

"Permanency is a bovine quality—or defect," he returned, amused.

"I know. But we Victorians—Victoriennes—require it. We have required bovine devotion ever since Europa selected her bull—"

They fell a-laughing.

"A progressive and lifelong succession of love affairs," he argued, "develops character and talents. Marriage paralyses and petrifies both. You'll see, some day, Leda."

"*You'll* *s*ee, some day, when you make an inventory and find in your old age that your only assets are a few marble figures," she retorted.

"And a number of charming memories," he added, mockingly. "God help those who have none to remember when it's too late to acquire any."

"More modern bunk," she said serenely. "Oh, Francis, you're such an enterprising ass, sometimes, that I'm almost sorry I'm not to be included among your 'memories.'"

Laughingly she moved toward the door toward which he politely accompanied her.

"It's never too late," he said, "for a charming girl to lay up treasures of memory for declining years—

"'Ghosts of the Past whose tender smiling features
    Console the wintry solitude of Age;
Were you my pupils then, or my sweet teachers
Who turned with me the sentimental page?'"

—he quoted; and kissed her gloved hand with mischievous and supple grace.

She came into Ellie's studio. The latter looked up, her greenish, gold-flecked eyes dazed from study.

"I had a chat with Francis," Leda remarked, flinging her hat and furs on to the bed. "He's such a dear. . . . Does he help you?"

"Yes."

"Much?"

"Yes, he does. I understand whatever he tells me. He lets me watch him at work, too."

"I didn't know that. When do you see him at work?"

"On Saturdays during lunch hour. I don't need any lunch. I saw him working on the Battle Monument. It was an education."

"Gosh," said Leda, "he had a man model posing, didn't he?"

"A wonderful model! Strangling eagles. There weren't any eagles there, you know. Francis will do those later. He'll make sketches from life at the Bronx, and at the Natural History Museum he'll have access to skeletons and skins. . . . I never was so excited in my life as when I stood in there and watched Francis building up those bones and muscles——"

"That's a darned disagreeable phase of your art—to have to look at a man with no clothes on," remarked Leda. "I suppose you don't mind it?"

"No, I don't. It was no surprise to me. Everybody has seen statues and knows what men look like. Only—what wonderful limbs and bodies and bony structure! and what muscles! I was simply wild to start a sketch; so Francis let me. It was pretty bad."

"Did Francis say so?"

"No. But when I looked at that model and then looked at my study, oh, gosh!"

"That's the proper way to feel, anyway," said Leda. She went over and examined the sketch called *Motherhood*—the child and Pan. After a while:

"It's in all girl-children, isn't it?" she remarked.

"The maternal," nodded Ellie. . . . "Anything to cuddle. . . . You know, I think, with girls it has a lot to do with their mushy parties. . . . I like it best to have a boy's head on my lap. . . . They're such children, when you look down at them. . . . Something about them that seems helpless and cuddlesome. . . . A girl gets blue, sometimes. And then, if that feeling comes, she just wants something to cuddle. . . . It isn't that she cares to be kissed so much. She wants something to fuss over. . . . I believe it's chiefly that. Don't you, Leda?"

"One thing is sure-fire," said Leda, smiling; "no man ever has really started anything with you. . . . Yes; there's more of the maternal in us than would flatter most men if they knew how we felt about them. . . . They don't like being fussed over, but that's pretty nearly all we want of them——" She yawned, stood stretching her limbs and gazing at Ellie.

Ellie yawned, too. "Gosh," she said, "this correspondence course is interesting, but I'd better go to bed."

CHAPTER XX

A BUSY man has little inclination for sentiment. A tired man none at all.

In the career of the average man how much of his lifetime has been devoted to love? A fractional percentage.

Love plays a very small part in the life of the normal man. The time devoted to it is but an infinitesimal proportion of the time devoted to other activities, other emotions, desires, inclinations, ambitions, motives. A quantitative analysis of a man's career would reveal love only as a "trace" among the elements and combinations which would compose his life.

The life history of the average man contains so little of love that one wonders why love is generally considered to be the world's motive power.

To normal man, in general, love never is more than an episode—a recognized malady, to be contracted, endured, and got over. And the business of life resumed. Which is to get on.

Whether the malady turnes into marriage or the victim continues sour and single, always, with comparatively brief delay, he takes up the business of life again. The "trace" only remains to flavour and colour, more or less, the span of time allotted him on earth. And this is the true importance and real proportion of love in the lifetime of the average healthy man.

At the age of thirty-five John Westall had given no

more time to sentiment than the normal and busy male gives.

At present the big power dam on Cat Creek occupied his thoughts—except when he considered the chances of another job on the Coast, and possibly another in Persia.

All his thoughts, ambitions, desires, hopes, concentrated upon the John Westall Construction Company.

To him, therefore, Ellie Lessing's letters were as fugitive as so many rose petals blown across the world. A moment's notice; a momentary consideration; brief consciousness of their frail fragrance; and then Westall resumed the business of life. Which is, always, to get on. To carry on.

In the first place he was not in love. Never had been. Never troubled himself to consider the popular malady, or his own chances of contracting it or of escaping.

In the second place—as far as Ellie Lessing was con-cerned—the current of generations stranded John Westall on the shore of one of the social puddles.

That puddle was one of many in this exclusive swamp. It was a rich and soupy puddle. His race had always squatted there. Never had investigated the vast, unknown morass outside or noticed its myriad inhabitants.

John Westall never bothered to think about matters that seemed obvious. Axioms he ignored as self-evident propositions. He took it for granted that species interbred naturally. That different species of the same genus did not naturally interbreed. But it could be done.

As for one genus rolling amorous eyes at another— it simply was *not* done.   .

For example, in puddle aristocracy, the Family of the *Ranidae* is one of the most unified families in its structural characteristics.

Now, it is natural for individuals of *Rana pipiens* to interbreed. All right to breed with *Rana ephenocephala,* too. Risky to philander with *Rena palustri*s or with *areolata, et al.* Eccentric to wander farther afield. Yet possible.

But as for the Genus *Rana* ever considering the Genus *Hyla* with a view to matrimony—it wasn't done; that's all.

"Homo sum!" . . . "Whatever concerns Batrachians is important to me!"

This, John Westall might have quoted had he had occasion. But he would have considered it unnecessary to add that *Rana* is *Rana* and *Hyla* is *Hyla,* and never the twain shall unite. Legally.

So much for Love. And for Ellie Lessing.

At Cat Creek all the preliminary work had been done —surveys, borings, plans, maps. Roads were under way; narrow-gauge tracks; shanties, barracks, storehouses, magazines. Several important gentlemen came and looked at Cat Creek, visualized the impounded waters; geologists, engineers, contractors; Government, State, county officials.

With all of these John Westall had speech. This was part of his business—a fraction. The remainder would have overwhelmed some men.

But Westall seemed to have plenty of time for everybody and everything. Even for Ellie Lessing, whose letters, like rose petals, came fluttering across a thousand miles of mountains and valleys before they lodged in the canyon of Cat Creek.

Late in the winter he replied to an odd, excited, distressed little missive:

My dear child, of course there is no serious permanent understanding between you and me. Merely the agreeable consciousness of a friendship. You owe me nothing. You are perfectly free.

Why do you ask? What perplexes you? You seem troubled about something.

If, as I suspect, some other man has strolled into your ken, that is what I predicted the last time I saw you. Didn't I?

If you have fallen in love, why not tell me? You know I'm your warm friend, and much interested in what concerns you. Don't think you have any obligations toward me. You've had many beaux. I'm only another one. I told you I expected to be superseded. If I am, I'll make the best of it without surrendering your friendship or my interest in you and your career.

Indeed, your development, your determination to better yourself, your almost hourly progress—judged by your letters—and your career now really in bud, and fascinating for such a man as I am to watch—all these, and your strong, clever, sweet personality could not fail to find in me a sympathetic and affectionate friend.

So if there is another man in the offing, you may say so to me quite frankly, if you choose. I know you are naturally affectionate, accustomed to being petted; that you like men; that often you are lonely; that yours is a nature that really needs affection.

As for your charming appeal to me to come back and give you what you need—I can't do that. Even if I did, I'd have to go away again.

You know, as well as I do, that ours is but a temporary companionship. Born of my diving ability. Nourished by your charm, cleverness, and intelligence, and my capacity to stimulate your mind. It was that, and the excited gratitude of a lonely child, that sent you into my arms that evening. That was the way you expressed the grateful emotion of mind and heart.

It took some resolution, too, considering that you believed me to be married. You funny kiddie!

Well, I won't tease you any more about that matter, Ellie. Contrary to your desperate conclusion concerning me, I'm not married and never have been. Moreover, I'm never likely to be. Did you know that I'm rather aged? Within a few months of thirty-five?

Therefore, my dear, go about your business of beaux at your own sweet leisure and with a calm conscience.

But I do hope you'll write me now and then and tell me about yourself and your progress in sculpture and general erudition.

And remember always I am your affectionate friend and ex-fella,

JOHN WESTALL

Two weeks later, as he was starting for the Pacific Coast, he had another letter from Ellie Lessing. He read it on the train, westward bound:

DEAR,

I don't know what is happening to me. Everything is confused inside my mind.

I have wanted you so much. Yet you seem more like a dream—more and more so. It is hard to remember exactly how you are—how your voice sounds—and how tall you are; and often your face is not clear when I try to see you with the eyes of my mind.

But sometimes, asleep, you are clear to me. And when

I wake up I've been crying, sometimes. Isn't that silly? I never cried about a man before, except Dad.

I'm confused, and lonely, and am beginning to realize you are not coming back.

I didn't expect we ever would be really in love. I didn't expect it when I thought you were married, and wanted you for a beau. You were my first well-educated beau. That thrilled me. I wanted to be with you. I wanted to be your girl, and be petted by you. I didn't think of love. I don't know anything about love.

The thing that attracts me in a man is his education, experience, and nice manners. And besides you are the best-looking man! You are a peach; and I knew it right away. All this went to my head. Then to my heart. I just needed you And you've been wonderful.

About another man—yes, there is one. I'm so confused. He isn't like you, except that he's the kind of man you are, socially.

Sometimes he fascinates me. There is enchantment about him. His vast knowledge dazzles me. It commands me. Not as yours did; yours inspired; his exhausts. I feel limp—no good for work after watching him.

It's terrible to say this to you, but I'm crazy about him. It's his knowledge, power—the genius in him. I try to separate that from the rest of him. Somehow I feel he doesn't want me to. It's terribly perplexing. I don't know my own mind. There is something in my heart and mind that always remains in communication with you. Vaguely—in a kind of dream—but always. I suppose because you were my first real man. A girl never can forget that. It's never the same with another man, I guess.

Well, I tell you, I've never been in love; but I never have wanted anybody as much as I have wanted you— except Dad and Mother.

I don't want this man as much as that. But, in some ways, I want him even more—I mean that part of him which is his power and experience and knowledge and skill. I am simply mad about these; it's perplexing to find that the man himself seems to be part of them—all mixed up with them.

I'd better tell you that he's that sculptor I wrote you about when I first met him. Francis Tolland.

As they say on Broadway, he's got me groggy. And, oh, the beautiful professional work he does! So powerful, so exquisite, so marvellous, so infinitely skilled! He is a great sculptor. And only twenty-eight!

Dear, I don't know what this new impulse really is; whether I'm just stunned, awed by his power, or whether I've gone plumb crazy over sculpture in general; but there is developing in me a kind of fever, a madness to plunge into it all, lose myself, live, breathe, strive for, and think only of this immortal art; and worship those who have the power to create it. And worship Francis Tolland.

Now, I have something most astonishing to tell you.

You know I wrote you in January that I had joined an evening class in modelling. That has helped me in a most amazing manner.

You remember I wrote to you about that little group I started called *Motherhood?* Old Pan with his head on the lap of a little girl? Snoring?

Well, I had enough money to hire models and pay Mr. Clay, our instructor, to help me with that group after the class was dissmissed.

We worked on it three times a week from eleven o'clock until one in the morning, all winter.

When it was done, it really was as much Mr. Clay's as mine, although I really did stick on the plastolene with my fingers.

Well, I took it to Shoreham's, not daring to believe that they would buy it.

Dear, they did! They paid me a thousand dollars down. They had it cast in bronze. I receive 25% on the price of every replica sold. More than that, they offered to consider everything I did. They urged me to do other small bronzes for them. They promised that, if they liked my next two figures or groups, they would pay me ten thousand dollars for the privilege of monopolizing everything I did for ten years; pay me fifteen hundred dollars down for the next group, with 25% royalty on every replica sold; sixteen hundred for the next, then seventeen, eighteen, nineteen, up to two thousand five hundred.

Dear, I did all this financial business myself. I think they are very, very generous, but didn't let them know I thought so.

I was rather clever. I saw right away that they were greatly interested in *Motherhood*. I heard one gentleman say to another: "It's sure a fine seller. That girl can do popular stuff. You'd better tie her up while the tying's easy."

They had gone behind a glass partition to talk. I didn't have to listen very hard.

I was terribly excited. I had no idea how much I ought to have for *Motherhood*. Mr. Clay told me to ask $250. So I asked two thousand. I was scared speechless when they said they could offer only a thousand. I could only nod. Mr. Clay said: "Take 10%." I nearly expired when they offered me 25%.

Dear, I never was so wild with happiness as when I saw my first bronze. It isn't very good, but I love it!

I showed it to the sculptor I've told you about—not Mr. Clay; Francis Tolland.

He *was* surprised. Said it was "quite nice." I don't think it pleased him to have me sell it. His ideals of technique are so high.

But, dear, I *had* to. I had to have money to go on. I've got to find leisure to work. How can I ever amount to anything if I spend every day from nine to five in a beauty parlour?

Just as soon as I dare I am going to leave Madam Felice. I need every moment of daylight to work in. I need every moment of evening to study in. Time is flying. I am now getting old very fast.

Dear, this is a long, long letter. Because it is to be a long, long farewell between you and me.

I shall write to you. I don't know what is going to happen between Francis Tolland and me. He is a master. His power commands. His work dazzles. He is a young man; quite handsome; very cultivated. There is a strange sort of authority even in his graceful, listless ways. He cares nothing for convention. Disregards matters which I consider important. I don't know—I don't know why I am so mad about him—about him, or his power—or both, perhaps.

But, dear, I'll tell you this: I don't feel reckless about him; only confused. But I *did* feel reckless when I supposed you were married; and flung my arms around you in spite of it. . . . Reckless, excited—and, oh, determined to be your girl —have you for mine, once, anyway—at *any* cost. . . . Dear, do you read clearly what I'm writing to you? I didn't *know* what might happen to me when I went into your arms. And I didn't care. . . . And *that,* dear, is the nearest I ever have come to being in love.

This new madness isn't that kind. I was drunk with excitement when you kissed me. I knew what I was doing with you; I didn't care. Now I'm drunk again, I suppose. The intoxicated *always* know what they are doing. But *this* time I *do* care what I may do.

Good-bye. You're so sweet not to be offended. If ever I fall in love I'll tell you, dear, first of all. . . . But—don't tell me when it happens to you. . . . I'm different. Not kind, like you. Don't tell me for a long, long time. . . . It isn't in me to take it—happily.

ELLIE

So much, again, for Love. And Ellie Lessing.

CHAPTER XXI

LOVE—and Ellie Lessing. . . . Or whatever it was —a species of love; or a sub-species; or a variety; or one of those undetermined phenomena known as "sports," by pomologists.

Fruit of what? Environment? Circumstance? One of those ghostly blossoms of the human mind? Spontaneous? Extraneous? Sown by the subliminal? Nourished by the occult?

Love? Or its mirage? Passionate enough—with the white-hot passion of the mind. Docile as a charmed bird! And as obedient.

One Saturday afternoon in March the seed split, disclosing a shoot as white and straight as a flame. Already pricking above ground. Everything, with Ellie Lessing, was always above ground.

Leda had her usual matinée. The Beauty Parlour remained open until five in winter; but Ellie had insisted on her Saturday afternoons; and neither Madam nor the "Doc" were now in any position to thwart her. But they delayed her all they dared.

Ellie came into Francis Tolland's studio in her smock and mules, still pink with annoyance.

"They're so darned mean to me," she said, "—always contriving to stick me with a customer at the last minute. . . . I'm too decent. That's how Felice puts it over on me. . . . Mewing and rubbing around. . . . Too damn confident that I won't walk out on her——"

She glanced at the model—a man—seated near the screen, bare of torso and foot and wearing a bath-robe only.

"Good afternoon," she said pleasantly. And then, to Francis again, and sorting out her handful of tools:

"They're afraid I'll leave and start a shop of my own. . . . About seventy per cent of our customers would follow me. Several have spoken to me about it, offering to start me. . . . Finance the venture. . . . Ours is a dirty, stuffy joint, downstairs. . . . But I'm not that kind of cat. . . . There isn't a great deal of cat about me——"

She looked up at Francis out of slanting, clever eyes: "—More about you, Francis. You incline to what is snug in life——" laughing at him with her greenish eyes, only, otherwise innocently grave.

He said, addressing the model: "All right, Luigi."

The dark young man, with the leisurely grace of an Olympian, let slip his drapery and stepped on to the model stand.

To his ankles he bound two short, white wings; Francis handed him his winged cap, and he fitted it as a young king might fit a diadem.

Now, crouching and picking up his caduceus, he extended it with its twisted serpents, while his impudently chiselled features suddenly glimmered with sheerest malice.

The bawling, helpless, baby-satyr whom Hermes was

tormenting was, for the present, represented on the model-stand by a pile of books.

Francis Tolland leisurely lifted a wet cloth from his study; twirled his modelling stand, lighted a cigarette, glanced at Luigi with that listless authority which had in it a hint of insolence.

He was working in clay. He gathered a wet handful, pinched out pellet after pellet, continuing yesterday's work without any hesitation—apparently without observation.

Ellie's fascinated eyes were aware of all he did, all he disdained to do—so sure his touch, so absolute his control, so utter his comprehension of the problem in hand.

The girl working in plastolene with her long, capable fingers; yet slowly; venturing; with method; and the greater portion of her labour was done with her clever eyes and concentrated mind—a passion of silent, intent observation.

During the first rest she studied the clay while Francis Tolland squeezed water out of a sponge and moistened it.

"Gee!" she said under her breath.

He smiled, easily, at the tribute. "Did Shoreham's man come to see you this morning?" he inquired.

"Yes."

"What did he say about your sketch?"

"He wants it."

He walked to the window and stood filling his pipe and looking out at the March sunshine. She followed.

"You've got to be careful," he said in a low voice.

"Oh, I know it—I know it, Francis. I'm scared and worried."

"That's not necessary. You've got to watch yourself.
. . . Take mental inventory every little while."

"Are you really afraid I'll think I know anything?"

He shrugged: "You know an incredible lot; that's the
deuce of it. . . . A lot; but not enough. . . . Nobody
knows enough. Nobody ever died knowing enough about
anything. . . . You, already, are beginning to make a
living without knowing enough to make one. . . . There's
the danger. If you'll look at it this way—if you'll continue to say to yourself: 'I don't know what I'm about
yet, but neither does the public!' . . . If you'll just understand that you're going to school at the public's ex-
pense——"

"Oh, I do understand that!—I really do, Francis!——"

"If you can keep your head," he said—and let his eyes
rest on her bright, bobbed hair as he spoke.

"I can always do that. . . . I can always keep my
head," she said. "You'll see. . . . I know I'm emotional.
. . . But you'll see, Francis."

He knocked out his pipe, placed it upon the sill. They
went back to their modelling stands. Luigi, eating a sand-
wich, laid it aside and rose like a young god.

At four o'clock Luigi dressed, received his pay for
the week, smiled his courteous, dazzling smile, and took
his leave, leaving behind a slight aroma of garlic.

Francis never lingered over his work; never loitered,
waited, hung around it with anxious solicitude.

He washed and dried his hands, resumed his pipe and
sauntered over to where Ellie stood in happy agony over
her study in plastolene.

She gave him a perturbed look: all of her secret hope,
secret distress, unfeigned perplexity lay discovered in
her eyes: all the indiscretion of her very soul, naked, un-
abashed:

"Is it bad, Francis? Is there *any* progress? Oh, God,
what terrible things are a man's bones and muscles! Always under the skin they *are*—whether you see them or
not. . . . Oh, Francis!"

He coolly twirled her study, pinched out a pill or two
of plastolene and stuck them here and there. Pointed out
what was illogical—detail of construction. Offered, in
his leisurely authority, a hint concerning handling; matter
of academic technique involving self-denial of self-
expression.

"Put a curb-bit on that cleverness. Do you want it to
run away with you?"

"Oh, no! I loathe it!"

"The public eats it up. I'm warning you again; look
out for your ensemble. Keep the whole thing calm and
simple. Don't cut it up. *Don't* cut it up. Block in your
long, unaccented contours. Pay no attention to texture
until you find you've got it without trying to get it. Never,
never forget your construction. Always remain conscious
of it."

"I tell you," she said desperately, "I've got to give up
that damn Beauty Parlour and join some class in anatomy! I've simply got to, Francis. It's necessary that I
dissect. That skeleton of yours helps, but not enough——"

She went to a small closet, took from it an articulated
skeleton, sat down in an arm-chair and took the thing
on her lap.

For a while her clever eyes devoured it from skull to shank; her long, smooth, savant fingers ran along the chalk-white bones, striving by touch to fix within her brain every detail of shape, measurement, proportion. The skull-topped cage of dangling bones seemed to endure the massage with grim complacency, seated upon this young girl's knees. Its subdued, ossified rattle suggested a sort of mortuary content.

She took it to the work-closet and hung it up again. Then she went over to the clay study and stood silent, entranced, suffering—not ungenerously nor with any ignoble envy.

He had told her that he was not going to use this study. He was doing it for her education; not insensible to her flattering and enraptured attention. For her instruction partly he was doing it—partly as an agile exercise to keep himself in technical trim. Daily dozen idea—the effortless exercise of conscious power. Careless authority, amiably disdainful. But with a lively appreciation of the worship in this girl's eyes.

. . . And yet, so far, so deep within him that he was barely aware it was there at all—yet, now, always conscious that it *was* there—remained in the depths of him a kind of surprised unquietness concerning this young woman. . . . Who had stepped out of nothing—out of obscurity—into a profession with which one does not trifle. . . . A young person who, ignoring the lower stages, had begun the Parnassian ascent half-way up. . . . Turning her lithe back to the stony, painful, untrodden path below—the path that all should tread—up which all ought to toil. . . . Unless one be some sort of

freak. . . . Prodigy. . . . Some unnatural Exception to
Rule. Outside law and tradition. Arriving cross-lots with
the impudence of ignorance. Solving uncannily but correctly, without figuring out the problem in detail. Not
needing the rule of three.

There are such people. But this young woman would
have a long, long way to go before she convinced him
that she was one of these. . . . A damned long way.

Meanwhile—apparently born immune to law—he had,
somehow, divined that she was, instinctively, law observ-
ing. Emotional, yet conservative. Impulsive, but clever. In
the stir and tumult of awakening intellectual adolescence,
passionate.

He picked up some damp rags to swathe his clay. She
sighed as she aided him to shroud it.

"You're tired," he remarked.

She nodded, went into his bedroom to wash; reappeared
presently, solicitous for her fingers. Plastolene is hard on
the nails.

Over her right shoulder her dreaming eyes caught
sight of the marble *Leda;* and, as always, the little shiver
of sheer ecstasy passed over her. . . . Power to create
beauty! Down on its marrow-bones dropped her soul to
worship. . . . This man was godlike who created!

And, turning her head, slightly, made no resistance
when he drew her within the circle of his arms.

When he kissed her she rested her long, smooth fingers
on his shoulders, her face averted, looking at the window.

"Do you care a little for me, Ellie?"—gracefully gentle.

"I'm quite mad about you."

"Will you kiss me?"

She put her arms around his neck and kissed him with the hot unrestraint of a child. . . . In reply to him:

"Love? I guess so. . . . I don't know. Shall we sit down on the sofa for ten minutes while you talk to me?"

He laughed very gently: "Ten minutes; that's your allotted time to a second, isn't it, Ellie. And I am to talk shop to you."

"But what else——" She reddened a little. "I—there's no point in pulling me about, you know——"

"I wonder," he said, "whether you are incapable of love."

"I'm not modern—if you mean that. You don't care what happens. You make no pretence of caring. . . . I'm sorry. . . . If you want to pet me, all right."

They seated themselves. His smile was good-humoured, yet slightly deploring.

On the sofa beside him, now, she rested her soft cheek against his shoulder. He had an oblique view of her clever profile; kissed it, presently, while her remote gaze remained fixed upon the *Leda* across the room.

"Tell me," she murmured—always her invitation for him to talk about his profession. A child's insatiable desire for tales of magic things. Wonder stories to muse upon; to pretend to be a part of.

And if she was aware of the charm, danger, grace, of this young man, it was inextricably mingled with the power of him, the mastery, achievement. His super-humanity embodied principally the creative authority; the godlike part. It was a sort of dreamy awe, impersonal content that his caress soothed in her. And if he solicited any response it came with quick, passionate decision, ardent of lip—like an obligation gracefully and swiftly fulfilled.

"Now, *tell* me," she pleaded, her cheek against his arm —and relapsed into excited silence, awaiting her wonder-tale.

Even in the thrall of this enchantment the girl was methodical; allowing herself no more than half an hour; anxious lest it be wasted in meaningless dalliance—what she called "pulling her about." A game at which this young man did not seem to weary, amiably interpolating, gracefully persistent.

"Oh, Lord," she said, "don't you ever get enough of kissing me? . . . I've got my French to do, anyway. Listen, Francis—*please* don't pull me about!—— Listen —I've got as far as this—I *declaim* it with gestures before the whole class:

> *"Dans Venise la rouge*
> *Pas un bateau qui bouge,*
> *Pas un pecheur sur l'eau,*
> *Pas un falot——"*

She twisted lithely out of his arms to her feet and stood poised, confronting him:

> *"——Et qui—dans l'Italie—*
> *N'a son grain de folie?*
> *Qui ne garde aux amours*
> *Ses plus beaux jours?——"*

"That," he interrupted with a wry smile, "is exactly what you lack—your *grain de folie!*——"

She laughed, took half a dozen dancing steps, pirouetted:

"Aren't you interested in my French?"

"Reasonably."

"Well, I'll tell you what I am doing this afternoon. I'm doing an English paraphrase of that poem. . . . Shall I declaim as much as I have finished?"

Vexation or excitement sometimes induces a yawn. For one, or perhaps both reasons, he was inclined to. But he said politely:

"I'm most interested."

"Well," she said, happily, "this is my paraphrase—my very first poem:

> *"In Venice the Red*
>   *The Carnival is dead;*
>   *No gondola in sight,*
>   *No lantern light.*
>
> *"Alone in the Square,*
>   *High on his lofty lair,*
>   *St. Mark's great Lion towers*
>   *Above dim flowers.*
>
> *"Where broken moonlight falls*
>   *On ruined plaster walls,*
>   *On marble stairways*
>   *And ancient quays.*
>
> *"Now, glittering afar*
>   *Like a rose-gilded star,*
>   *A stained window sparkles,*
>   *Glimmers, darkles.*
>
> *"There, among mossy tombs,*
>   *The spectral cypress looms*

Where, in their ancient bed,
Slumber the Dead.

"Alone in his tower,
Where iron bells toll the hour,
The aged Doge in his fur cloak
Counts every stroke.

"While we keep count, my Sweet,
As our young lips meet,
Of each kiss given,
Or forgiven!——

"While we number thy charms
Nestled within my arms—
A thousand years of bliss
In each long kiss——"

Leda knocked smartly; came in. Francis gracefully masked a yawn and got up. Leda's gay, careless glance enveloped them both—the *mise-en-scène;* all corroborative evidence.

"Hello, darling," said Ellie. "I've got to do my French, so you'll have to get your own tea——"

Her arm around Leda, she made her adieux to Francis —"Thanks a million times. I'm too grateful for words." And, at the door, laughingly: "I guess you don't like my poem. . . . Poor, patient boy!——"

When they had entered their own quarters and he heard their door close, he closed his own. And stood looking at it. Finally he yawned.

CHAPTER XXII

TIME had begun to gallop with Ellie Lessing. Only a rare letter from John Westall ever checked its swiftly increasing flight. But when one of these arrived, she felt the vague reaction, a dull sinking of her winged steed at the haunches. Time halted, wavered, moved on again, slowly. So long, so long had this man been away. . . .

In May she had a letter from him. On the eve of sailing he wrote her about some proposed construction in Persia, and that he was going; and that the journey alone would take many weeks.

He wrote cordially, even affectionately, but she seemed to divine the slight effort, the strain—something mechanical. . . . Due, possibly, to what she had told him about herself and Francis Tolland. . . . She realized, now, that intellectual separation might be traced to such conditions. That *something* was gently ending.

At such moments Time checked his galloping course. Halted. Waited while she wrote him in reply, wishing him every success; gaily yet wistfully resigning him to an outer world, infinitely distant and incomprehensible.

Always such letters made grave her day, and her mood tenderly aloof.

Well, with another sunrise Time was racing again—racing, even carrying weight—even handicapped with memories. Hopes exhaled in a light sigh, lost in the increasing glow and excitement of a new day, a new challenge, new adventures.

One morning in May her telephone rang just as she was leaving her quarters to begin work in the Beauty Parlour.

It seemed that Mr. Shoreham himself desired to talk to her that morning. "It's rather important," added the telephone operator in her pretty, refined voice.

"But I'm employed," said Ellie. "I could call after five."

"Mr. Shoreham is leaving for Europe this afternoon. He wished me to inform you that it would be to your advantage to call at his office before noon."

"I'll come now," said the girl.

Downstairs Madam Felice flatly refused to excuse her.

"Do you mean that if I go I need not come back?" inquired the girl.

"You can take your chances"—the shallow, yellow eyes became malignant—"I been on to you for the last month. You think you're tying us up. You're aiming to quit us cold and start business for yourself——"

"You're mistaken——"

"—And take our customers with you——"

"That would be rotten——"

"I don't put it past *you!*" retorted Madam Felice. "And don't think I don't get you—rubbin' around the Doctor the way you act——"

The girl gave her a pale stare, then the blood returned to her face and she began to laugh. Went out, laughing, into the May sunshine; signalled a taxi in gayest mood.

Sympathetic grins from the driver: "Is it that funny, miss?"

"Yes, it's even funnier," said Ellie. However, she gave the meter a clever glance before she got in. The items of life counted in these days where a sophisticated world was always trying to put something over on one.

On the way down-town she produced from her black silk bag a little memorandum book and jotted down in it all the personal property and the salary due her from Madam Felice. Then she drew a long, deep breath of happy anticipation. . . . If God would help her, now, a little——

On the top floor of the beautiful building devoted to the gems, silver, gold, enamels, and bronzes of H. Shoreham Sons and Company, Ellie Lessing was introduced into the private office of Mr. George Shoreham, one of the sons.

He was very polite; seated her; seemed surprised. It developed, humorously, that he had not supposed her to be so young.

However, he went directly at the matter pending:

"When my father accepted your first group," he said, "our firm made you certain offers. You perhaps recollect the terms, Miss Lessing?"

"Yes, I do."

"You submitted our offer to your attorney, Judge Barrett."

"Yes."

"Judge Barrett called on us. We discussed the matter. The Judge did not approve the contract we offered. We felt, at the time, that we could not offer better terms. The Judge was disinclined to let you make a long-term contract. So we agreed to take your first three groups."

Ellie nodded.

Young Mr. Shoreham looked grave, weighty—imitation of his ponderous parent.

He said: "Our judgment was correct. Our venture has been rather amply vindicated by results. Your work, Miss Lessing, is—to be quite frank—popular."

The girl's face flushed and her interlocked fingers tightened.

He said in his pleasant, serious voice: "A statement and cheque go to you on the fifteenth of this month. I think you will be gratified."

Her lips scarcely moved in a "Thank you."

"I'm going to be quite frank," said young Mr. Shoreham, tapping his palm with a gold pencil. "We want your work, Miss Lessing. We want to control it. We desire that those who wish to purchase replicas of your work should be obliged to come to us. Is that agreeable to you?"

"Yes."

He smiled. But when he had looked at her clever features for a few moments he became serious again.

"We propose," he said, "to open for you a drawing account with us. We desire you to give all your time to your work. At present you are otherwise employed, are you not?"

She knew it was not good business to admit that she was out of a job. But being honest, she admitted it.

There was a slight pause: "However," she added, looking out of the window, "I can always get another." Mr.

Shoreham's inspection of her clever profile satisfied him
that she could.

"What we propose to do," he said, slowly, "is to estab-
lish for you a reasonable fixed income on a basis to be
agreed upon. This would be in the nature of money ad-
vanced on account of royalties and other payments. Do
you understand, Miss Lessing?"

She nodded.

He said: "It would, perhaps, seem impertinent to ask
you what is your present income, but such knowledge on
our part might serve as a basis for an offer."

"Don't you know what I am worth to you?" she asked
naïvely.

After a while he smiled. "We don't know, Miss Lessing.
We offer to speculate. It is a legitimate speculation. All
business is a risk—or ought to be." This he thought
morally humorous, and smiled again.

"Well, then," said he, "perhaps you might suggest to
us what fixed annual income—what monthly drawing
account—might enable you to devote all your time to
your art with a tranquil mind and freedom from worry."

She considered, still gazing out of the window. And
the longer young Mr. Shoreham looked at that profile
with its lovely slanting eyes and contours, the more
certain he felt that Shoreham Sons and Company would
have to pay more than they desired to pay for the proposed
monopoly.

When he saw that she had come to a conclusion he
prepared to face the worst. But not quite in the manner
in which it came.

"I'll tell you, Mr. Shoreham," she said. "It's more

agreeable for me to be frank. I have a thousand dollars a year income from investment. I make about two thousand more in business. That is not half enough. I'll tell you why. I need a better studio, better quarters, better food.

"More even than these I need special instruction, and instructors. I need to travel, some day. I don't know the world or the people in it.

"As it is now I work all the time. I don't work too hard. But my daylight is thrown away——"

Again she turned her head to the window, her gaze absent, her mind engaged in matters remote.

Mr. Shoreham waited. Saw her teeth busy with her under-lip. Noticed the new colour in her face as she turned again to him:

"I have a friend," she said, "who has offered me an income and leisure for an education. I refused because I have nothing to offer in return. Now you make me a business offer of the same nature. That is quite another matter; and I am inclined to accept. . . . How much do you think I ought to expect if I make for you six figures or groups a year?"

On the basis of present sales of *Diana and the Dryad* and of *Motherhood,* he ventured to hope that she might count on more than six thousand dollars a year. He hastened to point out to her that she could increase this by any odd study dictated by impulse or fancy—or more properly, he added, by happy inspiration. Her remote gaze discouraged his smile. However, he mentioned probable orders for portrait busts—for fountains, garden ornaments—all these quite outside of their proposed contract. Except that replicas were to be made from any such works; the original belonging to her and with privilege of sale.

"About how many years would you want me?" she asked.

"Five. With option on five more on the same terms. . . . We are taking some risk, Miss Lessing."

"Yes, you are. I am, too."

He found nothing ready to say to that.

"I shall have to consult Judge Barrett," she said.

"Suppose," he suggested with a slight effort, "we offer you—well, say eight thousand a year."

"I don't think Judge Barrett would advise me to consider such an offer."

"Well—well, what——"

"I think," she went on, slowly—and so scared that her voice was scarcely under command—"I *think* that Judge Barrett might consider an income of ten thousand. . . . Although he is greatly opposed to my tying myself up for a term of years——"

"Will you sign with us on that basis?" said young Mr. Shoreham.

After a few moments she regained self-control.

"Yes, if he permits me."

"Do you remember his telephone number?"

"Yes."

"Will you call him up and tell him all about it? I am going to Europe to-day and I would very much like to settle this matter before I sail."

There was a private telephone in a small room adjacent. Mr. Shoreham bowed her in; closed the door; went and stood by the open window where the soft breeze of May was playing with the curtains.

After a little while the girl returned.

"Yes," she said, "I am to accept, subject to his approval of the contract."

He smiled broadly; offered his hand; said several polite things—something about mutual benefits—that sort of civility.

She went out so dazed that she could scarcely find her way to the elevator.

Young Mr. Shoreham sought his brother in an adjoining office:

"I've got her," he said.

"Cheap?"

"Rather cheap. . . . Yes, quite reasonably, considering that she's got the public started. . . . There's some indefinable *something* in her work that sells. Our public wants her stuff. . . . And the curious thing is that her work isn't bad. . . . Usually popular stuff is bad. Hers isn't. . . . Something about it, you see. . . ."

"Father says there's a hint of Falconnet about that *Motherhood*. . . ." He smiled: "—rather exaggerated, that. . . . How is it going to-day?"

"We're casting as fast as we can. We're raising our limit to four hundred. We had to. I've placed them all. They'll be selling at a big premium by Christmas. . . . I don't see why we can't arrange for a terra-cotta popular——"

His brother shook his head. "But," he added, "I won't neglect that in this contract." . . .

CHAPTER XXIII

BY the middle of June Ellie Lessing's life in West 86th Street was a thing of the past; Madam Felice and her beauty shop ancient history.

The shop was open, but no customers had arrived.

There was malevolence, defiance, and the ever-present threat, in Felice's yellow eyes when Ellie entered to collect her property and take her leave. Disbelief that the girl was not planning to start a shop of her own.

Miss Stella wept; kissed her; whispered gratitude and loyalty. Little Angelo's kind, brown eyes were reproachful, tragic; his inborn courtesy flawless. While she was making her adieux he bowed and bowed.

Her offered hand overcame him: "Whenever Miss Ellie want me——?" he murmured. And Felice, always watching, understood.

The "Doc," evidently, had been prowling the night before. His eyes and lips were unusually moist and puffy; his vocal chords ruined.

"Hey!" he exclaimed, hoarsely, coming in buttoning his white mess jacket, "what's all this foolishness? You ain't fixing to leave us, girlie, are you?"

Ellie, always indifferent to rancour, forgave him. He was just that kind of man-worm. It didn't matter.

"Good-bye, Doctor," she said; offered her gloved hand —as long as it *was* gloved—too happy to wound anything now; "—yes, I'm leaving."

Boisterous objections from him—inclined to further personal contact—to bluff, misleading, puffy familiarity. Cut short by Felice, always watching, slit-eyed:

"Maybe you'll want him, too, when you set up your new shop, Miss Eleanor."

"It isn't that kind of shop," said Ellie, good-naturedly.

The "Doc" became noisy again; attempted closer quarters; arm-pinching, skirt-twitching.

"Say, girlie," he croaked, "don't walk out on me like that!"—cut short by Felice, eyes suddenly aflame:

"You make your hands behave! What are *you* horning in for? Let her start anything she likes! She's grafted enough out of me to start a fancy house if she wants to——"

"Hey! Quit that line of talk!" bawled the Doc. "Come on, you two girls! Get together." He snatched at Ellie, but she brushed him aside on her way to the street door. As he followed, Felice blocked him; spat her parting venom:

"Let her alone! The guy on the top floor is keeping her. I don't want no kept women in my——"

Ellie stopped, astonished, her hand on the door knob. Turned; saw Angelo's shocked face.

Then her clever, slanting eyes rested on Miss Grayce, on Miss Stella. Not tactful to express contempt of such a charge to *them*. Their tragedy was *that*. . . . Keeper and Kept. The former's elaborate, youth-compelling make-up still smeared with tears. Revealing the dead youth underneath.

Ellie smiled at her, affectionately; smiled reassuringly at little Angelo; went out and upstairs, still smiling; confident.

Afterward, laying away her aprons, white uniforms, and white shoes, she remarked to Leda, who was still in bed:

"Felice meant Francis. . . . They all know I'm not that kind of fool. . . . I'll get your coffee if you like. Shall I?"

"Do you mind, darling? . . . What a filthy woman! I'd like to go downstairs and kill her!"

Ellie laughed, went into the kitchenette, started the coffee, prepared a saucer of strawberries, took the butter out of the ice-chest and placed two rolls in the oven.

"An egg?" she called.

"No! you little devil. And don't you give me anything to *eat*. Are you trying to ruin me! . . . You should have heard what Solly Katz said to the company last night about gaining weight!"

Ellie denied that weight came from a proper diet. Presently she brought in the tray. Leda sat up in bed and swore at her. Ate everything, swearing all the while.

"Rot," said Ellie. "There are only four things that'll get a girl; sugar, starch, booze, inertia. . . . I eat every darned thing I want, too. I do my daily stunts——"

She bent, placed both palms flat on the rug, turned over. Leda eyed her over her coffee cup: "Don't I dance myself to bits in the show and at rehearsals? Well, I've put on half a pound."

"Quit your cocktails and high ones with Francis."

After a while Leda handed her the tray; lighted a cigarette and leaned back on her pillows.

"Mentioning Francis," she said, "he's sulky about your leaving."

"Sulky?"

"Very. He called for me after the show last night. Talked about it all the time at the Club Fripon while we danced and had supper."

"You know," said Ellie, "I've discovered that Francis is a little spoiled. . . . I don't blame him. He's very marvellous."

"He seems to be crazy about you." Leda reached for the morning paper and turned to the dramatic page.

Ellie said, gravely, after a pause: "He is a little crazy about himself. . . . That's the real trouble. . . . And I'll tell you something; people who believe in what Francis calls modernism are no novelty in the world. They are people who merely wish to have their own way. At any cost. . . . No matter what it costs them. . . . Or others."

Leda looked over the paper. Looking: "Do you think Francis is selfish?" she asked, casually.

"I do. I've told him so. . . . Not that one can blame him. . . . He *is* a great artist. . . . In one sense, other people don't count compared to him. . . . I'm lenient with him. . . . But when he tells me that all law is out of date; that everybody ought to do as he pleases—isn't that pure selfishness?"

Leda rattled the paper; turned to the stock market.

Ellie said: "He says marriage is bunk. Love is bunk. Inclination and impulse are all that count. . . . Go on and live with whom you like. . . . And when you're fed up, go and live with somebody else who happens to suit you. . . . Yes; get everything out of life you can. Do everything and everybody you can. Don't miss a trick. . . . He says you'll never win out in anything unless you cut out the bunk and do what you darn please. . . . Did he ever tell you that?"

"I believe so."

Ellie laughed. "I wonder whether all great men have *something* the matter with them. . . . Maybe Francis and a few other geniuses could do those things. . . . Live that way. . . . But what's going to happen if the mob imitates them? . . . All that stuff. . . . Who the devil wants to?"

Leda glanced at her: "Haven't you ever wanted to do anything wicked?"

"Plenty of times."

"*Have* you ever?"

"Sometimes. . . . If you mean, have I ever been a fool with a man—no!"

"No temptation?"

"Not so far. . . . I don't know what I'd do if I were starving. . . . A girl never knows such things, I suppose. . . . But the way I've always felt, I'd rather die than let a man put over anything on me."

Leda, still reading the paper, remarked: "You've never been in love, have you?"

"No," said Ellie. "Have you?"

Leda flung away the paper: "Yes. . . . Once."

After a silence: "Well, you got over it."

"I don't know. . . . I thought so. . . . It's a poor line for a girl to follow. . . . I don't know whether you ever really get over it. . . . I suppose I'll find out before I walk out on the company for keeps——"

"*Darling!*"—in tender consternation. But Leda shrugged: "Oh, I could cure myself if I wanted to. . . . If I stayed away long enough."

"Is he *here?*"

"Around town, I believe."

"You see him?"

"Sometimes." She stretched her lovely bare arms; shook her hair loose; yawned.

"I'm happy," she said. "We ought to be happy, both of us. That show has put me on the map. And look at *you!* —my goodness, *look* at yourself! . . . And I'll tell you what Francis says about you: that you belong with that bunch of prodigies who play twelve simultaneous games of chess blindfolded and win 'em all! . . . You're like that seven-year-old little Jew boy who is ready for Harvard. . . . Like the little girl of ten who has just published a volume of poems and has started several novels——"

Ellie's laughter pealed out: "How rotten impudent of Francis! Probably he means my work is no better than that awful little girl's! . . . I suppose it really isn't any better. . . . I love it until about a week after it's cast. Then I begin to discover all the hideous faults in it. . . . Isn't the public funny? . . . To actually pay money for my things. . . . The way I look at it, I just thank God and promise Him to do better and better. . . . You see I *had* to have money to learn, Leda. God knew I had to. He knows I'll play square with the world just as soon as I can learn how to. . . . I'd like to be able to do one very perfect thing, and give it to the city. . . . You know— the way people send five dollars to the Conscience Fund in the newspapers. . . ."

"My Lord, what a chatterbox!" Leda covered both ears. "Turn on my bath, ducky; there's a dear!——"

Came a knock at the door; and Francis: "Anybody awake?"

"Don't come in!" cried Leda; but he opened the door and sauntered in.

"You darned jackass," she said; drew up her knees under the quilt and made a face at him.

"Prima donna stuff," he remarked. "How are you, young ladies, this merry June afternoon?"

"It's only eleven o'clock," said Leda resentfully. "You have much nerve, my friend, to walk in on us. . . . What are you smirking about?"

"Oh, nothing." But he was full of it, whatever it was; and continued to smile upon them both.

"All right," said Leda, "I'll ask you again, then. Why the brilliant matutinal blandness?"

It then transpired that, in the great Government competition involving the proposed Valley Forge Memorial group for the Federal Capitol, the job had been awarded to him.

"Oh, my dear!" breathed Leda, deep, genuine emotion in voice and features.

"But of course," said Ellie; "who else could it have been?" Radiant, she gave him her hand and a firm clasp: "Oh, Francis, it's so splendid! You'll have your great chance."

"I ought to. They've appropriated a million. That comes of sending two or three million Yankees overseas to look at Paris and the Place de la Concorde."

"We *are* waking up," said Ellie.

Francis, lounging on the window-sill, lighted a cigarette. To Ellie's enthusiastic inquiry he said he was gratified but not excited.

Leda said: "You miss the best part, then. I never shall forget how excited I was when I read the newspapers the day after our show opened——"

"My cue," said Francis; "show me your scrap book."

"You impudent thing—you get out of here, anyway. Ellie, push him out——"

"Not until I tell him again how I felt when I signed my contract with Shoreham Sons and Company. Listen, Francis——"

"No," he said; "what are you doing to-day, Ellie?"

"Why?"

"You said you'd give me a sitting when you had time."

"My dear friend, I will when I have time. I'm to meet a pink-faced youth from a real-estate office to-day and look at studio apartments."

"So you've really decided to turn us down?" he asked carelessly. But his dark eyes were a little sullen, now. Leda's glance rested on him; shifted.

"You'll have Leda," said Ellie. "Her show will run all summer, so she is going to take this dump off my hands——"

She glanced at her wrist-watch: "I've got to go. Why don't you clear out and let Leda have her bath?"

"When will you give me that sitting?"

"Oh, gosh!—when I get settled. . . . I'd love to, Francis; you know that. I'm flattered silly to be asked— but I've *got* to get settled——"

She was at the door, now; paused to look back:

"Oh, come on out of there! Leda's got to get up——"

"I want to talk to her a moment——"

Ellie couldn't wait any longer. As it was she now had to take a taxi to meet her pink-faced youth at the office of Stringem and Sloper.

When she had disappeared, Francis slid from the window-sill and seated himself gracefully upon a white-enamelled chair.

"I think," he said, "I'll go back to France and do this Valley Forge job over there."

Leda, resting on one elbow, regarded him in silence.

"I can do it better over there," he added.

"I think you'd better go," she said.

Perhaps he had not expected that; or it was something in her tone——

He had been resting both elbows on his knees looking down at his clasped hands. Now he looked up:

"You think I'd better go?"

"I do."

Again it was her tone.

"You take it cheerfully," he said.

"I have to."

"What do you mean, Leda?"

"What I say, exactly. I have to take things cheerfully. . . . Where you are concerned, everybody has to, Francis."

He seemed puzzled.

"My dear," said the girl, "you never are uncivil or unkind. You never quarrel. You have your way; or—you don't. But you are always polite about it. Charming. . . . Serenely persistent, but charming. . . . Gracefully al-

ways you pursue your own way through life. The *modern*
way. All effort artistically concealed; or, when artistic, *per
se,* revealed. But always gracefully."

He had sat quite motionless. There was, on his face, a
perceptible flush, now.

She said: "A girl doesn't quarrel with you, Francis.
Doesn't even resent, I think. You may become nothing to
her. Or, you may remain what you have been to her . . .
indefinitely, perhaps. . . . But anger? No. Bitterness?
Only against herself. . . . Which is why I say that one
needs must take things cheerfully where you are con-
cerned."

"Are you delicately indicting me, Leda?"

"For what?"

"For living life as it suits me? For being myself without pretense?"

"For doing what you wish to do at any cost? At any
cost—to *others.* Oh, no; I'm not indicting you. There are
some millions of others who subscribe to your beliefs.
Moderns." She smiled at him. "I ought to be tolerant: I
was one myself, you know."

The flush on his handsome features still lingered.

"Your ideas are no longer modern?" he asked.

"I'm sorry. Conservatism asserts its sway with us in
the end. Our ruling passion. . . . Submerged momen-
tarily, perhaps. . . . Temporarily in abeyance. Never
eradicated, my friend. . . . And sooner or later we all
come back. Immemorial instincts. Specific, my poor Francis. . . . The normal need of the conventional. . . . The
perfect safety of it. . . . Even if our souls, sometimes,
continue to wander outside."

He said that only the temporary was progressive. That nothing else was of any value. That permanency always foreshadowed death.

Leda sat up; twisted up her hair.

"You seem very much afraid of death," she said. "That seems to be your particular horror—that anything should die. . . . The sensation of the moment. Happiness. Passion. . . . Love," she added carelessly, still twisting up her splendid hair.

"Is there anything more tragic than the death of these things?" he asked.

"Oh, yes. . . . The death of self-respect. . . . If death comes to the other things—well, it's an honest end. . . . Please hand me that brush, Francis."

He rose, handed it to her. He sat down again, still flushed.

"Darn it," she said, untangling her hair.

After a silence: "I'm sorry," he said.

"About what!" She looked up, smilingly.

"About the way you feel. . . . I thought you——"

"No. If I ever said so I lied. . . . We all lie if we tell you that. . . . We never really change. . . . Sometimes we—experiment. Sometimes we get over it. Sometimes we don't. . . . But, at heart, and in our souls, we are always opposed to irregularities. There is, within us, a living hatred for them. . . . Even when we commit them." She combed out her hair and smiled at him. "Did you know that, Francis?"

He made no answer, studying his clasped fingers—firm, well-shaped, creative fingers that were about to add to the beauty and glory of the Capitol of the Great Republic.

Leda slowly combed her hair. "So I think," she said, "that you had better go to France. It will be well for you. . . . Perhaps for me"—she smiled at his bent head—"perhaps for Ellie, also."

The colour surged in his face. She saw it; looked away.

He got up, presently.

"You want your bath, don't you?" he said in his gentle, caressing way. "You've been so nice to me. . . . You always have been."

She laughed: "Always amiable," she said, "—even to a Swan! . . . Pull down that shade, ducky, before you go——"

CHAPTER XXIV

O F all regions on earth one would not suppose that a studio on Fifth Avenue would turn out to be the most reasonable quarters offered by Stringem and Sloper for Ellie Lessing's consideration.

However, that was the case.

On the south-east corner of one of the cross streets not very far north of Madison Square there lingers one of the old brownstone mansions of an era dead.

Externally and internally it is old-fashioned, shabby; but well and solidly constructed.

The Community Bank occupied the ground floor. The five other stories were given over to apartments, one to a floor. The entrance was on the cross street. A dingy, rickety little lift, operated by an old man, carried up the tenants. Or, they might walk up the dingy stairs lighted on each landing by gas jets.

Probably this relic of Victorian New York would soon be replaced by a zone law sky-scraper. Why it had not been pulled down long ago nobody seemed to know.

However, the fact that only a year's lease could be obtained, and a month's notice offered, proved that somebody was anticipating the early passing of this solemn old mansion.

It was a sad old house from the outside. Sad-looking windows pierced the sad brownstone façades. At some of these, dusty drab shades were lowered; at others, weedy lace curtains sagged.

It was no cheerier inside. On the ground floor the Bank had installed itself behind plate glass, brass grilles, and cherry-coloured mahogany.

But the floors above were massive and melancholy; heavy with lumpy old black mahogany; full of wasted spaces, dim hallways, obscure corridors. The walls were thick; windows deep. It was a very still place. Deathly still.

The top-floor apartment was very much more extensive than Ellie Lessing desired. But it was so much cheaper than any other studio apartment offered that she took it; signed the lease; hired a cleaner, and moved in.

She had no furniture except the garnishings from the 86th Street quarters.

These she installed—Leda deciding to refurnish with period antiques. Demanded expert aid from Francis Tolland—politely promised with symptoms of interest that seemed genuine.

So the furniture van engulfed Ellie's lares and penates.

These were indeed austere quarters of Ellie Lessing.

In a heavy, square bedroom with its massive mahogany woodwork, her white-enamelled bedroom effects and chintz curtains seemed almost grotesque. Like flimsy furniture from a dolls' house in some great, dull chamber.

The adjacent bathroom was full of black walnut and ancient plumbing.

Now, southward, stretched a vista of dreary, empty,

square rooms floored with pine and heavy with the aged black mahogany of San Domingo.

She had nothing to put into these. Gas brackets sprawled from the ceilings. There was no other furniture.

At the farther end of this musty vista was the studio with its fireplace, side and top light, and kitchen adjoining.

In the studio Ellie arranged the furniture, pictures, and books from her little living-room in 86th Street.

Here, also, she installed a coal-box, a model-stand and cheap screen; linoleum for the floor; modelling stands; a drawing-board, an easel; buckets—all the necessary paraphernalia.

The effect was austere to the verge of meanness. Only the summer sunshine saved this place, pouring in at all the deeply recessed windows. That, and the gay heart of the girl who went a-dancing hither and thither about the business in hand. Who sang at top voice while hanging curtains of dotted Swiss, or hemming them; or tacking up the two pictures of *Ormond* and *Man-o'-War;* or hanging on gilt hooks the portraits of her parents.

Judge Barrett dropped in on her to glance over the place.

"By golly," he said, "it's like the bowling alley in the old White Elephant!"

"Where was that?" she inquired.

"In the old Tenderloin—not far from Tom Gould's and the Hay—— Never mind, darling, but tell me what will I buy you for to contribute to this sumptuous chatoo?"

"You're such a dear! I don't need anything."

"You've no what-not," he said severely. "And devil a gold chair do I see——"

"I don't want any. . . . If you wish to buy me a coal scuttle——"

"Aw, listen to her !——"

"That's all I want. And a cedar mop."

But he sent her dozens of potted flowers for her windows; a gold table with pink marble top, and a standard lamp with a brilliant yellow silk shade fringed with purple. The effect of these in the nearly empty studio was almost immoral, giving it a bedizened allure.

But Ellie was far too happy to let it bother her. She had her heart's desire—time to work, and the means; and seemed oblivious to all else—conditions, environment— and to the vast noise of the Metropolis outside beating perpetually against her window-panes—now resonant, now raucous, now sonorous—a jazz sometimes; sometimes a diapason—clamouring, shaking, vibrating her windows—the vast, thundering rumour of the stupendous city that never rests from dawn to dawn.

Like the mighty crashing of an orchestra it stimulated the girl instead of disconcerting her. The powerful urge within these four walls preoccupied her; not the excitement, the joyous attractions, luxuries, delights, hazards, adventures suggested by the unceasing din outside. Yet she had loved gaiety, and bright places, and had been inclined to them—and to men.

But she was experiencing a riot of sensation within her own walls; passionately she made ready; passionately she flung herself into all that she loved—her modelling,

her studies, her books, her freedom—flung herself mind
and body into every happy detail of living—into housework, kitchen as well as studio, and lamplit sewing.

So far—and this again was August—there had been
no moment for parties, for shows, for a dance or a supper. Every hour was filled, pre-empted, dedicated; and
hours lacking still for necessary duties—shopping; matters domestic; requirements of dress.

She still wore black. She had not yet considered any
other colour, although the fashions were colourful
enough.

When, finally, she found time to realize that she was
almost shabby, she arranged to take enough time to rem-
edy the situation.

Clinging black—some gowns accented with white—
close little hats smartly turned up or smartened with a
great brush, or a cascade of plumes—black furs—one silver fox neck-piece—all else dainty, sheer, narrow cut,
slender. . . . And the slim beauty of the girl—greenish,
gold-flecked eyes, ash-gold hair; and the clever loveliness
of her face—smart always, yet humorously sensitive of
lip—tender, sensuous, childish lips which the swift smile
made sweetly shrewd. . . . And there were one or two
faint freckles near her nose. Visible. . . . Since John
Westall had approved, she had used no rouge and scarcely
a trace of powder and lip-stick. . . . Besides, the stench
of the Beauty Parlour was not yet free of her nostrils.

There came a day—she was awaiting the model, Luigi,
—and was thinking of Westall. The sketch in hand was
called *Laughter*—a harlequin convulsed, Pierrot dead at

his feet clutching a shattered lute. . . . Oh, very dead
and crumpled up in his dusty white—bony of face but
beautiful. . . .

Waiting for Luigi the girl's emotion suddenly became
acute, culminating out of nothing apparently.

She sat down at her little writing-desk and wrote:

DEAR,

It will be nearly three months before you receive this in
your Persian exile.

I have written you all about the great happiness that has
overtaken me; all circumstances and details; all about my
contract; my plans, my new quarters; the wonderful life I
lead. That letter, I think, is still on its way to you.

It is a sunny, warm day, here. I'm wearing only a sleeve-
less smock, short skirt, and mules. Oh, very sloppy. . . . I'll
tell you another thing; bobbed hair is out of date. But mine's
still like a curly-headed youth's. . . . You seemed to like it,
you know.

This morning—like every morning—I awoke with that
thrill of happy expectancy—a sort of eager, excited wonder
as to what the new day will bring!

It hasn't yet brought my model, Luigi—darn him! . . .
I've told you about *Laughter*. Oh, my poor Pierrot is so
very dead—so wasted with his devastating and immemorial
passion—just a delicate bundle of bones in his white smock.
. . . And that lithe, limber, soulless, laughing mask—all
heartless grace and diamonds! . . . The fittest *physically*
survive.

Mind, unsupported by the vigour of health, perishes. Old
and exquisite civilizations pass amid the empty laughter of a
brawny invader. . . . Greece falls. The Renaissance col-
lapses. Everywhere, like a shallow sea raging through
broken dikes, the proletariat surges in. . . . I've been reading morbid stuff, you see—all about survival, doom, the

down-crash of civilization, dead levels, dirt, the death of beauty. Modernism, you know, beginning to totter; impotent, aware of its own sterility too late, trying to use its fangs to the bitter end. Biting its own enervated limbs.

My dear, do you think me quite mad? Oh, I am, I guess —quite crazy with the joy of things in general.

On my window-sill, where I see them as I write you, there are some pots of old-fashioned fuchsias, clove pinks, and peach-coloured geraniums. . . . I should not give them too much water. Not too much plant food, or they run to leaf.

I write you at random, awaiting Luigi. . . . Always awaiting something with delicious expectation—not that good, polite Wop, in spite of his marvellous body and features; but events, generally:—new growth, new impressions, new ideas——

I'll tell you something—not to brag, my dear; but Leda was giving me some tea the other day in my old quarters— I had been in Francis Tolland's studio to sit for the portrait bust I told you about—and so Leda was giving me tea. And there came in some exceedingly interesting people— that charming actress, Marian Trafford, and her blonde sister who sings in concert; and there was with them the celebrated Frederic Daniells—our most celebrated theatrical manager, I suppose—so courteous, humorous, kind.

Leda told them that it was I who had done the *Diana* and *Motherhood,* and, oh, my dear, it was my first experience with flattery. . . . I *must* be careful not to like it.

But what happened was this: they were discussing the great French miracle play which Mr. Daniells is going to put on; and sometimes the conversation shifted into French; and I understood and could answer if I took time and spoke slowly.

"Miss Lessing," said Mr. Daniells, "when you speak in French your voice has in it something of the singing silver of Sarah Bernhardt's. Any talent is always a twin. Is your other talent musical or histrionic?"

I told him Mother had been an actress.

They all seemed to like my voice; asked me to recite something in French. I had been studying the "Chanson de Roland," as I wrote you. The lines recited themselves; being well-versed I let them flow, not conscious of declaiming:

Ami Roland, que Dieu mette ton âme en saintes fleurs
Au Paradis, parmi ses glorieux!

. . . . .

Ami Roland, tu as donc perdu la vie:
Que ton âme ait place au Paradis!——

—You know it, of course, my dear—you! source of all delight within me and my awakening. Tiens!—see what comes of *Roland,* and *The Romance of the Rose!*—phrases sentimental and romantic involving Monsieur Westall, engineer—a practical, sober gentleman. . . . Whom God accompany! . . .

Well, when I had ended the Emperor's burst of grief over Roland, and looked around for a chair, almost forgetting where I was, they startled me awake with hands clapping and hasty kind things said. . . . All about the "singing silver"—and Mr. Daniells said Sainte Catharine's face and body resembled mine—her hands like mine. Gosh, dear—it was not embarrassment but the difficulty of not losing anything so many were saying at the same moment. . . . Not a crumb of flattery must escape me, dear; I have an appetite for it all!

And the upshot?—my *dear!* Mr. Daniells's offer to take me on trial and drill me for the part of Sainte Catharine—the only speaking part in the miracle play—all else choruses, chants, and the solo aria of pretty Miss Virginia Trafford!

Excited, enchanted, I came back and sat down all a-quiver at my piano. It couldn't be, of course. But the sweet taste of it! I could bite flattery to the core! Am I not ignoble?

The dreadful doubt of it all is that *nothing* seems difficult to me. Always, always, since I started, what I seek comes swiftly—with a speed that scares me sometimes. Labour is pleasure; work, play. The hardest was to start—what with the sudden shamed comprehension of my infamous English —of the abyss of my ignorance!—now my mind races; my fingers, my blood—life is at full speed. Hope unlimited; ambition beyond bounds; self-confidence, cut down overnight, in full blossom again at sunrise!

Oh, my dear, my dear, what kind of creature have you started?

I hear that damn Luigi ringing my bell—an hour late. I'd like to murder him—only for the charm of my hour with you. . . . In the last analysis it seems to be you.

I go to admit and rebuke my Luigi!

Dear, may you walk the Orient with Allah!

Your,
ELLIE

CHAPTER XXV

I T was growing dusky in Francis Tolland's studio.

"Anyway," repeated Ellie, "I've got to go. I've dinner to get; I asked Virginia Trafford. . . . And I've some sewing to do; and a French comedy—the pupils in my class are going to do one at Christmas—I don't know where—but it's for the war-blinded."

He worked on in the dimming light of a late September afternoon. Watching him, always vulnerable to the spell, she sat in silence once more, seeing the masterly portrait of herself growing out of the wet, grey clay—an infinitely lovely thing. Virginal—not mindlessly chaste, but glowing, alive—an unspoiled thing of unawakened power; of dormant passions. Mind behind the beautiful slanting eyes; mind *within*—hidden, living, masked under crisp clustering hair that wreathed the little close-set ears to their lobes of Hermes.

"Francis?"

"All right," he said smilingly.

She came from her arm-chair to look. . . . There was nobody like him—nobody who worked to-day. Magic; wonder on wonder of loveliness commanded into being by the authority of his hands—by the celestial power of them—the irresistible will to create. Utter accord between mind and hand; absolute co-ordination—the one commanding, the other already divining; gracefully obeying.

He was washing those superhuman servants, now. When he came back she had her hat on; was drawing on one glove. Which he stripped; kissed the hand and her mouth—too close, now—almost suffocating:

"I'll have to go, Francis——"

And again: "I'm late, I tell you."

"Is that the limit of response in you, Ellie?"

"What response? . . . Well, then——" She kissed him with all the impersonal ardour of a child:

"—You're wonderful, Francis!—a master magician. . . . This marvel which you tell me is to be my portrait in marble bewilders me——"

"It bewilders me," he said, "—all that I am discovering in you——"

But she was becoming so restless that he released her slim body, his falling hand detaining hers.

They stood looking at the clay—a rather longish thing from crown to the first slight swell of the breasts.

"Marble," he said, "will transfigure this. . . . Marble. . . . Ellie?"

"Yes?"

"Leda told you that she sat for the *Leda* for me, didn't she?"

"Yes."

"You remember my idea for Diana and a wounded hound?"

"Yes."

"It's for the new fountain in Bronx Park."

"Yes, you told me."

"Well—Leda helped me, once. . . . Would *you?*"

"Nude?" she asked simply.

"That's necessary, as you know."

"Yes, I know. . . . I suppose I would, if I had time. But I haven't, Francis. I've got to get on. Good heavens," she said, impatiently, "—see where you are—and all that's already behind you!—all that I haven't yet even begun to learn!—No; I can't. I've got to think of myself. . . . I'm grateful; I always shall be; I've tried to repay your kindness—given you hours for this portrait bust—and if you think it was easy—well, I needed every minute I've given you—sorely——"

He took her into his arms again; she suffered his embrace—but would not suffer what he was saying to her. . . . Looked up to listen, surprised. Then, not interested, impatient of contact, freed herself. Walked to the door where he overtook her.

"You're too darned modern," she said, pulling on her gloves. She averted her head, then looked around at him.

"Haven't you courage to live your own life?" he asked gently.

"I have. But I'll be darned if I'll live *yours!*"

The moment she said it something about him struck her as humorous; and she laughed.

"I have courage," she repeated. "Plenty. But it doesn't require any to live my own life."

"You can't shake off the old, out-worn conventions, can you, Ellie?"

"Yes, if it suited me."

"You don't really care for me then?"

"I do. Yes. But I'm surprised that you should suppose me to be a fool."

"Do you think to be yourself reveals you as a fool?"

"I *am* myself. I'm doing what I wish, as I wish. . . . Perhaps, somewhere in the world, there is a man who could make a fool of me. One never knows."

"Because I am in love with you, does that make a fool out of either of us?"

"I won't discuss it. I'm not in love. I'd be a fool to play at it. A girl must be crazy," she added, pulling on the other glove,—"to take a chance like that. . . . Let a man put over anything like that—like some darned dumb animal——"

Something was gone in his amiable bearing—something missing of his careless grace. Not that he was disconcerted; not visibly vexed. But like one who encounters obstruction in the easy and familiar tenor of his way, pauses to consider other paths.

"If I believed marriage was anything but utter bunk," he said, "I'd ask you——"

Her quick, clear laughter cut him short: "My poor friend, I don't want to marry you!"

He managed to smile; but the girl's laughter was making a discord of the harmoniously attuned nerves inside of him. . . . Nerves long tuned in harmony with his creed and purpose in life. *Gloria mihi! Laudamus Veneris!*

The girl looked at him, laughed.

"Come," she cried, "you are a great sculptor! Dear Master, I salute you!"—and gave him her accolade—both cheeks, her gloved hands light on his shoulders.

Some of his grace returned as he saluted her hand— but it was mechanical—for he moved under the chill and thrall of a limitless and benumbing astonishment.

He had encountered a woman who didn't want him.

Even in marriage! There was a mistake somewhere. Because, surely, there was something that could be done about it. . . . Or—he could go to France and start the Valley Forge Memorial. . . . Or something.

It was quite dark in his studio, now.

He sat down; the poison of this girl burning in every vein.

But it was her indifference to opportunity that confronted him like a dead wall. Her callousness to advantage. Here was an impasse! . . . Was any woman ever born indifferent to social betterment? To preferment builded on brilliant marriage? Did this girl understand what she was, actually, and what she could be as the wife of Francis Tolland?

Did she realize that, no matter how he chose to live, his place in the social structure was fixed and definite? And most desirable?

Probably it was her poison, running now like fire in his blood, that started that threadbare idea of the marriage superstition. . . .

Well, if she had to have it that way——

He began to wonder whether she'd look like her mother at forty. He had seen the picture of Helen. . . . The trouble was he had seen Harry Lessing's portrait, too. . . . With his hair slicked up and horse-shoes on his waistcoat.

That poison!—that was an outrageous thing to get into the veins of a Tolland. . . . A Tolland who knew his own mind. Who knew bunk from fact; mush from modernism.

If only she hadn't *laughed!* Anything else—flushed an-

ger; white scorn; the hurt of it, and shame and tears—
but there's nothing to be done with laughter. . . . He'd
never before encountered that. Made no preparation. Invented no riposte.

Considering the matter, now, here in the dark and silence, he could discover no parry for her laughter. . . .
And there was her poison flaming through his veins—and
her incredible indifference to the condescension of a Tolland. Abysmal callousness to material advantage, social
preferment. And, added to all this, *laughter!*——

About eight o'clock the scorching poison became unen-
durable; and he went to the telephone and called her up:
"Ellie?"

"Why, Francis!" she exclaimed gaily.

"I wanted to ask you if you'll marry me."

"Oh! . . . Oh, *Francis! I couldn't!*"

"I'm very madly in love with you."

"I'm sorry——"

"Why?"

"Well, I don't want you to be unhappy——"

"I don't have to be if you——"

"Oh, I *can't!* . . . I know how wonderful you think
it would be for me—and it's so generous of you. . . .
I'm overwhelmed. . . . I"—she laughed uncertainly—"I
feel as though the Metropolitan Museum had invited me
to become its wife——"

He could hear her laughing; then she said hurriedly:
"I've a guest at table; I can't remain away any longer;
please excuse me, Francis; I am grateful; but I
couldn't——"

"Will you tell me why?"

"Because I'm too busy, and besides, I'm not in love with you. I *must* go——"

"One moment! Do you care for any other man?"

"I do."

"More than for me?"

"It's different. I don't know——"

"Are you in love?"

"No! . . . I don't think I am. . . . I know darn well I'm not. . . . I've got to hang up. Good night and many thanks——"

CHAPTER XXVI

WHEN a fencer thrusts, and his blade is parried, he not only ought to be thinking of the riposte and parry, but of his next thrust, and even of the thrust after that.

But the girl's blade had been poisoned and the poison was in Francis Tolland's veins; and it impeded him, made him clumsy, without skill to feint, without resources.

To be wounded at this stage of his career!—to be disarmed; and have his blade contemptuously returned to him!——

The deeply annoying feature of it all was that he could not be reconciled to his wound; could not comprehend that this girl meant it; that there was anything final about it.

The thrall of gratitude, awe, worship, held her still in a measure. Her liking for him, personally, had been genuine; still was. But the surprise of finding herself as intelligent as he—on an intellectual equality—made a difference. The creative artist still awed her; his power overwhelmed her; his authority humbled.

Of the man she was a little ashamed. He had taken his own measure for her. She was sorry he had revealed such undevelopment—such intellectual immaturity. Yet, it was that which saved him, too—the perverse selfishness which she mistook for wrong-headed boyishness. And this stirred the maternal in her—patience, solicitude, and an indefinable yet tender contempt.

But she would not endure the slightest physical contact with him, not the lightest playful touch or fugitive caress.

Not even when the Winter Academy awarded him highest honours for his marble portrait bust labelled, merely: "Portrait of Miss L."

He came that day to her studio to tell her about it. All that was basically hysterical in him made his face glow like a young god's—made his whole being radiant with the joy of authority and the passion of self-confidence.

Something of a scene finally threatened in the mutual emotion of the moment. But he carried nothing; swept nothing away; and his passion overwhelmed only himself, more weakly, unhappily laying bare the boy she was dealing with.

"I'll tell you something," she said, watching with impatient yet sorrowful curiosity the passion of him ebbing into pallor—the deathly, bruised look of him still slightly stunned from impact—"I tell you this, Francis; I've found out that physical familiarity between a man and a woman is a mistake. . . . All this petting and pawing. . . . Neither undersands it. . . . And men can't stand it and behave themselves. . . . As for marrying you; darn it! I have told you I'd as soon marry the marble Hermes in the Metropolitan Museum. . . . That's about what marriage with you would mean to me. . . . I never really wanted any more of you than to marvel over you. . . . Sit on my shins and look up to you. . . . I'm on my shins, still. . . . You'd better leave me there."

But the man was sick of love; sick of his want of her.

. . . Really ill. He kept his studio that winter. Worked little. Was deadly weary of a world which, for the first time in his life, had denied and flouted him. Maimed, distorted, aborted that gentle yet inexorable will which had quietly cleared for him his path through life—at any cost —to *others*. . . . The scythe of Modern Youth, sweeping through flowers——

Toward the latter part of mid-winter he took to dropping in on Leda Nieland. Not that he had a great deal to say. They both were rather silent. When other people came to tea he withdrew. After a while, however, he began to linger.

Leda's show was running to capacity through its second winter. There was as yet no talk of anything to follow; no activity except the assembling and sending forth of numbers two, three and four companies. . . . Some preliminary preparations for London in May arousing excitement among the casts.

Leda's number was conceded to be the feature of the Westchester Follies. When, unexpectedly, it turned out to be this, Max Mayer saw to it that it remained so, and that it gave the "punch" to the entire show.

Also, all auxiliary machinery was set in motion through paragraph, portrait and paid review; through magazine covers; photogravure supplements; smart weeklies pretending to social influence. All these featured, advertised, promoted Mr. Mayer's show through the medium of Leda's face and figure.

Leda Nieland! Nobody, now, had to explain who she was, or otherwise identify her.

Marian Trafford, playing in *Sainte Catharine,* Mr. Daniells's stupendous new miracle spectacle, asked Leda, one Sunday at luncheon, why she didn't set up more agreeable quarters.

"I'm saving my money," said Leda. "I know it isn't done in the profession, but I want a villa near Paris some day. . . . When I'm tired out. . . . When I'm all in but my shoe buckles. . . . Meanwhile"—she laughed—"a girl doesn't need much money in New York."

"I suppose," said Marian, "every pin-head in town is fighting for a nod from you."

"Well, you know how it is in *Sainte Catharine.*"

"Not so much. We play to the solemn and soulful; and to children. Johnnies don't bother much. . . . Virginia gets most of the mash notes. . . . We read 'em next morning, looking for a laugh, but they're not very funny. Middle-aged married men, mostly. Virginia is so bored. . . . Tell me, Leda, do you see anything of Francis Tolland these days?"

"He comes in now and then," she said carelessly.

Marian smiled: "You had an awful crush on him once."

"Two years ago. Old stuff, my dear."

"It's jolly to be friends, afterward," remarked Marian. "I like to get over a bad case and begin to be friends with a man. . . . Did you see his portrait bust of Ellie Lessing?"

"While he was doing it, yes. . . . I haven't seen the marble."

"It's the most beautiful thing!—Don't miss it. . . . Leda?"

"Yes?"

"That Lessing child is a lovely thing. Don't you think she's remarkable? So amazingly clever. Supports herself, you know. And, oh, Lord, what a worker! It isn't natural for a girl to work *every* minute. But you can't drag her out. I've tried. Do you know, she told me that she hadn't been to a show or a party this winter? That's all wrong. She'll get messy and sallow. She'll acquire a fixed expression and begin to dry up. . . . I'll tell you a curious thing about her: she doesn't seem to know anybody. Has scarcely any friends. You, me, Virginia, Francis. Who else? . . . Once, when I was in her studio, an exceedingly common young man called. His name was Lacy. She called him Jimmy. Didn't seem ashamed of him. . . . That's nice about her. . . . And once another man called —regular type of city politician—Judge somebody—Barrett, I believe. She kissed him; seemed proud of him; and he had all the refinement of an East Side auctioneer."

Leda said slowly: "I fancy Ellie Lessing's origin was rather modest. She is in the process of making. . . . She is the cleverest person I ever knew. She possesses real wisdom. She has a mind both courageous and generous; a heart both tender and valiant. . . . Gentle birth is no good unless it be endowed with all of these."

Marian said: "She ought to have friends." Meaning the sort that she and her sister and Leda were entitled to through the conceded social position of their families in their native city.

Leda remarked that there should be no trouble about that. Thought it rather necessary to Ellie's future career.

"She should know the sort of people who might become her clients. The sort who order portrait-busts, expensive memorials, garden decorations. The kind who present fountains, parks to their native communities."

Marian said: "Couldn't Francis do something of that sort for her? He's a New Yorker; he could if he'd take the trouble."

A very slight flush came over Leda's features. That was not the sort of trouble Francis Tolland was likely to take. But what would she have thought had she known of the conflict between snobbery and selfish sensuality? What would she have thought had she known that the snob in him had condescended to request legal alliance between a Tolland and the daughter of Harry Lessing?

Whether in excuse, or in the necessity of some answer to Marian—some comment:

"Men can't do anything socially for a woman," she said. "It's better that they keep out of it."

"Literally true," remarked Marian; "but there are roundabout ways. . . . It takes, of course, some little tact and trouble. It takes disinterested goodwill."

That evening Francis knocked at Leda's door. She was dining out; doing her hair at the moment. Inquiry through the door revealing who it was, she put on a lacy chamber-robe and let him in.

"Well, my friend," she said, re-seating herself at her dresser and resuming operations with a curling iron, "what's the news from Olympus?"

"Are you dining out?"

"I am. . . . Why?"

"I don't know; I'm bored. I thought we might dine together———"

"Do you think I want to dine with a bored man?"

"I wouldn't be, with you."

"Delicate. Very delicate." She was done with the iron; blew out the tiny flame; examined her reflected head minutely; curled a tendril or two over one slim finger.

"Now for my make-up, my dear," she remarked. "Gosh; I've *got* to hold my own to-night!"

He looked up with slight but sombre interest: "Who are you dining with?"

"There'll be some pretty girls there,"—unsheathing her lip-stick.

"Oh, is that why? Well, *you* needn't worry,"—resuming the study of the carpet.

"Delicater and delicater! Such adroit, elusive flattery!"

He looked up again. There seemed to be a certain carelessness, a new flippancy about the girl. He had noticed it before, rather listlessly. As a rule women were not careless about what he said to them.

"I suppose," he concluded, "I'd better dine at the club."

"You're not reduced to that, are you?"

"Reduced?"

"Yes. Where are all your girls, Francis?"

He smiled: "Where did you get that idea?"

"It's general———" She stifled a slight yawn: "—A new one every month. To be neatly labelled and laid aside. Milestones of progress. Pretty milestones for a pretty road. A girl every mile. Smiling."

"What the deuce is possessing you, Leda———"

"Nothing. Am I not smiling?—like the other mile-stones. . . . That's not *laughing*, you know——" She was using her powder-puff, now. "I don't believe any of your milestones ever laugh at you. Do they?"

She rose. "Great master," she said, "please proceed with majesty into the other room, because I'm going to dress."

He got up. After a short silence, he said: "Have I offended you?"

"No."

"There's some man, then——"

She began to laugh: "Why?"

"You treat me rather lightly——"

"Po-lightly?"

He reddened. "Rather derisively, Leda. . . . That our friendship was a firm one I took for granted——"

"You're accustomed to taking so much from a girl! You take everything for granted—take it anyway. . . . And plant another milestone. . . . Please remove your laurel-laden self; I want to dress," she added laughingly.

He went into the next room. There was a great soreness with him in consequence of his disastrous encounter with Ellie Lessing. Normally, perhaps, he would not have been sensitive to Leda's flippancy. But now, to him, there seemed an indifference in it amounting, almost, to disrespect.

She took her time about dressing. When finally she appeared she asked him to shake up two cocktails, "—and one for yourself, if you like," she said, smiling upon him and looking startlingly pretty in her jonquil-yellow and ermine wrap.

He was still shaking when a button-headed youth came in, shaved pink, all starch and shine and undergraduate cordiality. Very proud of calling so popular a celebrity "Leda." . . . The sort of young man who has a discreet but very new limousine waiting, with two men on the box. And he never had heard of Francis Tolland.

Well, she went away with him downstairs.

CHAPTER XXVII

HOURS flew like swift arrows; days flashed by betwixt two magic suns; week succeeded week; month after month vanished like mist at dawn.

The winter had raced away with Ellie Lessing and she could scarcely believe in the vernal symptoms now apparent—outrageous noises from sparrows on sunny window-ledges; whistle of starlings from sheltered cornices; sunshine gilding wet streets; forsythia abloom in parks; mimosa in florists' windows; degenerate compatriots of Homer selling daffodils and violets in city squares; love-songs of alley cats; battle-hymns of back-fence cats; May-parties; soft-shell clams.

So intense had been her winter's pleasure and concentration that it seemed incredible another spring was here; another summer impending; another year threatening her with its challenge to achieve.

Time leered at her; catechized her concerning progress and accomplishment.

Time! There was her master and her enemy! Her tyrant. Therein lay her peril. The volley flight of hours and days almost frightened her—that this crazy creature, Time, should gallop so recklessly with her—with her who needed only leisure, now; who had so much to make up of wasted years—years spent in ignorance, days unenlightened—all these to be retrieved; opportunity speeded; chances seized; every moment made the most of.

She kept her health. She kept her freshness, and what generally was called her beauty. Those happily employed suffer nothing from effort, where driven industry and self-denial leave their marks.

Years of running wild as a child had builded her to endure. Her studio was no prison—not even a cloister. Her activities were not penances—not even duties or obligations. How could the joyousness of it all mean isolation or confinement? Where was the austerity with every passion exercised; given full range and sway?

Time was the only spectre at the feast. Time alone limited her; denied her. She had found no opportunity for her music, so far. None for Italian and Spanish, so far. None for a thousand exciting, seductive pursuits, glimpses of which she had at moments—flashes of enchanting possibilities for the human mind to compass. It was Time that always interfered, forbidding, menacing, even while reproaching her, scourging her on.

Nearly two years, now, since she awoke to the terrors of Time. Two years since she found herself earth-bound, struggling with frantically beating wings. . . . Beating wings! Oh, how well *he* knew! And how would she seem to him some day? She who could fly a very little, already? Her wings, no longer beating wildly, impotently, already had carried her above the earth. Not very high. But it was real flight. She was wild for him to see her try her wings.

It now had been nearly two years since she had seen John Westall. She had not seen very many other men in the interval. His image was still fairly clear. Perhaps somewhat magnified. A little topheavy with attributed virtues. Ideally overloaded. Prismatically visualized.

She had had one or two letters from Persia. On Christmas he had sent her an old illuminated Persian manuscript. Rather valuable; very beautiful; very Persian. Her one antique treasure, pored over, caressed—source of mad temptation to study the Persian language. Brooded over it, sometimes, aware that Time was leering; mocking her. Persia obsessed her.

You dear, dear man [she wrote], to send me such a gift! It's so wrought me up that I've had Persian books from the library by the dozen; and I'm tempted to buy a Persian cat and use Persian powder on her—— Is that a crude joke?

But, dear, I've made the belated acquaintance of Omar; and I've started a group. Do you recall the seventy-eighth quatrain?—Eros terrified by dread of Hell?

Well, my sketch shows Love shrinking like a frightened butterfly; and a young girl fairly writhing with mirth behind a mask of Medusa which she holds up to terrify Eros.

I'll tell you a funny thing about it. Mr. Shoreham, senior, came to the studio to look at it.

He's a dear old thing. A little inclined to fluff.

"My dear," he said, "isn't this a trifle salty? Hum-hum! Yes, a trifle. Yes; Attic salt! Hum-hum! Ironical. Yes? I think so. Yes. Hum-hum!"

He walked all around it; turned the group on its pivot.

He said something about Clodion. And why didn't I do some work on my own bronzes. Learn how to use gold.

Oh, gosh! I caught fire at that! It doesn't take more than a spark to set me afire.

Dear, I tell you so much that's trivial. I suppose I'd tell Mother instead if she were here. That was my habit. I seem to have no reticence if there's any outlet. You seem to be the only one, now.

Well, I'll tell you also about business. I think Francis Tolland's marble portrait of me has given me some publicity. Several notices speculated upon the identity of the "Miss L." There's been a little talk about it—oh, very limited.

But it stirred up young Mr. Shoreham. He's one of those keen, enterprising men who talk business to people in terms of art.

So when the identity of Francis Tolland's "Miss L." was being discussed in the papers, young Mr. Shoreham had an article written revealing me as the original, and—oh, my dear!—giving me such flattering publicity on account of *Diana* and *Motherhood* that I couldn't read it for my blushes.

That same day he came to my studio and told me that there was a steadily increasing demand for my work; that all the limited sets of my groups had been sold; that now was the time for some carefully planned publicity.

My dear, I've been photographed and photographed— smock, street gown, evening effect—and so has my work. Sunday supplements and smart periodicals are beginning to publish Francis Tolland's portrait bust of me; pictures of my work; photographs of me; paragraphs; puffs, paid for—I am *certain*—by the Shoreham people.

I'd tell a deliberate lie if I told you I didn't like all this. Dear, don't scorn me; I adore it! Every bit of it. Even the vulgar papers that dwell on what they call my personal "beauty." Describe my clothes. I am enchanted. *I* am the vulgarian, I suppose.

But I hope there will be something more to it than my flattered vanity. I hope somebody will give me an order. I could make a pretty fountain, I think. Not the fountain part —I mean basin and pedestal and all that. No; an architect would have to do that for me. Show me how, anyway.

One more thing and I'll have mercy on you, dear. Mr.

Shoreham—junior, I mean—suggests that I try for Autumn Academy. Oh, if they *would* let me in!

So I am going to do my

"O threats of Hell and Hopes of Paradise"

for the Academy—to try humbly—oh, so humbly!

That, above, is not, of course, a quotation from the seventy-eighth quatrain—but it describes my poor Eros all of a shiver with the conflict within him—and that lovely little wretch giggling behind her Medusa!——

Dear! *Would* you let me tell you one thing more?

It's only this. When Mother and I lived in the Bronx we had a black maid-of-all-work named Smilax.

She has a daughter named Rose.

Rose is a naturally refined coloured girl, dainty about her person, exceedingly pretty and with the most beautiful hands and feet and figure I ever saw.

Once—it seems very long ago to me—Rose said she would like to be my maid when I could afford it.

And once I saw her undressed; and I told her that some day I would make a "statue" from her. How long ago that seems! And I never dreamed I was ever to have the opportunity.

My dear, I have it! Rose came to see me two weeks ago. I *had* to have somebody. It saves time.

She does everything—the housework, the fine linen, sewing, dresses and undresses me. I feel like one of those horrid helpless ants that would perish unless fondled, washed and fed!

But it does save so much time.

And now I'll tell you the secret. I've made several studies of Rose. And this summer I am going to take a little cottage studio near Cross River, in Westchester County. Young Mr. Shoreham suggested it. He owns it. It is a tiny cottage. The rent is tiny, also. So there I am going to make my first life-size figure. Rose will be my model. It is to be called *Africa*.

And I say very humbly and very much scared, "God help me and overlook my audacity!"

And now I add: God walk ever with you in Persia. And, wherever you stray, God accompany you.

From your "girl,"

ELLIE

CHAPTER XXVIII

THE reaction to gaiety is sadness. Like a pensive shadow, melancholy follows mirth.

So it is with prolonged excitement in a vigorous young mind. And, for Ellie Lessing, the inevitable reaction was overdue.

It came in June, a languor, disinclination; a gently restless weariness.

Not prone to retrospection, the girl began to indulge in it now. Lay later in the mornings on her sunny pillow, thinking, conscious of indefinable unease.

She had attempted a great deal in the last two years. Had accomplished incredibly. Measuring listlessly, now, the distance between the years, she began to have some vague comprehension of the distance she had covered; something of the transformation wrought; of her development.

For a little while, now, her work had not gone well. She was becoming conscious of effort, of the demands on her—her own; of the burdens which every hour carried —happy burdens, yet obligations still.

Rose, bringing her bedside chocolate, said to her one morning:

"You're so young, Miss Ellie——" and stood hesitating and smiling.

Ellie gave her an amused look: "Why do you remind me?"

"When I get enough of a thing I like," said Rose, "I know I've had too much."

Ellie laughed: "And what do you do then?"

"I let it alone."

Ellie sipped her chocolate.

"Now, I like to go to church," continued Rose, laying out Ellie's bath-robe and shower-cap; "but when I've had enough church I've had too much. So I go to a show. . . . And when I've had too much work I go to a party. And when I've had too much dinner I skip a meal."

She drew the bath; gave it the proper dose of bath-salts; spread a freshly laundered mat; laid sponge and flesh-brushes handy.

Ellie brooded over her chocolate. Unaccustomed mental inertia made her uncommunicative.

Presently she pushed away the tray, slid to the floor, laid aside her pyjamas, and went through some supple exercises—made a silvery arch of her body with feet and palms flat on the rug; stood on her head, her slender figure a line of beauty; raised and lowered herself six times; sprang upright, and began to bend and swing and sway like a sapling in a gale of wind.

Her bath was hot; her shower a chilly one. Rose pulled off her red shower-cap, dried her, partly dressed her, and lifted the curling-tongs from the brazier on the dresser.

Recently Ellie had loitered over her dressing. Something unusual. Now, half dressed, the magnet drew her; she went into the studio and wandered about in chemise and stockings, lifting a wet cloth here, twirling a wax sketch there, inspecting some new plastolene, fiddling with an armature, with pliers, wires—fussing, pottering about like an old lady in a rag-littered work-basket.

Once or twice she seemed inclined to mess about with plastolene; Rose brought her smock to pull over the curly head; but Ellie shook her head in silence.

As a matter of fact, the saturation point had been reached. She had had enough. And the depression characteristic of over-mental stimulation was taking possession of the girl.

It was not weariness; she was all a-quiver with vigor; felt its heat and surge. Wondered impatiently, nervously, at her mental inertia.

"Spring fever," remarked Rose. "I've got it, too. I'm glad there's a dance at the Armory to-night. I need it."

Ellie went to the window and looked out. Her ardent restlessness was exasperating her. She could not understand why her mind made no response.

The mind was tired; the restlessness physical. Bodily vigor clamoured for some outlet. Mind pined for pleasure without effort.

She sat at her piano; played for a few moments, broke into jazz—some imbecile "blue" song, two years out of date. Rose was airing the room, taking graceful dance steps now and then as she drifted about the place.

"Rose?"

"Yes, Miss Ellie."

"Get Luigi on the telephone—and the little model—you know?—the little Williams girl. I don't want them to-day. Not until Monday anyway. Tell 'em I'm mailing them cheques."

She idled at the piano while Rose was telephoning; played scraps of Puccini—associated themes—tragic, passionate, repeating arias dimly involved with love and death.

"Is it all right?" she called over her shoulder, still lingering in the dissolving dissolution of Mimi.

Reassured, she drifted into the hair-tearing finalities of the little Nipponette. Left her lying with obi red and wet. Turned carelessly again:

"Please call up Miss Nieland!"

When Leda was on the wire:

"Did I wake you, ducky?" she asked guiltily.

"It doesn't matter——"

"I'm so sorry. . . . May I reconsider, and go to your party, darling?"

"You bet! It's high time you came out of your cell!"

"Will it be hectic?" inquired Ellie.

"Far be it from me to dash your pious hopes——"

"I *do* hope so. Something's tripping me up. I'm crazy to go on working and I can't——"

"You've gone flat, my dear. Nobody can travel on a flat tyre——"

"Darn it, I haven't time to frivol, either!"

"In every lifetime," remarked Leda, "there comes a period when one makes the highest speed by standing still."

"Quoted?"

"Yes; Francis."

"How is he?" asked Ellie.

"All right. He'll be at the party. . . . Gosh, I'll be

glad to see you forgetting how clever you are for a couple of hours——"

"You impudent thing!—Oh, Leda, *am* I getting ponderous?"

"Not yet. But if you go on you'll become an infliction —one of those earnest young seekers——"

"I'm going to be an earnest young devil to-night. I'm going to turn myself loose. My dear, I haven't danced for months and months. I haven't laughed at nothing for years and years."

Leda said: "There'll be plenty of *that* to laugh at, darling. The youths are pin-heads, bless their hearts! Two girls in my show, Marian, Virginia, you and me. My personally devoted button-head has taken charge. It's the Primrose Salon in the Hotel Rajah. Francis can bring you——"

"No, I'll take a taxi; and Rose, if I need her. Now you may go back to bed, ducky——" She hung up; and, to Rose: "You lock up the studio and hide the key where I can't find it! Don't give it to me until Monday. No matter whether I swear at you——"

Rose laughed.

"I'm going out," continued Ellie. "You've the rest of the day. You're going to dance at the coloured regiment's ball to-night, aren't you?"

"No, Miss Ellie."

"You said you were."

"I'd rather take you to your party——"

"No! You go to your party and I'll go to mine."

All the same, at eleven o'clock that night Rose came

in to care for her mistress, bathe, curl, and dress her. She
herself was extremely fetching in rose tulle and silver;
and there was certain to be some excitement in the 15th
Coloured Infantry.

The girl had no gloves and no fan, and Ellie gave her
both, and a dainty handkerchief.

"Sleep as late as you please," she instructed the girl;
"I'm going to."

When Rose had dressed her she sent the girl away to
her Armory ball and sat down at the piano for half an
hour. Then she rang for a taxi.

When she left the house the spire of the grey church
across the street was snowy with moonlight.

Into the Primrose Salon at the Hotel Rajah Ellie
Lessing came, almost dancing, her lovely arms extended
right and left as she encountered those she knew with a
silvery: "Hello! Hello!" to Leda, to Virginia, to Marian,
to Francis, and added a vigorous shake to the airy contact
of greeting.

She smiled enchantingly upon a Miss Linton and upon
a Miss Vane of the Westchester Follies; upon other young
ladies temporarily unidentified with jobs but, apparently,
not worrying on that account; upon Leda's particular
button-head; upon assorted, well-groomed, nice-mannered
pin-heads.

She wore a primrose gown, the bodice of which glimmered like pale April sunshine. Physically she looked her
best. Felt exquisitely reckless.

They were dancing, already. There were cocktails and
champagne and hunger and thirst-provoking morsels; and

flowers everywhere. And a band of niggers, and galvanizing, dance-inciting rhythms strummed and drummed and tooted and rattled and slam-banged about——

She danced with pin-heads, button-heads; with Francis Tolland now and then. With every one she flirted—excepting with Francis—leaving each in the to-be-continued-in-our-next state of mind which started him prowling in her vicinity in hopes of the next installment.

She wouldn't drink; didn't need it; declined to be a "good fellow"; jeered the frequenters of the bowl and their necessity for such recourse.

At supper she demanded plain water and plenty of it; ate with a thorough knowledge of calories; but avoided nothing else—no sentimental perils of the infatuated and pin-headed; no inflammatory declarations; no whispered vows; no amorous gaze. It was neither cocktail nor champagne that started the local blaze around her; it was she; and she was aware of it. And blew it into a conflagration with every breath, every glance, with every silvery laugh that parted her lips.

Her clever, slanting eyes were now all golden with daring; now dim with sympathy, now a soft and bashful green, now veiled with mischief—but ever the devil was lurking in their gold-flecked sea-green depths, ready for pin-head, button-head, bone-head—yet hiding instantly when Francis looked her way.

Well, they danced and danced. One or two youths became noisy; one led Ellie aside and wept when she declined to be kissed. He was so young and nice and unsteady that she was inclined to take him on her lap and cuddle him.

He wept on. So she kissed him on both cheeks and made Francis send him home in somebody's car.

Leda, watching her in action, marvelled, wondered, adored her. Let her take away her own cordial and particular button-head—that nice youth so fresh and clean and shiny of hair, and whose discreetly appointed car carried two men on the box. It is true that the exchange gave her Francis.

They danced; they danced. There were plenty of pinheads to go around. It was gay. Marian, mistress of the art of laughter, swayed everything. Virginia of the brown eyes and golden locks remained steady to glass and foot. Pin-heads might rock; turn incoherent. Not Virginia of the golden locks.

Breakfast was to be served at seven. In the cloak-room Ellie flung both arms around Leda and kissed her ardently.

"I'm grateful, darling. I needed it as badly as Rose needed the Armory ball. . . . Have I behaved indecently?"

"You're a thoroughbred, dear. That Hildreth boy was a beast to you——"

"He was too enterprising. It's our fault, too—fifty-fifty—I guess. . . . Ducky, I'm going."

"Wait till after breakfast——"

"I couldn't. I'm going to sleep until two this afternoon. Then I've something to do. . . . I've had the kind of time I needed. . . . You're so sweet to me, Leda——"

CHAPTER XXIX

WHEN Monday came Ellie did not ask Rose for the key to the studio. After Leda's party the same restlessness, disinclination for work, returned. As an outlet the party had been a failure, apparently. Or, did she need more parties? . . . Answered her own question in the negative. No; another would bore her intellectually. That her mind did not require that sort of rest seemed evident.

However, she tried it.

Like stock characters in old plays—first murderer, second murderer, third murderer, or sometimes they were grave-diggers—Leda had her first button-head, second button-head, and third button-head.

Number three she didn't value much; he had scarcely a speaking part and no business in her life's comedy. His name was Hildreth—the same who had wept at the party and who had been sent home in somebody else's car.

Leda called up Ellie:

"Do you want to bother with him? All he can talk about is you—the treacherous hound! But he's bought both your bronzes."

So Ellie let him come to see her. He was pink, young, sentimental, sensitive. Demonstrative, but timorous as a pup. Likely to be all over one if encouraged.

She made him take her to Coney Island. She had been thinking of Westall and a vanished year.

Somehow the blazing beach, the noisy throngs, the brilliancy of sky and sea, unutterably depressed her. Besides, this boy couldn't swim very well. And he was white and woman-smooth. And too darned devoted.

She could scarcely eat her soft clams at Villy's. And the boy got moist when he danced—breathed audibly, sentimentally.

He wanted to marry her; become a nuisance on the telephone; wept at their final interview. Of these are the callow ranks recruited; food for powder—and lip-stick. Medium for healthy distribution of unearned wealth. Back it goes to the workers. And gold-diggers.

Something in his spineless sentimentality seemed to have infected Ellie Lessing, for she took a taxi one day, drove slowly along the Grand Concourse looking out upon familiar things—upon what had been her universe——

All had been solidly built up with endless acres of brick and stucco—an illimitable perspective, now, stretching into Westchester.

The Lorelei Fountain was a blow to her. She could scarcely believe she ever had thought it beautiful. She looked at it sadly; looked at the big tree, the sentry box, the solitary policeman. Averted her head.

The apartment house where she had lived seemed squalid; shabby and very small. Once, to her, its towering storage tank had seemed to sweep the clouds.

She stopped her taxi and got out. The janitor, now, was Jewish; scarcely conversant with the English language. All the tenants, she gathered, were Jewish. . . . No; she couldn't be permitted to see apartment forty-seven because the children there were ill with measles.

She got into her taxi and drove away toward the Botanical Gardens.

A vast new hotel—Somebody's "Arms"—reared its brick walls where she remembered a vacant lot in which ailanthus trees grew.

At Fordham new ecclesastical edifices of very new grey stone faced the noisy street.

As for the domed greenhouses in the Gardens which once, to her, seemed like vast glass castles piled up against the clouds—well, they needed paint and repairs.

Beds of flowers were in bloom. She left her taxi at the fountain opposite the Administration Building and walked across the grass where the pines already had grown so big.

After a little while she came into sight of the vernal little valley where the brook flowed. And it was then she realized that she had not only been following the familiar trail of her childhood; but that it, also, was the trail along which she had once guided John Westall. . . . So long, so long ago——

Here, finally, on this shady bank, beside the grown flowing stream, they had sat. She remembered the scarlet bird with black wings. . . . He had told her it was a Tanager. He had told her so many things that day. . . . The first man of his caste she ever had met. . . . The first man who ever had made a friend of her mind. . . .

And on that day of all days—the day her mother died.
. . . About half-past four in the afternoon. Alone, except for the nurse——

She rested her face between her hands. The wound
was not yet scarified. Its soreness did not permit her to
dwell very long upon her mother. Not yet.

She brooded on her until throat quivered and lids
burned with gathering tears. . . . Turned her thoughts
resolutely to Westall. . . . Like her mother, now lost to
her. . . . Almost as irrevocably.

Scarcely more in touch with her by letter than was
Helen by prayer. God is far; and so is Persia.

Birds were vocal everywhere in the woods and thickets.
She remembered that some must be thrushes; tried to dis-
tinguish the colours on the flashing wings. . . . The man
with whom she had idled here on that happy yet sadly
sacred day—he knew. He knew these birds. He knew their
voices; he knew these black velvet butterflies powdered
with turquoise. He knew a great deal; a great deal. . . .
Even how to swim. And dance. . . . And how to make
a friend of a young girl's undeveloped mind.

And it had been she who had suggested anything less
intellectual; never before having had to do with any man,
any liaison where the physical had been in abeyance.

Thinking, her face burned a little with chagrin. Grew
hotter in spite of chagrin, thinking of that last few moments together. . . . The first voluntary caress that ever
she had offered a man. . . . Lord, Lord, how young she
had been! . . . As though she could have hoped to hold
between her ardent arms all that her starved, blind mind

was craving—all that it began to suspect, divine, perceive——

Like snaring sunlight in a silken net—to hold this man between her arms; plead her passionate need upon his lips. It had been instinctive. . . . The only way she knew how to convey her necessity to him.

She brooded. Other wisdom had come to her since. Comprehension, without the understanding of experience. Chaste, yet troubled acceptance of facts. Concerning herself, still impersonal; not to be analyzed. . . . If ever to be self-applicable, vague, incalculably remote.

But—men? . . . She brooded between gloved fingers framing her clever face—Men? . . . And the darker aspects of their emotions. . . . Between her arms—in the hot gratitude of possession—in the swift ardour of her lips—*what* had he thought? . . . Whither could he have carried her, had it been his will? Had there been any limits to her virginal passion of possession?

She brooded, wondering, shivering slightly, visualizing all that she had been—what she might have been. . . . "Yonder, but for the grace of God," goes Ellie Lessing!

It was sunset when she returned to the drinking fountain and got into her taxi.

An expensive afternoon.

CHAPTER XXX

"AND I'll tell you another thing," she said to Leda who was seated on a steamer trunk packed for Europe, "—these hectic parties are no outlet. There's no satisfaction in them."

"Aren't they sufficiently depraved to satisfy you, darling?" inquired Leda.

Ellie laughed: "Depravity? That's not the outlet for me. It would bore me. Do you know I don't like what is irregular? I like what is usual. Customary. I seem to have a passion for respectability. I seem to have been born for it. . . . Order and quiet; the tranquillity of familiar things. . . . I don't like change of procedure or of environment——"

"Do you expect to be an old maid?"

"I don't give a darn. . . . It's all right to be a maiden, isn't it?"

Leda glanced out of the window: "Quite all right," she said.

Ellie rose and pulled on one glove: "How's Francis?" she inquired politely.

"A trifle sulky."

"Why?"

"Objects to being abandoned." Leda got up from the steamer trunk: "Francis, you recollect, complained of your leaving. Now he is injured because I'm going to London. Pretends he'll be lonely in New York. . . . It won't harm him if he is."

"Why doesn't he go about with his own sort of women?" inquired Ellie.

"After all, I'm his sort," remarked Leda, amused.

"Yes, that's so. . . . But even *you* don't go about with your own sort——"

"You are my sort, also," said Leda, taking the girl's gloved hands. "Don't you know that?"

Ellie flushed slightly: "You're so sweet to me. But you know the kind of people I mean. Francis has a definite place in this city. In your own city your family is of social consequence. Mine was not. I don't know anybody south of the Bronx."

"Would you like to?"

"It would be pleasant to know educated women. That would be a real outlet; not the kind of parties I have to go to—or see nobody. . . . And I wonder why men like Francis spend so much time with us? Why he complains if we desert him?—when he knows so many educated and cultivated women."

Leda said: "I know a man who has a fine old house in town, and who never lives in it. His pleasure is in knowing he has it. But he prefers irresponsible hours and temporary hotels. Most men do."

"Are *we* human hotels?" asked Ellie, laughing.

"I think we represent desirable and possible lodgings to the men who frequent us. . . . Our charm is our irregularity and impermanency. . . . That's what they think, anyway."

"Probably that's why they bore me," said Ellie. . . . "—always hopeful of a night's lodging——"

They both laughed. Then Ellie kissed her good-bye.

"Darling, it's so wonderful for you. I hope your show goes over in London. I've sent some little gifts to the steamer. *Please* write; I *do* love you."

They clung together for a moment.

Then Leda accompanied her to the head of the stairs:

"You're going to Westchester for the summer this morning?"

"Yes; my taxi, baggage, and Rose, are waiting out-side. . . . Good-bye!"

Passing the open door of the Beauty Parlour, she noticed Madame Felice who gave her and her pretty apparel a look of malignant accusation; which left the girl serenely wondering if, by any chance, she really did look like a "kept" person. It was the first time she had worn colour since her mother died—just a white and peach-tinted sport suit which gave to her slender body, bright bobbed hair, and unspoiled face the touching charm of the school-girl.

All the way to the station, and during the hour's trip on the train, increasing happiness at the prospect of re-suming work preoccupied her.

She and Rose already had made this short journey two or three times to look over the tiny studio-cottage; install her town furniture, all of which except the piano had been sent up in a van; make new sash curtains; and arrange for food and necessaries with the several trades-men at Bedford Village. Her new studio was not very

far from Bedford. One continued straight northward,
passing over the Cross River viaduct, and taking the first
right-hand road. A mile farther on, near the brook which
runs north through tangled woodlands and wild meadows,
stood the tiny cottage owned by Mr. Shoreham, junior,
with its bedroom, maid's room, kitchen, and studio. A
stone-embedded path led from the highway to it; tall old
tulip trees, and one enormous elm, stood near it; a grassy
hill behind it was crowned by woods.

To the left, the brook rushed sparkling out of a little
grove into a briar patch, and, thence, through weedy
meadows to Cross River half a mile away.

A big yellow farmhouse, built more than a century
ago, stood near the junction of brook and river. Here
dwelt Ellie's nearest neighbours—a farmer, wife, and
numerous barefooted progeny.

There were no other houses near. But two miles eastward was the old, Revolutionary village of Three Lakes.

Here were fine old estates and some handsome modern
ones; and a country club, and golf links, and miles of
private trout fishing on a lovely little river—all the stig-
mata of expensive, extensive social insulation.

Ordinary lightning was not supposed to strike in Three
Lakes. Ordinary folk were not supposed to poke their
ordinary noses inside any of the great pillared gateways,
to intrude on private domain, park, club property, or
preserve.

Which was quite all right. The great, great, great grand-
parents of some of these people once lived in these old
houses. Some of them rode with Baylor's Light Horse;
some with Moylan's Dragoons; some marched with the

infantry of Colonel Thomas, when Tarleton ravaged the region; when Bedford and Pound Ridge went up in flames; and the British musketry crackled from New Castle to North Castle.

Well, Ellie Lessing did not know any people who lived at Three Lakes. Had no idea she ever was likely to know them. Had other things to think about.

There were mental adjustments to make first of all. Here was considerable country and some remnants of a wilderness—as she interpreted wilderness.

She was not a country girl. The jungles of Pelham Park had been her limit of rural remoteness.

But here there was need of self-reassurance when she walked at noon as far as the tangled woods; when she prowled, soft-footed, through dewy grasses around the house and under the great tulip trees by moonlight.

Also, by night, there were noises. Noises to be investigated, analysed, understood—winds in the trees; in the more distant woods; stirrings in thickets; unaccountable splashes in pools; the interminable chanting of wild birds by day; of frogs by night; odd, smothered croaks and flappings of unseen, nocturnal creatures; rustling of feathery wings, of foliage; smothered squeaks from bramble patches; and, always, when the west wind blew, a far rumour of flowing waters.

To a girl who had been born amid unnumbered miles of brick buildings, and had passed her existence there habitually deafened by interminable and outrageous noise, the silence of the country was startling. Such stillness seemed unnatural; suspicious; left her unquiet, at first; nervously alert; inclined to listen in bed.

Indeed, so still was the starlit world about her that, from her open window, she could hear the far, dull stamp of horses in the farm barn; the muffled plaint of cattle; the crowing of some distant cock deluded by a brilliant moon.

All this passed—these excursions and alarums. After the first few nights, the strumming of the frogs no longer kept her awake; winds in the woods no longer disturbed her dreams after a day of healthy labour and the happy lamplit peace of evening.

During the first week she missed her piano. Next week she had her own sent up from New York.

When it arrived Ellie had finished her *Love in Dread of Hell*; and the Shoreham people were having it cast.

The main and exciting work, now already in preliminary stages, was the projected life-size figure in clay—the long-dreamed-of *Africa*—the first consciously conceived creation of her youthful mind—born of an ardent, impotent brain so long, so long ago.

And now it was to *be!*—God aiding her, she thought, slightly frightened at her own temerity.

Yet it was delicious to recall the magic moment of her first conception—the flash of celestial intuition; the naked, charming figure of Rose; the lamplight playing over her golden body; the swiftly imagined and gorgeous parrot on her slender wrist; the lifted forefinger and intent features!—Africa!—and Ellie remembered her own childish, breathless words—"Not because you are a coloured girl—but—I know what I mean!——"

She *did* know. A flicker of insight of the quality of that salty wit which Shoreham, senior, had labelled "Attic."

Africa!—the eternal parrot; teaching its fellow its intellectual limit; the Art of Mimicry.

Ellie had made from "Chic" a dozen or fifteen sketches in plastolene; from Rose half a dozen little studies in the same medium.

One Sunday she had Luigi come up to help her with pedestal, pivot, armature, and the heavier tubing and wiring. All day they worked at it; and when Luigi went away there was yet much to be done.

On Monday, however, the farmer, Hugh Strawn, who lived near the river, took several hours off to help the girl with her construction. She gave him three dollars; he presented her with a dozen eggs and a quart of new peas.

By the middle of the week Ellie was up to her dimpled arm-pits in wet clay. The studio's stone floor glimmered all aslop; buckets, sponges, heaps of clay, piles of damp cloths pervaded the place. As the studio also was her living-room and dining-room, mid-summer weather alone averted pneumonia.

It was her régime to rise early, help Rose with breakfast, help her with housework, then seize her and lead her to the model-stand.

Until lunch-time she worked in a fever; then she and Rose got something to eat; spent another hour in preparing for inevitable dinner; or in mending; or in other domestic discussions and duties.

Then back to the studio; Rose to the model-stand; Ellie, well smocked, to her clay and her dripping sponges.

At five, tea. At six, baths. Then fresh aprons, the

kitchen; pots, pans, kettles; table to lay; dinner to be served and eaten. And, after that, lamplight; book or piano. Or a chair on the porch; star-gazing in the fragrant stillness; or a wandering quest of nothing, perhaps, over dew-wet grass. Then candles; bed; dreamless Nirvana.

CHAPTER XXXI

YOUNG Mr. Shoreham telephoned her one morning to inquire whether she was comfortable in her rural quarters.

"Perfectly, thank you," she replied happily.

"I thought you'd like to know," he went on, "that your *Love in Dread of Hell* has been cast."

"I'm crazy to see it!" she cried. "Did it come out well?"

"We think so. . . . Our people are doing some tool work on it. . . . By the way, wouldn't you like to have a set of your three bronzes in your new studio?"

"You are so kind, Mr. Shoreham—I'd love it!"

"I shall see that you have them. . . . How is your *Africa* coming along, Miss Lessing?"

"Oh, darn it, I don't know. It's on such an appalling scale—such a colossal undertaking for me."

"Are you discouraged!"

"Oh, *no!* But I become confused; bewildered. It's the handling of such masses. And the physical effort is surprising—it seems as though I were handling tons of material. . . . And then I'm unaccustomed to the scale; and to climbing up and down step-ladders, and across scaffolding. . . . But I'm not at all discouraged, Mr. Shoreham."

She could hear his polite, well-bred laugh: "How far along is it?"

"It's roughed in. I'm pointing it up."

"That's astonishing," he said. "You should be a little careful not to overwork."

She laughingly denied that there was any danger.

He said: "Any time you are ready we can start our bronze replicas from your wax study. How soon would it be convenient for you to let us cast it in plaster?"

There ensued a discussion of ways and means, terminated by his suggestion that he should call some afternoon in person.

He arrived one cloudless day in July—a nice-looking, clean-cut figure in his golfing togs.

Rose, naked, hastily got into bath-robe and slippers and fled to her bedroom; Ellie plunged her long, smooth fingers into a bucket, dried them, and, unrolling the sleeves of her blue smock, went to the door to welcome him.

They shook hands. He followed her into the studio.

"It's messy," she remarked. "We were at work."

"I'm afraid——"

"It's all right. I'm glad you came—this chair is clean and dry——" She drew up another for herself.

What always was to be agreeably noticed about young Mr. Shoreham was his extreme neatness of person; his agreeable deliberation of speech; his keen but pleasant grey eyes behind the gold-rimmed glasses.

"So," he said, "you are quite comfortable here?"

"Entirely."

"I think," he said, "that I shall add a wing to the place —from the kitchen end. Don't you think that a dining-room and a living-room would give you a little more elbow room?"

He smiled discreetly, his mild joke pleasing him.

"Wouldn't it take all summer to build an addition?" she asked.

But it seemed he had already planned for two sections of a portable house to be added to the kitchen end of the cottage. It would not take much time. There was a contractor now working on a new barn of his at Three Lakes who could send down a gang of men and put the job through in a fortnight.

"I didn't know you had a country house at Three Lakes," said the girl.

"My family originally came from there. I hope to be able to show you the place this summer."

"I'd love to see it!"

"It's rather interesting. In the last century it was known as Trinity Manor. The name came from the three ponds known as Trinity Lakes." He adjusted his glasses, turned to look up at the clay figure on its revolving pedestal, rose and walked toward it. Ellie rose also.

"Oho," he said in a modulated voice.

"It's very rough," she explained.

"I understand."

Keen-eyed, leisurely, he examined the figure from one angle after another. He seemed to understand the arrangement of the mirrors, too; and studied the reflected figure in them.

Roughed in as it was there was, already, an exquisite grace in its supple, loose-limbed repose—a sort of exotic languor, youthful indolence.

"I see," he nodded, as though speaking to himself.

"Would you mind criticizing?" she asked diffidently.

"I'm scarcely qualified. . . . I should say that your construction is sound. . . . A firm, logical bit of work. . . . Of course you'll go on studying it. . . . The pelvic basin; and the knees——"

"I know. Both are troubling me. My model has such narrow hips—like a child's. . . . Her knees are lovely. But I've *got* to make one *know* that the bones are there underneath. I think the only way is to work out the bony structure in anatomical detail, over-lay it in detail, then, some day, when I know all about it, absolutely simplify it with merciless decision."

He nodded: "Cold blood does it."

"I know," she admitted; "I'm too excitable and ardent to practise self-denial easily. Beauty affects me so—so sharply——" She laid her long, smooth fingers against her throat—became conscious that her smock was unbuttoned, repaired the oversight without embarrassment.

Young Mr. Shoreham was now examining the small-scale model in wax.

"Her hips and knees are all right here," he observed.

"I'm glad you think so. But you see I'm accustomed to working on that scale."

He understood. He strolled about inspecting studies, sketches, a beginning of a bas-relief—her first—some charcoal drawings of a grey African parrot.

"Where did you do these?" he inquired.

"In a bird store, last April."

"I have a grey African parrot at Trinity Manor. He is quite gentle. Let me send him over to you."

She was enchanted; inquired about the bird's food and the care necessary. They walked together to the porch. His grey sport-car stood on the road beyond.

"I'm going to play a little golf," he said. "I shall be at Three Lakes over Sunday. . . . I wonder whether it would disturb you too much if I brought some people to see you? . . . It might possibly be agreeable to you to know a few people at Three Lakes."

She said, rather shyly, that it would be agreeable.

Then he shook hands with her in his pleasant, rather solemn manner.

After a few minutes she went into the house.

"Rose! Rose!" she called joyously, "we're to have a most wonderful parrot!"

CHAPTER XXXII

THE three bronzes arrived. When they were unpacked, Ellie hung over them, torn between maternal love and exasperation at the shortcomings she could now perceive in her offspring.

"Darn it all," she said to Rose, "if I had a chance I'd never again do things *that* way. . . . I've gone ahead of those things. . . . I realize that. . . . Stick them around the studio——"

She sat down and hammered out her impatience on the piano.

Half an hour later a man-servant, driving a dog-cart, arrived from Three Lakes with a gilt cage containing one grey African parrot.

The parrot, whose name was Don Juan, walked calmly out when Ellie opened the door of his cage, looked first at Ellie, then at Rose: then, deliberately preferring the latter, stepped upon her extended finger, slid up her arm, tucked his pastel-coloured head under the girl's chin, and began to make soft, dreamy noises of satisfaction.

"Rose!" exclaimed her mistress, "the bird has fallen in love with you at sight!"

It seemed to be the case. The attachment was immediate; Rose was enchanted. All day long she carried the grey and scarlet bird about on her shoulder, except when posing for Ellie. It was even necessary that she reassure and control the bird while Ellie made preliminary studies of it in plastolene. All day Don Juan rode on Rose's forefinger or shoulder, or, if put down, waddled tirelessly after her wherever she went.

Gradually the accomplishments of Don Juan were revealed. He could whistle several bars of "Nancy Lee"; he could shout in a hoarse voice: "Blow the man down! Blow the man down!" He had a most degraded laugh ending in hag-like shrieks. He could say in a mincing tone: "After you, my dear!—after you." And, "Why do the roses fade?" Also he could mew like a hungry kitten, and make a vast variety of indefinable noises besides.

One morning in August Rose, returning from the Post Office at Cross River, brought to her mistress two letters.

Ellie saved the one as a child saves the biggest bonbon for the last, and opened the other letter.

When she had read it she said rather blankly to Rose: "They're going to tear down our place in town. This is a month's notice to move out. I think you'd better go down this morning and have the pictures and rugs sent here."

Pictures and rugs sounded like *objets d'art*. They consisted of several chenille mats and the coloured prints of *Ormond* and *Man-o-'War*.

Ellie went to her desk, drew a cheque for the last rent she ever was to pay for the ancient Victorian dump. Then, seizing her letter from John Westall, she hurried out to the shadow and seclusion of the tulip trees and flung herself full length upon the grass:

There is always in your letters the same indescribable charm that I remember about you yourself. From your letters and what you tell me of your life I can only surmise what changes there are in you since I have seen you.

Certainly, also, the photographs you sent me reveal a rather bewildering beauty developed out of what promised in the fresh and engaging features of a very young girl. You're very stunning, Ellie.

But what vastly interests me, and what I can scarcely keep pace with, is your amazing progress in self-cultivation and in an art which now so entirely seems to have become your own.

It is admirable to have done what you have done. I won't say incredible. Because there *are* people of your species in the world. A few. Not to be measured by prevailing standards.

The photographs of your extraordinary bronzes stand on my writing table. I am still trying to comprehend that you are their creator and executrix. . . . It seems only yesterday when you came back from your first enchanted visit to the Metropolitan Museum.

This is a strange, medieval country. We white folk never will understand them. Never, never will they like us. Looking at them in the streets and bazaars, sometimes I find myself wondering how soon they'll break loose on us and obliterate us. Of course fear is their only deterrent.

They're a lazy, cheating, untruthful lot; and my work drags and drags. What's time in Teheran? What's time to any Persian? There's no money in the entire country except in official pockets. Grafted out, flogged out of the population.

But, oh, Lord, the potential wealth here! And the Bolsheviki are very much aware of it. And the situation is more than sinister.

My dear, I'm tired. I'd like to see you. I'd like to go home.

I've sent for a man to come out here from Paris. If he is what I expect, then, perhaps, I may be able to get away by the first of the year. It would be jolly to see you, Ellie.

But I rather imagine you've another "fella" by this time. The latest of many. Yes?

By the way, what's become of your former idol, Francis Tolland? I rather imagined you might become seriously sentimental over him.

But you never mention him any more.

Well, dear, you're so grown up, so superior, now, that I suppose you'll not want me for your "fella" any more. Probably it will be three years before we meet again. And three years in a young life are three centuries of development. Probably I'll scarcely recognize you when I see you.

And I suppose you'll no longer care to dive at Manhattan with me or dance at Villy's some Saturday evening. Or guide me through the labyrinths of the Bronx parks.

Or, in short, "see more or less of me."

Alas!——

JOHN WESTALL

She jumped up, ran to the house and wrote:

It was different with Francis Tolland. I am still your girl. I'll write you this evening.

ELLIE

She stamped and sealed the note, walked, hatless, to Cross River and mailed it, returned through the sunshine, singing across the fields, waving her hand to the farmer's children who hailed her with shrill acclamations of rustic devotion; and went about the house, still singing, to finish the housework and be ready for Rose on her return.

About one o'clock a horrid burst of excitement from Don Juan announced the return of Rose from town.

By two they resumed work in the studio—Ellie continuously vocal and Rose's lovely African voice joining in *The Joyful Blues*:

"I'm so happy when I see things blue,
The soft blue skies,
Your deep blue eyes—
Blue blood, blue eyes, and a heart true blue,
That's you, baby doll,
That's yu—h!
Underneath the yaller moon,
With my yaller octoroon,
Gimme room, baby doll, gimme room!
Kiss me quick,
Kiss me bold,
Kiss me sick,
Knock me cold!
Yaller baby doll with eyes so blue,
That's you!
That's yu—h!——"

Thus, progress in the most chaste of all the arts; immortal Greece saluted by the velvet voice of Africa and the happy carolling of a youthful Yankee. Punctuated by the ignoble laughter of Don Juan.

One morning during the first week in August young Mr. Shoreham called Ellie on the telephone, saying that he was at Trinity Manor for two weeks and might he pay his respects to Miss Lessing that afternoon and bring some people to see her.

Ellie came back from the telephone, and, looking up at Rose on the model-stand:

"They'll come about five," she said. "We'll give them some tea."

They knocked off work at half-past three; mopped up the studio. Then Ellie bathed and got into a pretty gown, ready to help Rose. But the girl had the tea-tray ready, and several platters of those squashy confections which women like.

Young Mr. Shoreham and his people arrived about five o'clock. Mr. Shoreham shook hands formally but firmly, and, formally but pleasantly made his presentations.

There was an elderly woman, a Mrs. Weymiss, whose inspection tinged the girl's cheeks with pink. There was a very young woman, a Miss Stanley, whose manners were impulsively cordial. There was an elderly man, Captain Atwell, who shook her hand with the smiling decision of a gentleman who knows a pretty girl when he sees one, and who had no doubts about this one's qualifications.

Rose served tea on the porch. Conversation began easily, amiably. Mrs. Weymiss thought it so interesting for a girl to choose so solitary a cottage for her work. Miss Stanley thought it "wonderful," and "plucky."

"Shouldn't you have a police dog?" inquired Captain Atwell.

Ellie had not thought of it.

"There *are* tramps, you know," said Mrs. Weymiss. "Haven't you any protection?"

Ellie mentioned her neighbor, Mr. Strawn; dismissed potential peril with a smile.

"I've a dog of sorts," suggested Captain Atwell.

Then, finally, Mr. Shoreham, with the slightest hesitation, admitted that he had a man to watch the place ever since Miss Lessing had occupied it.

Ellie flushed surprise; her embarrassed gratitude; regret

for causing inconvenience concentrated upon her the intent inspection of Mrs. Weymiss.

Mr. Shoreham assured the girl that he always employed a watchman to keep an eye on the cottage whether occupied or empty.

It might have been true. Mrs. Weymiss was uncertain. She was, however, becoming rather certain concerning Ellie Lessing.

"George," she said to Mr. Shoreham, "I think you are perfectly right to employ a watchman." And, to Ellie: "You should be a little cautious in Westchester, my dear."

Jane Stanley said impulsively: "Wouldn't it be safer for you to stay at the club and come here every day? I could put you up."

Ellie laughed, thanked her, and said it was not at all necessary. Captain Atwell thought it was necessary. They all discussed it; were still discussing it when they went into the studio.

Jane Stanley instantly became exclamatory over the bronzes. Art was unsafe ground for Captain Atwell. He maintained a demeanour indicating serious approbation.

But Mrs. Weymiss, who was no fool, and who had knowledge and taste of her own, stood looking very intently at the *Africa* for a long time. So did George Shoreham.

After a while she turned to him, careless as to who heard her.

"This is rather remarkable work," she said.

"That is my opinion."

She said to Ellie: "Yours is an unusual talent. This

is a most interesting beginning. It promises extraordinary beauty."

Ellie flushed brightly under the praise: "It is kind of you to say so. . . . I am so troubled about it."

"Why?"

"Because there is so much to learn; so fearfully much I don't know. I have never before attempted a life-size figure."

Mrs. Weymiss smiled: "I have the pleasure of owning your charming *Motherhood*," she said. "Mr. Shoreham has promised me the first of the *Love in Dread of Hell*. You see, my dear, mine are no empty compliments."

She smiled at Ellie, slipped one arm around her: "Come; show me all your studies," she said, turning away toward the various works in progress.

Mr. Shoreham and his party took their leave, presently.

Mrs. Weymiss took Ellie's hands in hers—not unaware of their loveliness—and, holding: "When you are at leisure will you come to me at Ridge Hill for a week?"

"I'd love to. . . . Is it in Three Lakes?"

"Near there. . . . I know enough not to interfere with your work. But George Shoreham tells me he means to make an addition to your cottage. Come then, if it is convenient. You need merely telephone me."

"Do you play golf?" asked Jane Stanley.

Like other urchins of her age she had swarmed over the Van Cortlandt Park Links at unoccupied hours and, with the caddies, had picked up the sort of clever and natural skill that extreme youth alone can master.

Thinking of it she smiled at Jane Stanley and said she did play a little.

"I'd like to show you my kennel," said Captain Atwell, abruptly, "—if you're int'rested in pointers."

Ellie was interested.

As they went away across the grass toward the waiting limousine, Mrs. Weymiss took George Shoreham's arm.

"Your protégée," she said in a low voice, "is perfectly beautiful."

He reddened, slightly, but said nothing.

"Are you pleased that I asked her to Ridge Hill?"

"You are always more than kind——"

"My dear, I *like* her."

"Thank you," said young Mr. Shoreham—not quite aware of what he said.

After a while Mrs. Weymiss laughed. But young Mr. Shoreham did not notice it.

CHAPTER XXXIII

NOW there began for Ellie Lessing, and for the first time in her life, a natural and wholesome career; balanced rations of work and pleasure where the vitamines and calories necessary to healthy development of mind and body were properly adjusted.

About the middle of August she went to Mrs. Weymiss at her ancient seat, Ridge Hill.

There, every hour of the day was occupied. There she rode every morning with Mrs. Weymiss and a groom. Not that she knew how to ride. She told Mrs. Weymiss so, but added with characteristic self-confidence that she'd like to go.

Jane Stanley's coat, breeches, and boots fitted her. A gentle, well-schooled nag was promised.

After the first half mile Mrs. Weymiss laughed—that odd, sophisticated, amused laugh—intimate self-communication. The girl was born to the saddle, that was as plain as a pike-staff. . . . It was her hands. Those long, light, capable hands. And a perfect co-ordination.

But it was a sore girl that day; sore for several days. Witch-hazel and talcum helped. And Ellie continued to ride every morning with Mrs. Weymiss, rain or shine. After that, bath and breakfast. After that golf at the club.

At luncheon and at dinner, too, there always were

people. Guests, sometimes, from the outer world. Mostly neighbours.

After luncheon Mrs. Weymiss kept to her room and Ellie did what she chose. There was plenty to choose from.

Jane Stanley haunted her like a bright shadow, too infatuated to endure a day's separation.

Captain Atwell had every pointer in the kennel out for her inspection. He taught her to hit clay targets from concealed traps; he took her trout fishing and taught her to cast. In about ten minutes she learned to cast a fly nearly as far as he could. With a greenhorn's proverbial luck she raised and hooked into the notorious and almost legendary "big trout of Red Rock Pool."

A most terrific commotion ensued; splashes like a wallowing horse; shrieks from the reel; hoarse instruction from the fearfully excited Captain, intelligently obeyed by the bewildered girl.

How in the world the fish ever was brought to net neither she nor Captain Atwell could clearly explain.

Everybody in Three Lakes came to view the defunct on exhibition at the Club. He was a monstrous fish. But what, to the anglers of Reedy River, was far more monstrous, was the taking of this fish which had flouted them all for years, by a young girl who never before had caught even a minnow. However, such—almost invariably—are the people who do such things under the noses of outraged experts.

It was a heavenly two weeks for a girl who never before had known such people, such pleasures, such surroundings.

Almost all the women she met, young and old, were

amiable to her. All the men were. Much was due to her own simplicity and charm. However, it was not wise for anybody to be sniffy about anybody Mrs. Weymiss befriended.

There was dancing in the evenings at the Club or at several of the larger houses in the neighbourhood. Mrs. Weymiss adored dancing. So Ellie had an amazingly happy time of it.

Every day after tea she and Mr. George Shoreham motored over to see how Rose was getting on, and to examine the clay figure of *Africa* and be certain that it was properly dampened and wrapped.

Also there was the new addition to the house to inspect. A gang of Italians, spurred to unaccustomed activity by extra pay and a padrone with a violent voice, had dug a cellar, set forms, poured concrete, installed lighting wires, plumbing and heating pipes, and a furnace. Upon the concrete foundation the portable house was erected complete.

But Ellie was troubled when, on the last visit before returning to occupy the place, she discovered that Mr. Shoreham had furnished both rooms in quiet but excellent taste.

"I ought to have done that," she said reproachfully.

He reminded her with a smile that it was his house. Neither his smile nor his explanation quite satisfied her. Always she had had an indefinable objection to having men do things for her.

It seemed ungracious. But it was an ingrained aversion. And always she had endeavoured to balance any obligations incurred between herself and any man. . . . That was why she sat for Francis Tolland. Why, so long ago, she had rejected aid from John Westall. Why she insisted on a bill for legal services from Tom Barrett. . . . Although she got merely a tongue-dressing and no bill at all from that legal luminary.

The day before she left Ridge Hill for her own cottage she could have remained for the season in Three Lakes had she chosen to—with Mrs. Weymiss, with the infatuated Jane, with any one of several interested and friendly people whose amiability had become kindness, and, in some cases, warm cordiality.

The evening before she left, Mrs. Weymiss suggested that they dine at home by themselves. Her hostess's maid being ill, a hairdresser from town had been telephoned for that afternoon. To find one, in August, was difficult. Finally the housekeeper located one by consulting the classified directory. Mrs. Weymiss sent a car in for her.

When the woman arrived she was conducted to Mrs. Weymiss's dressing-room.

Ellie, in silk robe and slippers, passed her as she entered. The woman was Madam Felice.

Madam opened her satchel and proceeded about her business with her usual ability and loquacity.

Mrs. Weymiss was paying her very little attention. Had no notion what she had been saying until she had finished and had been paid.

Then she said: "Thank you, Madam. It is very nicely done, indeed. I think Miss Lessing is waiting for you in her dressing-room."

Madam laid away the last of her paraphernalia; closed her satchel with a snap; slowly, smilingly, turned the yellow evil of her eyes on Mrs. Weymiss.

"I don't do servants' hair," she said.

Mrs. Weymiss stared at her: "What do you mean? Miss Lessing is my guest."

"She was my maid, once," said Madam Felice. "When I found out that a man was keeping her I fired her."

Mrs. Weymiss remained still as a stone. But after a moment, something about her made Madam Felice nervous.

"If you don't believe me," she said, "I can give you the man's address——"

Mrs. Weymiss rang. A maid appeared.

"Show this disreputable slut out," said Mrs. Weymiss.

When Felice had disappeared, hastily, with her satchel, Mrs. Weymiss stood motionless until the flush had died out on her cheeks.

Then, suddenly, she laughed. To redress the misery of the world, God created humour.

She knew, really, nothing at all about this Ellie Lessing.

She guessed, however, that young Mr. Shoreham was seriously in love with her. And if it were true that this girl had been a hairdresser's maid, and, furthermore, had been somebody's mistress, what about the overpowering respectability of Mr. Shoreham?

Mrs. Weymiss laughed.

"Well," she thought, "I don't care if George Shoreham doesn't. The girl is utterly lovely. . . . And somebody ought to do her hair——"

She went to Ellie's door, knocked, entered. Ellie was curling her own gold-brown ringlets; rose, still holding a shining strand of hair with the iron.

"I came to do your hair," said Mrs. Weymiss, smilingly.

Ellie looked at her calmly, but there was a bright flush on her cheeks.

"That woman was Madam Felice," she said. "I was once employed by her."

"How interesting," said Mrs. Weymiss pleasantly. "Tell me about it, Ellie."

She seated herself; Ellie sat down again before her mirror; and while she continued to curl her hair she told Mrs. Weymiss about her mother's death, the necessity of employment, the experience with Felice.

The girl's candour was entirely convincing. Besides, she never had made the slightest pretences concerning herself. She had not even been reticent when casually questioned concerning herself.

"I imagined," said Ellie, "that Felice would not come to my room. She had a most horrid husband who annoyed me, and that, I think, accounts for her hatred of me. . . . I suppose she told you I am an unmoral person?"

All Mrs. Weymiss's doubts suddenly dissolved into a ringing laugh:

"My dear," she said, "if you ever have been, it doesn't make you any less adorable. You've got the honesty of a little boy and the heart of a little girl. And the cleverest mind that ever I have known in anybody between your age and mine——"

She checked herself; the girl's eyes were brimming with tears.

"My dear!" exclaimed the older woman, "I didn't believe it!"

"It isn't true," said the girl, "—what she said about me. . . . If it were I'd say so. It would be contemptible to deceive *you*——"

She bent her head and laid it between her long, smooth fingers. The tongs fell clattering to the floor.

Mrs. Weymiss leaned forward and drew the girl's warm, fragrant head against her breast.

After a while she smiled to herself, thinking it no wonder that the heart of young Mr. Shoreham was already so seriously involved.

CHAPTER XXXIV

MRS. WEYMISS was a weary old woman with nothing to do.

Physically she was rather a good-looking widow of sixty, active, always thoroughly groomed, still resolutely carrying on in that last forward movement toward trenches that never can be taken, and where all bones at last must lie.

In the saddle, on the links, on the dance floor Mrs. Weymiss was still going strong.

At heart she was through, had shot her bolt. For her, life had been lived; the irony of it analyzed; its illusions and delusions collected and catalogued.

She was no more selfish than another; too wise to be cynical—aware that it is the unusual that usually happens —which no cynic believes, even when it does happen.

If any trace of bitterness ever had starched her, it was converted into sugar now—that grape-sugar of the human mind: humour.

So, to laugh, genuinely, at life—not too unkindly—still amused her; and satisfied within her that modicum of malice latent or active in us all.

Here was a case which amused her. The case of Ellie Lessing.

She understood it now from A to Z, filling in from

experience and intuition the skeleton of facts which the girl's utter candour revealed at every tactful question.

There was less humour in it than Mrs. Weymiss had almost hoped for: George Shoreham was not solemnly in love with a hairdresser's assistant who had been some man's mistress. . . . Which was God's mercy, too, considering the youth and the need of her, and considering the character of Francis Tolland whom Mrs. Weymiss knew very well indeed.

But George had fallen heavily in love with the orphan daughter of a bookmaker and of a variety actress. This was mildly funny. Because there is always humour in the solemnity of ponderous self-deception.

Mrs. Weymiss, in her heart, didn't care any longer what anybody had been—excepting herself. She had lived through all that dreary Vere-de-Vere era and into a modernism which was more or less indifferent, perverse, and inclined to accept anybody qualified to amuse it.

Also, there was a piquancy in putting Ellie Lessing over. Something to do. Something that always would appeal to her humour; to the human malice in her.

And the material she had to mould, if she chose to, was fresh, unspoiled, fine, pliable, and interesting.

Without any except pleasurable effort she could do, for the girl, anything she chose to do. Materially. . . . Countenance her; place her; play games with her future; extract from her both pleasure and amusement.

Now, after Mrs. Weymiss had considered all these things in the case of Ellie Lessing; analyzed her own motives in the matter—Ellie, apparently having no motives of self-interest for Mrs. Weymiss to analyze—she came to the reluctant but faintly amused conclusion that there was, probably, another motive—possibly a basic one —that suggested her intervention in behalf of this young girl. And there was humour in this motive, too—humour of a certain sort. And the pith of it was that there was, in her heart, a tenderness for this girl, born neither of pity nor of sympathy. But born out of sheer respect.

This, probably, was the basic motive. Doubtless the girl's beauty—her physical loveliness—her talents, her cleverness, candour, transparent honesty,—doubtless all these solidified the basic motive of Mrs. Weymiss.

But tenderness born of respect is the firmest of all foundations. On it must be builded all friendship.

Yet, here again were all the elements of humour. And Mrs. Weymiss laughed, now, at herself, and no longer at George Shoreham, or at the impregnable ranks of the elect whither she now had decided to conduct the daughter of a Bronx racing man.

She drove over to see Ellie one golden afternoon in October; found her all stained with clay—all flushed and lovely with exertion; and the *Africa* a supple, sinuous, exotic, exquisite thing—an enchanting creation of purest delight.

The older woman was no fool. There was shrewdness as well as the æsthetic quality in her appreciations and appraisals.

"What are you expecting to do with this, my child?" she asked abruptly.

"I thought I might venture to offer it to the Salon——" The girl smiled uncertainly at her own impudence.

"You've done it as the central motif of a fountain, I believe?"

"I thought so. . . ."

"How would it look in the centre of the great circular lawn inside the entrance gates to Three Lakes Park?"

Ellie reddened to the blonde roots of her hair.

"—Banked up to the basin with a riot of blazing flowers?" added Mrs. Weymiss. . . . "Suppose I put it up to the board of governors? . . . Could you give me any idea at all as to what sum we should appropriate?"

"I hadn't thought——"

"What is the Palisades Club paying your friend Francis Tolland for their new fountain? Did he ever tell you, Ellie?"

"Y—es."

"In confidence?"

"Oh, no. But that is so very different——"

"It gives us something to figure on. What did that young man get?"

"He is to have a hundred and fifty thousand dollars. That includes his expenses, of course—casting, delivery —everything."

"How much will he clear?"

"About a hundred thousand."

"Very well. Suppose we assume all expenses and offer you twenty-five thousand?"

The girl seemed bewildered; stared up at her clay creation in silence.

Mrs. Weymiss said: "I can get that much. They usually do what I suggest. . . . If you wish to hear my opinion of your *Africa*, I think it is one of the most seductive and enchanting creations in modern sculpture that ever I have seen. . . . I don't suppose there will be any question of the Salon accepting it. . . . And, Ellie, I don't believe you will ever excel this figure—no, not in all the coming years of added skill, experience, and knowledge.

"Often that happens, my dear—that what is to remain immortal is conceived and accomplished in early youth.

"These years, now—years of inexperience but of fiery inspiration and divine youth—years of hot impulse unclogged by chiller knowledge—years of ambition unafraid!—My dear—these are the years—*your* years. And all the coming craft and skill which make for nobility and permanency cannot gild the lilies that are growing in this hour——"

She hesitated; then she laughed outright at her own warmth; and came and rested her gloved and bony hands on the girl's shoulders.

"To-day," she said, "you must do a dollar's worth of work for a penny: to-morrow you shall do a penny's worth for a dollar. That is the fate of all genius. . . . Will you kiss me—a dollar's worth for a penny?——"

The girl flung her clay-stained arms round her neck and hid her bobbed head on her breast.

They were taking tea on the veranda, later, when George Shoreham appeared—vastly to Mrs. Weymiss's amusement.

For one thing, she meant to eliminate him if she was to undertake the social creation of Ellie Lessing.

Marriage, giving in marriage, was to be no part of it

for a good long while. Nor was this type of man to be considered when the girl could be received anywhere and be qualified to pick and choose anybody.

It occurred to her to put up that trespass notice now, and drive a nail in it.

She said blandly and carelessly to Ellie: "As long as you've given up your quarters in town, why not come to me when you leave here?"

"I'd love to for a few days——"

"My dear, I mean for the winter. I've a big, ugly, empty house. We can hunt up one of those cat-alleys, or mews—whatever they're called—and rent a studio for you; and you can drive down every morning and back every afternoon——" She smiled on Ellie, rose, and, leaning lightly upon the girl's arm, walked leisurely across the grass toward her waiting car.

"These are the years, my dear," she said. "Don't neglect any opportunity. Don't fetter yourself either; don't handicap yourself. Keep care and responsibility at arm's length as long as you can. . . . And keep men outside the picket fence. . . . Draw *that* dead-line *now!* There will be time enough, later, for the Only Man on Earth."

Ellie laughed: "I don't believe I ever shall have time for him."

Mrs. Weymiss, with a sardonic smile, turned toward the cottage and waved a gloved and bony hand in adieux:

"Good-bye, George," she called across the grass.

CHAPTER XXXV

ELLIE LESSING worked all day long.

In November the rains set in. It rained for a week. It rained and rained. The meadow brook was out of its banks; a lake spread between the studio and the Strawn farm; Cross River was a surging torrent.

Great winds came, lashing the woods with rain. Everywhere dead leaves were flying; flocks of wind-driven crows beat heavily to leeward; a dense, opalescent obscurity enveloped the world.

Ellie worked on. Songful, the greater part of the day. Or at the piano. Or, when Three Lakes folk called, gay and loquacious as a magpie, unfolding, revealing herself, expanding, maturing into a radiant thing with the spontaneous delight of a strayed creature restored among its own kind.

Yet, such as these she never before had known. Not in this incarnation.

She heard, sometimes, from Leda; wrote her often.

It appeared that Francis Tolland was stopping in London, also.

"He really seems lonely," wrote Leda, "—even with all his friends—if he chose to frequent them—all his activities, his successes, his laurels.

"Usually he comes to the theatre for me. . . . I'm getting so afraid of hurting his feelings that I hesitate to make engagements or go to parties where he has not been asked. Not that he's morbid or melancholy, but he seems like a perplexed boy whose inclination is to stick around as though in hopes you would solve his difficulties for him.

"It's a phase of him I never before have seen. I never before knew him to depend upon anything or anybody—not even upon himself—yet, self has been his god.

"For his is a detached soul, unstable, nourished on chance, born of drifting elements, taking protean shapes. . . . Essentially lonely, this soul of his. Drawn hither, thither, only in hope of cure. And there is none; and never shall be on earth. A cure for others; yes. No cure for the sick god of self."

Snow came in December. Followed a week of bitter cold. Great excitement and solicitude in the studio caring for the clay *Africa;* keeping up warmth and moisture.

But the freezing weather softened into fog, then pouring rains once more.

Ellie worked on, singing her joyous song of youth triumphant, arrogant, unafraid.

It was in January that she heard from John Westall. He sent her, from Constantinople, a Herez rug of glowing sapphire, ivory and rose; very ancient.

"In years to come," he wrote, "you are to sit upon it and reflect how famous you are."

She replied:

Upon it, there is room for two—in our old age. . . . Then if I am still your girl, we can squat there and tell each other how wonderful are the ways of friendship. . . . And praise Allah for the magic gift we share between us.

My friend, I can't transport this clay called *Africa* to New York. If I could I have no time to go there and hunt up a studio.

So I shall remain here until my *Africa* is ready to be cast in plaster.

Don't ask me how long that is to be. I don't know. I work and work and work; and I don't know.

I am not lonely. And if there were no people to be polite to me at Three Lakes I should not be lonely. I'll tell you something: there is no loneliness in me. There was grief for Mother. Not loneliness of soul. Not for you, either, when you went away. A very youthful and tender sorrow. But mine is not a lonely soul. Within me there never could reign solitude.

Desire? Yes. Every emotion, probably, except only loneliness.

I think my soul must be a comrade, and no unknown; and that is the true reason.

Which does not mean I haven't missed you. The acute unhappiness has gone, bridged by memories and our letters. But you are Habit; your origin was necessity. And if you return and go away again always you will be missed. Wanted. Regretted. Awaited. . . . My dear—and welcomed—married or single!

Is that indecent of me? But I haven't really changed since I told you the same thing—so many, many ages ago.

My dear, do you know it is going on three years since I have laid eyes on you?

I've told you about Mrs. Weymiss. She doesn't know you. I've asked her. I'm rather sorry I did because she continues to mention you at times, and I think she believes I am sentimental about you. Well, I am. But not in the degree she might suppose. Not that way. Of which I am now convinced I am incapable. The love of men was born in me. But not the passion for any one among them. Love, but not "profane" love. Rest easy, my friend; my only overflow is what I offer you.

In January—if I cast—I shall go to New York for a few

weeks and stop with Mrs. Weymiss. I hope I shall be ready for many people—for gaiety and lights and theatres and dances—for music and the opera and every pleasure designed by God and man.

But there is a bond that ever must draw me back to quiet and leisure and the freedom I can no longer live without. Work! That, to me, has become the only meaning of life. The one immortal pleasure.

And I am determined to take up Italian this coming year, and a course in architecture at Columbia—I've *got* to know how to design a fountain, at least!—and I *need* a course in comparative anatomy, and—oh, Lord!——

And, despite all these absorptions and demands upon me, my dear, I always shall have time to swim with you at Manhattan, and dance with you at Villy's and show you the secret glades of the Botanical Gardens—our Eden of an afternoon—and thence driven forth until this day of grace, and half the world between us!—Poor Eve! Poor Eve!

Who is your missing rib, called

ELLIE

Toward the end of January she wrote him:

The die is cast and so is *Africa!* A thrilling success! But it nearly killed Rose and me.

Oh, my dear, the Three Lakes Club has bought it. And on this day of miracles I also have bought something. Six per cent bonds with gilded edges, to the value of twenty-five thousand dollars!

I am strangely calm about it. Indignant, however, when I consider my income tax. Otherwise, of a marble tranquillity. Very tired, also.

I go, now, to Mrs. Weymiss for a few weeks. She is very kind—good, amiable, and kind.

But, somehow, when we are together, if I listen hard, I seem to hear the faint jingling of a pair of handcuffs in her

wrist-bag. And wonder who they're for. . . . Am I ungrate-
ful? God knows. . . . But if the price of freedom were a
stable and a handful of clay I'd have to pay the price.

It is snowing, my friend, and I am going to walk to Cross
River Post Office and mail this letter to you.

And to-morrow evening, in New York, the pink lights are
to be turned on for me. . . . A party! For *me!* Oh, my dear,
if only you were there to teach us all what dancing really is
—give the world one perfect lesson with

Your girl,
ELLIE

On the morrow, young Mr. Shoreham came up from
town to close the cottage and receive the keys.

He seemed, to Ellie, unusually polite, formal, attentive;
unusually pale, too.

While Rose was packing the bags in the bedrooms, he
and Ellie stood on the veranda looking across the snowy
grass at the car which Mrs. Weymiss had sent up for her
from town.

She was thinking of nothing in particular—a pleasant
expression on her lips—her clever gaze shifting over a
snow-covered landscape—when, in a modulated, polite,
resolutely controlled voice, Mr. George Shoreham asked
her to marry him.

It was her first serious declaration—not considering
Francis Tolland's, nor the emotional and excitable offers
of the pin-head species.

She was much too surprised to have any other feeling.

She said, rather wide-eyed: "Why, I am not in love
with you, Mr. Shoreham."

He was so nice about it; so serious, so courteous.

Hoped she might come to care for him in time. . . .
Realized that she had not thought of him in that way.
. . . But, perhaps, now that she had been made aware of
the sentiments entertained toward her, possibly she might
—in time—consider him more favourably——

No such possibility could ever happen. She knew it.
And, presently, she told him so. Most politely and very
gently.

No man ever is absolutely convinced that his congé is
final.

Mr. Shoreham lifted her hand a little way and bent
very far over and touched it with his lips.

Her fingers closed quite firmly over his in friendly sign
of understanding. Nothing further was said. He took off
his glasses, polished them, set them again upon the delicate bridge of his nose.

She gazed into snowy distance.

CHAPTER XXXVI

IN the average human life there is no plot. It begins as an incident in the lives of others, and ends as an unfinished and rambling episode with no story to it, or scarcely any.

The exceptions are the lives that are written about. Actual or manufactured stories—the latter usually the more popular because of a definite beginning and end. A plot and an ensemble. A finished piece of work.

But life is not that any more than realism consists in the use of crude words. There are far cruder words in real life. Far more romance, too, than the modern school of gloom and whine admits or understands.

There is no realism in art. The phrase is a paradox. The two nouns deny each other.

Only a paraphrase of Truth is possible. The degree of skill employed to produce it is the degree of its worth as a work of art.

To some such conclusion Ellie Lessing had arrived. The perplexities of such arguments did not seriously disturb her. She was too young. Too intent upon creation. Only prematurely aged minds fight over such bones. Only the impotent snuffle and nose among such débris. The virile and creative mind has no time to lose among academical hoop-skirts and tin cans. There are more appetiz-

ing pastures where no goats roam. No mongrels. No fur-
tive alley cats. No critics.

Ellie's *Love in Dread of Hell* had been accepted by the
Academy and was on exhibition there.

Critics either neglected it or mentioned it as a sugary
bit of playfulness evidently inspired by *feu* Clodion.

Mrs. Weymiss had asked several of this embittered
tribe to tea—thinking it prudent that Ellie should meet
and placate them and that they should view some of her
other work. They appeared.

They were not offensive; not enthusiastic, either. Theirs
seemed to be a low-grade intelligence inclined toward the
distortions and incoherence of modernism. Bolsheviki of
art; ratty; secret; sullen; not averse to a moral stench;
roaming by preference near Slavic sewers and the Teu-
tonic-built latrines of Scandinavia.

They signed their articles. They were of great importance.

It turned out to be a pretty tea. Quite a number of gay
people. And Ellie was very lovely and looked no older
than a child.

It was she—and the food and drink—that interested
the critics. "Yess—Yess——" they said, examining the
bronze replicas—"Yess—yess!"

And took high-balls instead of tea.

Well, vermin are vermin; a louse is a louse whether
he calls himself Minkley or Pascoe or De Pester or
Sylvester. Whether he inhabits the head, body, or other
sections of literature, art, or music, always his name is
Pediculus.

It was after all guests had departed and Mrs. Weymiss and Ellie were discussing the affair, that a card was brought in by a servant. Two cards; one for each.

"Oh," exclaimed the girl, brightening, "'it's a family friend! Do you mind?"

On the contrary, Mrs. Weymiss was interested.

When "Judge" Barrett came in Ellie placed both hands on his shoulders and kissed him. Then she presented him to Mrs. Weymiss.

The Judge was immaculate to a degree of perfumed shininess that made him and his attire radiate bay-rum and light.

"Ma'am," he said with that confident bow that had hypnotized many an East Side jury, "—I have, perhaps, ventured too much in presenting myself at your sumptuous threshold unbeknownst to you——"

"I am flattered and happy," said Mrs. Weymiss in her liveliest manner; "and it is most gallant of you to include me in your inquiry."

"Ma'am," said the Judge with another bow that no jury ever polled could have withstood, "how could I pay my respects to a star, however bright, and take no notice of the moon beside her?"

Mrs. Weymiss, who was brimming with mischief and delight, arose and made him a lively curtsy; and the bow that matched it would have corrupted the Supreme Court.

She made him sit beside her. She prophesied that he would prefer Irish to tea.

She laughed with him; consented to sip a little herself. And the gallantry of Judge Barrett blazed and scintillated;

and he told stories and jokes; and they laughed and laughed.

When he took his leave Mrs. Weymiss gave him her hand and asked him to come again.

Ellie kissed him; walked with him to the door; kissed him again before two flunkies.

"You're well, darling?"

"Wonderfully," she said.

"And famous!"

"Oh, no——"

"Y'are that! . . . And heart-free—God bless you?"

"Only for *you!*——"

"Y'little blarney! That's the Irish in you, and I'm an old fool to believe you! I am that. . . ."

A servant handed him the shiniest top hat that Ellie ever had beheld.

"Good-bye! Good-bye!" she cried as he left the house.

Mrs. Weymiss was entering the lift. Ellie stepped in, pulled the lever.

When it stopped she opened the door and followed her hostess.

"I wanted to thank you," she said.

"My dear, your friend is delightful!——"

"Yes; he is. But you are very sweet to me——"

"There is," said Mrs. Weymiss, "an aristocracy which is unconscious that it is one. Not many belong to it. But you are one of them, my child."

The girl gave her a diffident, confused look, standing there in the brilliantly lighted hall. The elder woman laughed, moved on, turned again, still smiling.

"You'd better dress," she said. "It's *Tristan* to-night; and you wanted to hear it all——"

There was no rest for Ellie Lessing during those weeks with Mrs. Weymiss. She needed none.

A dance was given for her at the Colony Club. After that she was asked about, generally. At one of the junior parties she met several of the pin-heads of Leda's party— among them the particular one who had been sent home in somebody else's car.

It was he who blushed, not she. And in her friendly fashion she gave him her hand as reassurance, apparently unconscious that she needed any from him.

Afterward, in the cloak-room with his fellow: "My God," he said, "I didn't know she was a deb on the loose when I met her at Leda's!"

"You gotta watch out," said the other; "you never know where you'll bump into your own sister these balmy days——"

If there was any talk about the matter at all none came to Mrs. Weymiss. And it is probable that leeway was conceded to this very popular genius—nobody being familiar with the breed; none other being known to have originated from the several social puddles represented.

The débutantes thrilled to her; the more experienced— if there be any—took her curiously, seriously, sympathetically, suspiciously, as their several natures prompted.

But nobody remained indifferent to Ellie Lessing. And there was one woman socially well known, who was a sculptress, and who, at least, had done one fine thing; and this woman, with charming simplicity, offered Ellie her friendship and the fruits of her own experience with the ways of the most ignorant public in the world.

She met, that winter, other women in her profession; a great sculptress of animals who offered her a quiet hand of welcome; a yellow-haired, slender, delicately beautiful girl whose portrait bust of a young opera singer was the sensation of the winter exhibition; and who, also, offered Ellie a pleasant, unfeigned welcome to the ranks.

The odd feature of these days was that Ellie had so instantly and so easily become merged in all that she had never known—so instinctively a part of it, without effort, without awkwardness, unsurprised, unflattered, and serenely, as of a right. Like a travelled child returning to her own, interested, enchanted, curious only because it had outgrown her infant recollection.

Much was as she had visualized it; imagined it. Much was strange, but in a stimulating, friendly way that offered itself as frankly as the girl approached it, shyly confident that it all was part of a happy everything that concerned her.

They located, finally, a barn-like studio—not in Cat-alley, or The Mews, but west of Lexington in the Fifties.

With it was connected a master's room, a maid's room, a dining-room, a living-room, and a kitchenette.

Mrs. Weymiss fought against it. And, sometimes, the girl, listening, thought she could hear the faint jingling of handcuffs in the silk wrist-bag.

There was no use. She required the freedom she was instinctively seeking. She was going. Mrs. Weymiss realized it. Comprehended that to let her go was the only way to retain her at all.

Perhaps the elder woman understood, too, that she never could retain her. That nobody could. That the girl had been fashioned for independence of mind and soul and body. And, so far, had abused none of these.

Mrs. Weymiss was loath to let her go. . . . There was a boy; not more spoiled than another. . . . Women spoke of him as "the sweetest thing." . . . His was a fortune already; would be a vast one, some day.

Every mother in town was more than cordial to him. His own parents more than careful. Bland; and very careful.

He and Ellie had met at several parties. Had not been particularly impressed with each other.

So far, in his career, he cared only for polo. And plenty of it. There did not seem to be any common ground between these two except the dancing floor. Over that they slid together joyously enough when chance and propinquity suggested it. And went, as happily, out of each other's lives.

And now the girl was going partly out of Mrs. Weymiss's life. She was a tired old woman. She had not given her affection easily.

After the last party before departure she came in and sat on the edge of Ellie's bed after a maid had tucked the girl in.

"Have you liked it?" she asked.

"It's been heavenly," said the girl. And reached out of bed and took the elder woman's hands. Lay there, caressing them; their load of jewelled rings; their bones; the fingers ridged with chalk deposits.

After a silence Mrs. Weymiss got up, turned out the tiny night light.

In darkness she said in a low voice: "Love me a little. . . . Will you?"

"I do."

The elder woman bent, felt for the fresh young face, kissed it, then went her way in darkness.

CHAPTER XXXVII

BY April the new studio in the Fifties west of Lexington, and the apartment, too, began to look as though Ellie Lessing had lived in them for years.

In the first place the rooms, one and all, had that austere look which, hitherto, had characterized the girl's quarters.

Not that she was insensible to the beauty of environment. She loved it dearly; loved harmony of effect, loved ease and comfort; but was not going to be dependent upon these at this stage of her career. Had no intention of spending money for such purpose. Not yet.

So Rose had been summoned from the purlieus of Harlem; once more a van brought from Westchester Ellie's lares and penates; including the portraits of Henry Lessing and of Helen; and those equine but mechanical masterpieces, *Ormond* and *Man-o'-War*.

It brought, also, all her studio effects and paraphernalia. It brought the old Herez rug—sapphire, ivory and rose.

Mr. Shoreham's furniture in the portable wing remained. The parrot, long since, had been returned to the aristocratic confines of Three Lakes. But the May Salon was to behold the bird, immortalized. *Africa* had been accepted. The incredibly joyous news had come; and Ellie sang in her studio while she worked; played whirlwind jazz on her piano; went into the kitchen a dozen times to tell Rose about it and examine the layer cake she was baking.

Other moods succeeded; she left her clay; came and stood before Helen's portrait and gazed dumbly at her mother. . . . Not that, in the girl's mind, there was any question that Helen knew about the Salon. . . . But—if she could only have told her——

However, she could write about it to John Westall. She went to her bedroom desk and started the letter; and was interrupted by an amiably correct call from George Shoreham, partly civility and congratulation, partly business—inspection of her new sketch for a bronze to be handled exclusively by Shoreham Sons and Company.

They went together into the studio. The sketch in wax was called *Untameable*—a wild little girl Dryad and a wild little boy Faun playing with a wildcat and her kittens. An untamed, untameable company. Free, they flourished; caged, they perished. It was all there, the passionate plea for freedom—eloquent in the wild, laughing boy with his pointed ears and his twig of oak leaves; in the wild, lithe girl on tiptoe behind him, curiously poised, ready to fly at the stir of a shadow; in the sinuous cat of the forest, on its back, twisting to pat at the teasing twig, playful, yet snarling——

Mr. Shoreham discussed it with her in a modulated voice and solemn; always unmitigatedly the gentleman.

Taking his departure, presently, he ventured to suggest another group in addition to this one. All the replicas of *Love in Dread of Hell* had been sold. . . . As per statement with cheque enclosed, due May fifteenth.

"Thank you so much," said Ellie.

"*We* thank *you.* . . . And, would it be too much to ask you to consider another group—say somewhat after the manner of Clodion? My father mentioned it——"

She repressed a smile: "*Attic,* you mean?"

He thanked her and took his departure solemnly. And Ellie went back to the kitchen and seated herself on the table and laughed and laughed.

Rose turned from her oven and laughed too. She laughed easily and melodiously. All coloured girls do. It made no difference to her that she didn't know why her mistress was laughing. For that matter, even Ellie herself scarcely knew.

She may have surmised however, for presently she said: "It's shameful to laugh at anybody! It's perfectly outrageous." And as the apartment bell was ringing she started toward the studio once more, eating a slice of chocolate cake, and wiping her long fingers on her smock.

"I'll answer the bell," she called back over her shoulder to Rose; "it's probably my blue gown from the cleaners'——"

She placed in her mouth the last morsel of chocolate cake, ran her spread fingers over her smock, opened the door, and found herself looking at John Westall.

She made an odd, whimpering sound; clutched his sleeve and drew him through the door.

Dumb, she held fast to him, swallowing hard—cake or emotion—not letting go of him.

He began to laugh; saw the green-gold eyes glimmering; saw the rush of tears.

"My dear," he said gently, "are you really glad?——"

"I'm weak with it. . . . Let's go somewhere—no, not

the studio. . . . My room. . . . I was writing to you.
. . . You can see the letter——"

She had hold of him still; realized, now that she was
dragging him about; slipped her fingers from his sleeve
to his hand and drew him with her.

"You see?" she said, "I was just writing to you. . . .
This is very merciful. . . . And kind of you, too. . . .
Will you please sit in this chintz chair? It is my chair——"

She took his hat and stick and the light coat he carried
over his arm—as though afraid he might go away. She
seemed in fear of that—kept watching him, her eyes still
glimmering with tears.

"*Africa* has been accepted for the Salon," she said.
"I've just heard. I was writing you."

She laid his hat, stick and overcoat on her bed, watching him over her shoulder. Came back swiftly, pulled
a stool from before her dressing-table and seated herself
before him, knee to knee, her hands enfolding one of his.

"You won't go away again?" she asked.

"Not for a while. . . . Why, Ellie!——" He fell
silent, conscious of the girl's emotion; unprepared, after
three years——

"—For a few moments," she murmured, "let me realize
I have you here. . . . I didn't know how I was going
to feel. . . . One can't guess—just by letters. . . . I
know it's three years. Do they matter to you?"

"Of course not—if you mean——"

"Yes, that. Our friendship is the same, isn't it? Mine
is. More, even. . . . I scarcely know what I'm talking
about. . . . You *will* stay with me, now, won't you?"

"Certainly," he said, deeply moved at the dread in her eyes. . . . "I didn't know I meant as much to you——"

"I didn't, myself. . . . I'm not sure whether I knew. But I do now. . . . I've got you back; that's all I am very clear about. . . . Tell me, are you hungry?"

He began to laugh: "No," he said, "are you?"

"Oh, no; I've had some cake. . . . I don't know what I'm saying. Shall we sit here for a while? I'll begin to tell you things by and by. You'll see the studio——"

She kept gathering and pressing and soothing his hand as though she were absently caressing a kitten; but there was a splendour in the eyes which never left his—a concentration probing, plunging into the depths of his as though close to penetration.

"*You* are no stranger," she said. "I was afraid."

"I'm quite the same. But Ellie, *you* are changed. . . . No stranger, either. . . . But——"

"Am I not what you remember?"

"You've developed out of what I remember."

"Is it—agreeable to you?"

"Charmingly agreeable."

"Well, then"—she played absently with his hand—"I think we shall be happy together. . . . I'll tell you something; I'm going to rearrange everything. . . . To suit us both. . . . All my engagements. Shall I?"

"Have you so many?" he asked, smiling.

"Oh, yes. They're merely social engagements. Well, until five I usually work. . . . However, any time you want to come——"

"My dear, you should not let me interfere——"

"Darn it!" she cried happily, "you've knocked the whole 'sorry scheme of things entire' into the dustbin! I've got to rearrange *everything!* I *want* to!

"I'll tell you; this is the best way: you'll be busy until about five, won't you?"

"Except Saturdays and Sundays——"

"Oh," she cried, "could we *always* have those? I mean, if you want to, too——"

He began to laugh: "You'll get awfully fed up——"

"Don't *you* want to?" she persisted.

"Yes, but—isn't that rather different with you now? I mean, you have rather a definite position among friends of consequence——"

"But I told you I'd have to rearrange everything, now!"

"Certainly you're not thinking of sacrificing anything——"

"There's no sacrifice."

His smile faded to a sort of serious curiosity.

She said, gravely: "Is there any objection to our 'seeing more or less of' each other?"

The almost-forgotten phrase relaxed the tension and they smiled.

"Well," she insisted gaily, "*is* there? And I'll tell you something; after all these years without you I'm not going to let anything stop me now!"

He was still laughing: "Villy's for us every Saturday and Sunday. Is that it, Ellie?"

"It is if I'm still your girl. Am I?"

"Don't ask *me! Are* you?"

"Oh, I always have been!"

They still were laughing; but impending reaction shadowed her eyes already.

"As to that," he said, lightly, "you've admitted at least one relapse."

"Francis?"

"I believe that is the demi-god's name."

She smiled.

"Well," he said, "that seems to dispose of him. . . . Who else, Ellie?"

"There never has been anybody else. And that includes Francis."

"What! With your confessed inclinations?"

She smiled. "Oh, those? They subsided when you went away. Besides, there was too much to do. . . . I'll tell you this; when one is agreeably busy all day, work satisfies. There's nothing wanting—no inclinations, such as you accuse me of——"

"You *said* you liked men."

"I do. . . . Not that way any more."

"Since when?"

"Since you left. . . . I didn't want to, with Francis. But you know how it is. Men are sentimental. Well, I'll tell you this; it's terrible to me *now!* . . . I don't know how I ever let him touch me . . . when I look at you. . . . It didn't mean *anything!* Do you believe me?"

"I do. But aren't you taking it rather seriously?"

"Yes, because I was afraid you might. . . . All I care about anything is that"—she laughed—"you say that I'm still your girl."

"You are. That's settled. Now, go ahead with your plans."

"I'll tell you," she continued gaily; "until five, on week-days, we'll be at work. After that, I'll fit in my engagements to suit you——"

"My dear, you can't!"

"I *will!* When you don't wish to come here or take me out, then I'll go to their damn parties——"

She checked herself: "I'm sorry. I forgot. . . . But I'll tell you this," she added; "they swear a good deal more in some circles than we ever did in the Bronx——"

His laughter rang out in the little room.

"You're the sweetest thing!" he said; "certainly the swearing in Flanders was something awful!—— "

"*That* quotation," she exclaimed triumphantly, "is entirely familiar to me!——" She suddenly pressed both his hands convulsively between her own: "John Westall," she said, "I have been developing into what *you* started! Oh, *tell* me! You haven't, yet! Tell me about myself!"

"Tell you that you are very lovely to look at?"

"Am I? That is accident if I am. You *know* what I mean."

"I do. . . . It seems impertinent——"

"*Tell* me!"

"Well, then, yes, you have made good. . . . Is it three years? Is that all? It seems that it was in you from the beginning—all you are, and shall be. It's different for me —it seems presumptuous to say more——"

"Am I what you wished for me?"

"I dared not wish you all that you have become," he said. "Why do you care what I say to you when everybody is aware of your popularity and talents? What you are is amazing enough. But the miracle is that you are unspoiled."

"By what?"

"By fortune; by flattery. . . . By these people who have become your friends. . . . I should say that, to-day, you may go where you please, receive whom you choose. . . . As for your work, it is recognized. More than that, it is marketable. You've stood on your own legs from the first. Now, if you like, you can seat yourself in a solid gold chair."

She said: "I'll tell you something; I'm tired standing on my two legs." . . . She laughed: "You picked me up once. I'd like to have you do it now. Pick me up, to rest my legs, and carry me into the studio. Will you?"

"Now?"

"Will you?"

They both laughed when he leaned forward, lifted her, held her cradled.

She said: "This is the first rest I have had since you went away."

He balanced her, swung her gently, smiling down at her upturned face.

"Oh," she sighed, "this is so wonderful. Will you carry me?"

"To the studio?"

She nodded. In the corridor she extended her arm to point the way, then rested it on his shoulder.

In the studio he held her for a little while, still, before setting her upon her feet.

After a silence he released her. She took his hand and led him about, excited, now, happily loquacious, thrilling at his praise; enchanted at his surprise; confiding to him all the myriad details of hope and disappointment, worry and elation, for which until he came there had been no outlet.

She talked and chattered and laughed and demonstrated; she poured out the accumulations of a dammed-up mind for him; opened the locked gates of a flooded heart.

In the midst of it all she was suddenly possessed of the obsession that he was hungry, and rang for Rose and tea.

"Why," he asked, "do you insist that I need nourishment?"

She didn't know why. Probably it was the maternal in her, instinctively desiring to stuff the object of affection.

"It's funny," she admitted, "it's *funny,* but somehow I keep noticing the boy in you. You *are* a boy! I felt that way about you long ago. . . . That night you went away——"

There was a silence; then they both spoke at once: spontaneous effort to make light of something suddenly pictured. Their parting on that night three years ago.

A slight flush lingered on his cheek-bones for a while, even after her gay voice had dispelled any lingering visions that seemed to have no longer any meaning to either.

Rose came with tea, toast and cake. She smiled at Westall, who smiled at her.

"My Rose," said Ellie, "is so wonderful! If there were any justice in the world the Salon would send her a medal."

At which Rose laughed outright and retired, giggling.

Ellie said: "I'm coming, slowly, back to earth. Slowly.

I have a dinner-party to-night. I can't decently get out of it, can I?"

"No; that's a thing you can't do."

"No; they might not fill it. Oh, Lord! You'll come to-morrow at five, anyway; won't you?"

It seemed that he was tied up.

"Darn it!" she said, "this is likely to be a wasted week. I'm involved. But I won't be after this. And we have Saturday and Sunday, haven't we?"

He began to laugh again; and her clever eyes seemed to divine the source of his amusement. Of a sudden she blushed brightly; strove to laugh with him:

"You're thinking I'm behaving as though we're in love! . . . People might think it of me if they heard me planning. . . . I oughtn't to, I suppose."

"Yes, go ahead," he said coolly.

"I know, of course, you understand——"

After a moment: "I do. Proceed."

"You *do* understand all you mean to me, don't you? You realize that what I am, to-day, you began three years ago—out of nothing—*nothing!* Out of a lump of ignorance! Out of a perfect fool! . . . You *know* that! Why shouldn't I care for you? . . . Next to my mother?"

"Do you?"

"Yes, I do."

After a moment: "That's fine, Ellie," he said quietly.

He got up and began to walk to and fro. Serious. There was a certain detachment in his glance.

"It's all right," he said under his breath. "But I didn't know. . . . I didn't know when I was coming back here."

"What are you saying to yourself?" she asked lightly.

He halted:

"What time is it?" He glanced at the studio clock: "You have to dress. I'd better be going."

She did not rise.

"My hat's on your bed," he said.

She rose. They walked from the studio to her door. She did not go in: rested; leaned against the wall. She seemed suddenly tired. Drooped a little.

As he stood waiting, she said: "Don't you want to remember?"

He knew perfectly well what she meant.

"I do remember."

She rested still, leaning against the doorway: "I mean —do you *wish* to remember?"

"Yes," he said gravely.

For a few moments she remained as she was. Then she turned toward him. Came a step toward him. In his embrace she looked up at him, awaiting his kiss; welcomed it with a slight sigh.

Then she put both arms around his body and strained him to her. . . . The same child's ardour; her whole heart hotly embracing him in an overwhelming impulse of gratitude and affection.

She had become "his girl" again. She laughed up at him. She dropped her head back to look at him.

There was no smile in his eyes. Suddenly, in her own, the smile died out, and her face flamed.

In his eyes was voiceless reassurance. She understood it; understood that her fate was upon her.

Then, in this girl, leaped the first pale flame of passion,

kindling her cheeks and lips, and her breath with a vague, hot fragrance.

He was saying something to her about love. She already understood. She might have known what it really was. Always had been. Always, always. In the very beginning. Now. Always.

She drew a deep, uneven breath. Her mind was on fire; her heart; her mouth. His body was burning her.

"John Westall," she said faintly.

And, again: "I didn't know——"

She let him kiss her; melted to his lips. Left what was done to him; in his keeping and discretion. Her supple limbs yielded, not offering any more, not holding.

The studio clock struck. A door opened; Rose's voice: "Miss Ellie, what gown will you——"

She said to her lover: "I've an hour to dress in. Will you lift me up in your arms?"

"Darling, hadn't I better go and let you——"

"No. Carry me into the studio. . . . How can I dress for dinner *now!*"

And, in the studio: "I'll tell you this: we've got to re-arrange everything, now. *Everything!* . . . You poor boy! What are you planning to do with me?"

"Not a thing, except marry you."

"Oh, Lord! Did *you* know that this was going to happen? I never dreamed it. . . . You don't *have* to hold me, darling."

"I'll carry you to your room."

"Don't go!"

"You'll have to dress, you know——"

He walked back to her bedroom, still cradling her.

The half-hour struck.

"I'll tell you this, darling," she began; but:

"You tell me to-morrow morning," he said firmly. "I can see your scandalized maid peeping from the kitchen." He kissed her. Her mouth was like a rose afire.

"Will you come to breakfast?" she asked. "You'd better get used to it, you know."

"You mean, for life?"

"I do."

He kissed her.

After he had gone her maid came in on tiptoe.

Ellie, partly undressed and all flushed with excitement and impatience, was tearing at her hair with her comb.

"Hurry and turn on my bath!" she cried; "I've got to go to that darn dinner! And I'm trying to think what he might like for breakfast! . . . And that's the only important thing in the world! . . . What he would like. . . . What he wishes. . . . I'll tell you something, Rose; I'm not twenty-two! I'm an hour—what time is it now? A quarter to eight? Well, then, I'm an hour and a half old. . . . Is my bath ready? Please pull off my stockings. . . . An hour and a half old!—How long has Mr. Westall been gone?"

"About t-twenty minutes," faltered the bewildered Rose.

"He's home, then! Call up Hamilton 6996! Ask Mr.

Westall if he'll speak to Miss Lessing. . . . Is he *there?*——"

She sprang to her feet and caught the instrument from Rose:

"Mr. Westall? . . . Oh, *darling!*—is it *you?*——"

(1)